Forest Of The Dark

Palvi Sharma

Forest of the Dark
By
Palvi Sharma

Chapter One

At eleven-thirty at night, everyone was either going home or to a late night party. The city was quiet and the streets were quickly emptying as the traffic lessened. The stall keepers were closing down and counting the earnings of the day before they too would return home.

Sitting under a building on a wooden bench, Preeti watched an old man put a wad of notes in his shirt pocket and get on the bicycle. He would go home where his wife and children were probably waiting for him. That image added to her despair.

Only a month had gone by since Abhi had broken up with her. He had been the love of her life, unfortunately, she hadn't been his. They had been together for three years and he had professed his love for her every day, along with sweet promises of marriage. She had even found a ring in one of his drawers one day while cleaning out his room.

When a week passed by and the proposal hadn't come, Preeti had become restless and had asked him straight up if he intended to marry her. Then to her horror, not only did Abhi refuse to do so but also admitted to having an affair with another girl.

She couldn't say anything as he told her how moving in with her in the first place was a big mistake and his parents would never agree to their marriage because of her *open-mindedness to have a live-in relationship.* She had just stared and said nothing for a while. When he started to walk away, she had grabbed his arm, whirled him around and slapped him hard on his face.

He had been shocked at first and before he could open his mouth to vent out a tirade, she had screamed at him and thrown him out of their house. No... hers.

The month she had spent without him had been pure agony. Her heart was broken and the will to eat or sleep or do any of her regular activities, waned. Then last week, came yet another blow—she was fired from her job at the call center.

That had been the last straw for. She had gone back home and cried her heart out. Her friends had called her numerous times, but she had no strength to attend to them they even sent her texts and when she read them, she had felt more miserable.

One of her friends, Aksh, had finally become a doctor and wanted to celebrate. Her friend Maya also told her that Aksh was getting engaged to an affluent girl. Seeing her friend's lives better had filled her with jealousy and misery. Here, her world was falling apart and there, her friends were progressing in theirs.

Maya had texted her about a promotion she had gotten in the newspaper office she worked in. Dhiraj had made it to the badminton championships and her photographer friend, Rudra, was dating a beautiful model.

Preeti had thrown her phone on the nearby couch and wept into her pillow. When they were all in college, Rudra had proposed to her in front of everyone. She had declined and told him that she was looking for someone else who shared her ambitions. Now look where she was.

She had wiped the tears from her face. Perhaps, she should have given Rudra a chance; he wouldn't have cheated on her like Abhi had.

The phone had rung again and Preeti had finally given up trying to ignore her friends. It was Aksh and he told her that he was arranging a get together at his parent's farm house and that she would have to come. Preeti had tried to make excuses, but Aksh assured her that he would break the door of her house and drag her out.

That had made her smile. She couldn't imagine her scrawny friend dragging her much less breaking open a heavy wooden door. But he was smart and she was sure he would find a way to get to her.

Now here she was, waiting for her friends on a dark and windy night. She imagined if Rudra was driving, he would no doubt be late. Then a thought occurred to her. Aksh had confirmed that it was a friends-only get together, but what if Rudra was bringing his girlfriend to flaunt in front of her?

Preeti took out her phone from her pocket and drew her small grey trolley bag, closer to her. She was about to call Aksh when she saw the wallpaper. The one thing she still hadn't been able to do was get rid of Abhi's pictures. She missed his smile and the way he always made her special and tell her he loved her.

Taking a deep wavering breath, Preeti went into her photo album and started to delete all the memories that were nothing but lies. She didn't want to remember how he had held her hand when they had gone to watch a movie, she didn't want to think of the moment he had asked her to be his girlfriend at a lavish restaurant. She couldn't bring herself to remember that perfect day on the beach when he had kissed her just as the sun was setting.

The water under their feet had been cold and so was the wind, but his touch had filled her with warmth and that was when she knew she had wanted to be with him for the rest of her life.

When a teardrop fell on the screen, Preeti realized she had been sobbing out loud. She turned to see the security guard of the building, watching her with hesitance. He obviously wanted to ask her if she was okay, but like the neighbors, even he knew that she had just broken up with her boyfriend.

"Madam..." he said.

Preeti raised her hand. "I'm okay, Suresh."

Suresh nodded and went over to tend to his dog. "Haven't you eaten yet?" he cooed to the dog.

The black dog barked happily and walked to his dish. With the security guard now also gone, Preeti was all alone on the lonely street. The winds were getting colder and the trees surrounding the building were swaying. The branches brushed against a glass window and made a screeching sound.

Preeti jumped and tapped the phone in her hand. She hoped the Suresh would come back soon. Picking up her phone, she started to dial Aksh's number when she saw her phone had no service.

"What the hell?" she muttered to herself. Raising the phone she found she still had no signal to make a call. "They'll be here any minute," she said to herself and put the phone away.

The wind brushed against her and she shuddered. It was getting colder by the minute on this moonless night. The clouds were gathering up, promising a storm later on. She hoped that they would be further down the road and away from this impending storm.

"Where are you guys?" she shivered and then slowly jogged on the spot to provide her body with some warmth.

A tap on her shoulder made her gasp and when she turned, she saw no one. Suresh's cabin was still empty and she couldn't hear the dog anymore. Preeti grasped the handle of her suitcase and looked all around her. She was certain the touch on her shoulder felt like someone's hand, however with the wind strengthening, there was a possibility that a twig may have...

When there was a tap on her shoulder again, Preeti let out a cry. She turned, but again there was no one.

"Is anyone here?" she asked. She took a few steps forward toward the road and looked both ways. There were no cars on the road, so the chances of her friend's playing a prank on her was unlikely. Besides, Maya knew the state of mind she was in. She hadn't talked to her friend, but had messaged her about the break up in two lines.

Maya had responded in concern and kindness. She had told her she would call her when she was ready to talk and for now they would have a fun weekend to forget all their worries. It was only later that Preeti had wondered if perhaps Maya was going through something as well, based on her melancholic tone.

"Hello?" she called. Looking down at her watch, she saw it was midnight. Where were her friends?

Something touched her shoulder and Preeti froze. Holding her breath, she tried to recognize if it was a twig or a plastic bag that had clung to her shoulder—but the touch felt like a hand, and that meant someone was behind her.

She counted to three and turned, but again there was nothing. "Who's there?" There was a loud crack and she turned to see a broken branch landing on the ground. Preeti stepped back instinctively and a gust of wind brushed against her.

"Don't go," someone whispered in her ear.

Preeti let out another cry and turned all around her. "Who is it?"

A loud blare of horn startled her and Preeti stumbled to the ground. The car was speeding toward her and all she could do was stare at the bright headlights.

The car came to a stop, just inches from her and she swallowed.

"Preeti?" It was Rudra's voice, as he climbed out of the jeep. "Hey, are you okay?"

Preeti gazed up at him. He had combed back his wavy long hair and was dressed in a black jacket and white t-shirt with black jeans.

He offered his hand and she took it, wondering absurdly if he had dressed neatly for his girlfriend.

Her friend Maya too came out of the car. In this cold weather, she had donned a brown mini skirt and a brown jacket with an animal print scarf. Her short curly dark hair was covered with a black cloche.

"Preeti? What are you doing in the middle of the road?"

Preeti stared at her, trying to collect her thoughts. "I thought I heard..." Then when she realized how foolish this incident would seem to her friends, she took a deep breath and lied. "I just tripped. Clumsy me." she smiled.

"Let's go!" Aksh said from the car. His usual friendly voice was a bit harsh today and Preeti blinked at him. Aksh should have been happy after finally getting his medical license, yet he seemed perturbed. His hair had thinned quite a lot since she last saw him and he kept pushing up his glasses in annoyance. Dhiraj was sitting behind him, but he was lost in his own thoughts, gazing out the window.

"I have to get my bag," Preeti said and ran back to the bench. She grabbed her suitcase and saw Suresh standing in his small cabin and looking at her. She put up her hand to wave at him, but he didn't respond.

He only stared at her while the dog started barking. Preeti saw the dog looking at her and growling. Shaking herself, she dragged the suitcase behind her and tapped on the car. The trunk opened and Rudra helped her put her bag in.

"All set?" he asked.

Preeti smiled. There was no one else in the car apart from them; he hadn't brought his girlfriend. "Sure, let's go."

Chapter Two

As they left the city and headed to the highway, Preeti gazed out the window, staring at the night sky, lost in her thoughts of her failed relationship. It was only after a drop of rain hit the window that she snapped out of her reverie and realized that no one in the car had spoken a word.

Aksh was driving and he had propped up one elbow against the window and clutching his forehead. For someone who had just achieved his dreams, Aksh appeared withdrawn and tense. Rudra was sitting beside him and he was glued to his phone. No doubt his girlfriend was texting him.

Preeti felt a twinge of jealousy and dismissed it immediately. She had no right to be jealous of someone else's relationship just because hers had failed. In fact, she dreaded revealing her breakup to Rudra who would be amused since she had rejected him in college.

She felt Maya's hand clutch hers and she looked at her friend.

"Are you okay?" she asked in a low tone, intended only for her ears.

Preeti nodded, making sure Dhiraj who was sitting on the other side of Maya, hadn't heard. She needn't be concerned as Dhiraj was listening to music on his phone. When he saw her looking at him, he removed a earphone and raised an eyebrow at her.

Preeti smiled and shook her head. More rain splattered against the windows and windshield, but it looked like it wouldn't turn into a storm after all. Aksh was a cautious driver, so they really had nothing to fear about skidding on the slippery roads.

As more minutes passed, and no one had said anything, Preeti squirmed in her seat. This would be the first time that the friends had met up and not created the revelry that was usual for them. At first she had thought Maya must have briefed them about her breakup, but the way her friends were acting, it seemed everyone was entwined in problems of their own. She longed to ask them about it, but then she would have to reveal hers as well.

Unable to bear the silence anymore, she pushed herself forward.

"So where exactly are we going?" she asked. "I mean, where is the farmhouse?"

"Uh... it's in the countryside," Aksh replied, distractedly. "It's a two hour drive."

"Oh," Preeti said in a small voice. "What is the name of the place?"

Aksh seemed annoyed with her persistent questions. "In Diladar."

Rudra, who was sitting beside him, suddenly slammed his phone on the dashboard and punched the side door.

Aksh turned to him. "Hey!"

Rudra picked up his phone and shoved it down his pocket. "Sorry, man."

"Are you okay?" Aksh asked.

"Yeah." Rudra looked over and pointed at the indicator. "You're running low on petrol."

"I'll make a stop at the next petrol station. After that there won't be another one until we reach Diladar," Aksh replied.

Preeti sat back, watching the rain slowing down. Somewhere in front of them was a couple on a motorcycle. Only the man had the helmet on while the woman was shielding herself from the rain with a scarf. They made a right and were gone, leaving their jeep the only vehicle on the long road.

Maya leaned her head back and closed her eyes and Preeti decided that her friends were probably tired which was why they weren't their usual selves. She decided to get some sleep too, when Aksh made a sharp left turn.

Sitting up straight, she saw the bright lights of the petrol station and decided to get out and stretch her legs while Aksh filled the tank. When the car stopped, Preeti opened the door and found herself being pushed out by Maya.

"Sorry," she said. "I was feeling a bit stuffy in there."

"You could sit by the window when we get back in." Preeti offered.

"Thanks," she said. "Let's get a bottle of water from the mart."

"You girls stay here," Dhiraj said. "I'll go get it."

Everyone got out of the car while the attendant opened up the tank and inserted the nozzle.

As Aksh and Rudra made their way to the small mart, Dhiraj was coming out with two large bottles of water in his hands. "Here you go."

"Thanks." Maya broke the seal and uncapped the bottle. "Want some?"

Preeti shook her head. "You go ahead."

Dhiraj stood with his hands in his pockets, looking around at the station and then back at them, as if hesitating to tell them something.

"You seem distracted," Preeti told him.

"Yeah, just some stuff. And other people's stuff as well." He turned toward the mart, indicating Aksh and Rudra.

"What do you mean?" Preeti asked.

"Hey!" Maya said. "I thought we guys decided not to discuss our problems."

Preeti was leaning against the wall and straightened, looking at her two friends curiously. "What's going on? All of you look so serious."

"It's nothing." Maya took another gulp of water.

"We're all friends here. If we can't tell our problems to each other, then what's the point of our friendship?" Preeti said.

"All right, then you go first." Maya challenged, putting the bottle down on the hood of the car with such force that some of the water spilled out. The attendant looked startled but kept to himself.

"What's your problem?" Preeti asked. "Why are you so irritated?"

Maya twisted the cap back on the bottle and took her hand. "I'm sorry," she said. "Look, all you need to know is that something happened and we all needed a break. We need to have some fun and forget all our problems. After the weekend, I promise we'll talk about it. Until then, please..."

"Okay," Preeti said. "Just one question: is it serious? Are you guys in serious trouble?"

Dhiraj patted her back. "Nothing we can't handle." He smiled. "It's a bit of an ugly coincidence that we all have gotten ourselves into trouble at the same time."

"Nah, mine has been brewing since I was born," Maya said. "It's just become unbearable now."

Dhiraj watched Aksh and Rudra come out and frowned. "For some, the problems have been created by their own hands."

"What are you talking about?" Maya asked and Preeti was relieved to know that she wasn't the only one who didn't know what was going on.

Dhiraj shrugged. "After the weekend is over, remember?"

Preeti took a swig of water and stared at Rudra wondering if Dhiraj was talking about him. After seeing Rudra's outburst in the car, she wondered if it had something to do with his girlfriend. Did they break up as well?

She chided herself for being smug about it. Just because hers hadn't worked out, didn't give her the right to be happy if someone else's relationship wasn't working out.

"Ready to go?" Aksh asked.

"Yup," Maya said, returning to the car. Preeti offered to let her sit by the window again, but Maya declined and sat between her and Dhiraj.

They all resumed their places while Aksh paid off the attendant. Then he got back in the car and started to drive.

"It's finally stopped raining." Preeti tried to make idle conversation. Anything was better than the eerie silence from her friends.

"Hmm," Rudra said.

"You guys want to listen to some music?" she asked.

"I'm trying to sleep," Maya snapped. Preeti frowned but didn't argue with her testy friend. They drove in silence again and Preeti took a cue from Dhiraj and took out her own earphones from her purse. She wasn't sleepy yet and plagued by her troubled thoughts anyway.

Inserting the earphones in her ears, she scrolled down the playlist to play soft instrumental music that reflected the beautiful night. The clouds had finally parted and the moon made its appearance. Twinkling stars littered across the inky blanket that was the sky and Preeti felt a glimmer of peace settle within; enough to sedate her to go to sleep. She rested her head on the window and closed her eyes, savoring the music playing in her ears.

This was her favorite part. The piano gave way to the violins that evoked a feeling of peace within her. She started to fall into the deep dark pit of sleep, when suddenly she was jolted violently from it as the car came to a screeching halt.

"Watch where you're going!" Aksh screamed at someone.

Preeti felt her heart pounding in her chest. The music in her ears turned to a shrill cry and she plucked the earphones from her ears and thrust it aside.

Beside her, Maya too was sitting up straight while Dhiraj let out a cry and pulled out his earphones. He rubbed his ears and Preeti realized he had heard the shrill sound too.

Staring ahead, she saw an old bearded man dressed in white, walking toward them. He was limping and supporting himself with a thick stick. When he drew closer, Preeti clutched the headrest of the front seat.

The man looked to be about eighty-years-old at least and his eyes were green and milky. He knocked on Aksh's window until he finally relented and opened it.

"What are you doing here late at night?" Aksh scolded him. "Walking down the middle of the road... I almost hit you!"

Preeti swallowed as Aksh screamed at the old man. Since when had her docile friend turned aggressive? Troubles sure changed people, she thought.

"Don't go," The old man said in a wobbly voice

Preeti gasped. She remembered how she had a whisper in her ear when she had been waiting for her friends below her building. Hadn't the voice sounded the same?

"What?" Aksh said rudely.

"There's danger ahead." The old man warned.

"Is the road closed?" Rudra leaned over.

"Don't take the forest road," The old man told him. "It is dangerous."

"Why?" Preeti asked. "What's happened there?"

"Death strolls the roads," The old man said in a mystical tone. "Many have died in the forest road."

"Forest road?" Aksh asked incredulously. "There is no such road. Unless you mean..."

"Don't even speak its name!" The old man said. "It's cursed. Anyone who travels it meets only despair and death. It's haunted by ghosts that have never found peace. They seek revenge and prey on anyone who crosses their path."

"He's crazy," Maya murmured. "Sir, please go home. Does your family know you're out here?"

"Don't go ahead." The old man shook a finger.

"Just drive," Maya said, tapping on Aksh's shoulder. "He's a senile old man."

Aksh drove off and Preeti turned to watch the old man standing in the middle of the road, staring at them.

"That was spooky," Preeti said. "Which road was he talking about?"

"Didn't you hear him?" Maya laughed. "The mere mention of the name will kill you!"

Everyone started to laugh except for Preeti who only smiled. At least her friends were happy, and that made her feel a little better, even though it was at the expense of the poor old man.

"Darkwood Road," Aksh told them.

"That doesn't sound too scary," Preeti said.

Rudra turned to her. "Oh that's not what the people call it. It's called The Haunted road or The Road of Death, as the old man said."

"I have never heard of about it," Preeti said.

"You must have heard about Tina Sulekhna," Maya said.

"Yeah, the daughter of the businessman who went missing two years ago." Preeti said.

"Uh-huh, apparently rumor has it that she was raped and killed here and her body dumped in the woods that run along Darkwood Road," Maya told her. "Some say that her spirit has been seen, but her parents refuse to believe their daughter is dead. They still hold out hope she'll return to them."

"That's so sad," Preeti said. "Didn't the police investigate leads? I mean if people saw her spirit, maybe they actually saw her, lost and roaming around to find her way back home."

"The police did come and investigate. But they found nothing and as night fell, they returned," Dhiraj said. "The horror stories of that place frighten even the police."

"What else happened there?" Preeti asked.

"Apparently years ago, the woods were a haven to the criminals. They buried their enemies there—sometimes alive."

"Whoa!" Preeti gasped.

"Yeah and I heard a disgruntled failing student murdered his teacher and hung her on the tree," Dhiraj said.

"Oh and there was a woman who escaped from the mental institution and found a home in the woods," Maya added. "Legend has it that to date she roams the woods and the road in search of her children, which she'd murdered."

"Okay, guys stop!" Preeti said. "This is really scaring me."

"Two lovers committed suicide there," Rudra said. "Their parents were against their marriage, yet they married and their families chased them out of town."

"Oh no," Aksh said, finally breaking his silence. "The families were hunting them down. They chose to kill themselves in each other's arms rather than be killed by hatred."

"That's disturbingly romantic in a way," Preeti said. "Okay guys, you have me convinced. We are not going down that road. I don't want to run into any ghosts."

"But that's a shortcut to the farmhouse," Aksh said in an expressionless tone.

"I don't care!" Preeti said.

"Yeah, I don't think I would be very comfortable either," Maya said. "We'll take Shirin Road instead."

"You girls are afraid of everything," Aksh said in a temper.

"Hey, if they're not comfortable..." Dhiraj started to say.

Aksh turned around, his eyes wide and wild. "We are going by Darkwood Road!" he screamed.

"Aksh..." Preeti was suddenly scared.

"Hey just relax, you're scaring them," Rudra intervened.

Aksh glared at her and Preeti averted her eyes. When she saw a blinding white light ahead, she gasped. "Aksh... look out!"

Aksh turned around, but it was too late.

Chapter Three

From the very beginning, Dhiraj was used to a strict regime set by his authoritarian parents. He was to wake up at five in the morning and made to take a lap around the whole garden ten times, after which his Father would make him do cardio exercises for half an hour followed by a healthy breakfast of fruits and milk. Only then, he would be sent off to school.

In the weekends his parents would take him to a multi-sport club, where he would be exposed to various games. His parents were both tennis players and wished for their son to master any that would take him to the world championships.

Dhiraj never knew if he ever wanted to be someone else. He tried tennis, hoping he would be a natural at it like his parents, but somehow his skills felt lacking. He tried football and basketball, but nothing drew his interest until one day he played badminton in school. He took an instant liking to it and when he told his parents they seemed a tad disappointed but also relieved that he had finally picked something.

Dhiraj practiced every day in the evenings after his studies. His parents didn't seem to mind that he brought only average marks in his tests and exams; all they wanted for him was to be a sportsman. He went on to win school tournaments and then club tournaments. He was finally selected for the national team—a day Dhiraj thought would never come.

His coach made his train every day and Dhiraj defeated his opponents effortlessly. Then a week ago, while performing a serve, he twisted his wrist. He had ignored the pain at the time; he had been so close to winning. But later, after the adrenaline rush of victory had waned, he had been in unbearable agony.

The doctors advised him complete rest after informing him that he had severely sprained his wrist. Dhiraj was in dire pain, but he hid it well from his parents by continuing to perform his usual training activities. Then yesterday, the doctor told him what he had feared- he had torn a ligament in his wrist and would be unable to play for the championships.

Dhiraj tried to persuade the doctor to do something about it and administer some medicines, but the doctor had refused and advised him to put no more pressure on the hand or else it would cause further injury, which could require surgery.

Replacing his wrist band, Dhiraj had left the doctor's office feeling dejected. Not only would his career suffer but his parents would be so disappointed in him. They had persevered with him and he had nothing to fall back on. His grade reports in college were dismal and he had never wanted to work in a cubicle anyway.

It was over.

Aksh's message couldn't have come at a better moment. He told them about the get together and Dhiraj decided that before he would tell his parents, he would spend one weekend, enjoying the few moments of his life, before he decided to deal with his problems.

He had been leaving the club when he had run into Sumit—his opponent. His injury was no secret to him and much to his chagrin, Sumit began taunting him, reminding him that his position in the team was replaceable and he was next in line to claim it.

Dhiraj wanted to ignore him; he really did try to, but when Sumit kept prodding him something inside him snapped and he punched the bully hard on his face. Sumit suffered a broken nose and needed stitches on his upper lip.

Assault charges had been pressed and he had to call his family lawyer for help. Mr. Mathur was asked to be discreet and not reveal this to Dhiraj's parents. Mr. Mathur complied and Dhiraj was released on bail. This was yet another secret he would have to keep from his parents.

His wrist hurt as did his pride, but nothing hurt worse than the thought of his career going down the drain. As he left the police station, Sumit taunted him some more. He was one hell of a relentless bastard, he thought abysmally.

When he met his friends, he pushed away every one of his troubled thoughts and greeted them with the same friendliness they were accustomed to. It didn't take him long to notice how withdrawn each of them looked. Upon Maya's insistence, they had decided to not discuss their problems this weekend, but looking at his friend, Dhiraj wondered what Aksh was hiding in the first place.

They hadn't talked about the incident at the hospital and Dhiraj wasn't sure he wanted to bring it up. He had just gone there to get his wrist checked on. He hadn't expected to see what he had and encouraged himself not to let his thoughts run amok especially when he didn't know the whole story.

Nevertheless, he promised himself to enjoy the weekend. Preeti thought he was listening to music; he wasn't. He was listening to a meditation tape that helped his relax before his matches. Right now he needed it more than ever considering the bubbling anger inside him.

He hated his injury, he loathed Sumit and he despised his luck. He had been immersed in his gloomy thoughts when the car had screeched to a halt and he had heard Aksh's voice interrupt his tape. Pulling out the headphones, he heard Aksh scream at the old man.

After that bizarre encounter, he found himself relax a bit as his friends returned to their normal selves by talking about the horror stories of Darkwood Road. He had a few to share too.

Then suddenly Aksh turned moody again and before he knew it, Preeti was screaming.

"Look out Aksh!"

There was a strange blinding white light that enveloped him. He covered his eyes with his hands and then all of a sudden, the air around him started to get thicker. He pushed against the side door, dimly aware that the car had stopped.

He heard someone cry out and before he could reach out to his friends, the door had opened and he fell out. The smoke dissipated and he crawled blindly to the side of the road, gasping for breath. His lungs seemed to be full of smoke and he coughed hard.

After a few moments, when his breathing became easier, he looked up to see that he was leaning against the tree and that the car had gone.

"Hey!" he called. Using the tree trunk for support, he staggered to his feet and coughed again. "Guys? Where are you?"

Had they left him?

"Hey! Aksh! Rudra!" He coughed again. "Preeti? Maya! Where are you all?"

He turned around to see an empty road on one side and the dense woods on the other. He saw someone running behind a tree and raised his hand.

"Who's there? Hey!" he called, but received no response. He ran into the woods, seeing the figure duck under a branch as he ran. "Aksh?"

The figure clearly belonged to a man he determined. He ran behind him as fast as his legs could carry him, keeping his eye on the flitting figure, hidden behind a veil of fog.

"Stop!" Dhiraj called. He grabbed a tree branch and panted for breath. He had run faster and run miles ever since he was a kid, but tonight it was as if the energy had been zapped away from him. He started to feel dizzy as he tried to catch his breath.

The fog was making it impossible for him to breathe. He saw the dark figure make a jump and then disappear behind some undergrowth.

He was about to chase after him, when he heard a loud click behind him. His feet froze as he felt a twig snap. Then cool metal pressed against the back of his neck.

"Make one move and I'll kill you," A hoarse voice whispered.

Chapter Four

The only thing Maya had always cared for was the approval of her mother. When she was barely six, her father had left home. She still remembered that fateful night. She had been in bed, cuddling her favorite doll, when the screaming had begun.

Her father had used a word to describe her mother that her young mind had been unable to comprehend. Then the door had slammed and she had heard her mother sobbing loudly. Maya had not wanted to move from her bed.

Clutching her doll in her arms she waited for the sun to rise, after which she crept out of her room to find her mother smoking in the balcony.

"You're up already?" she had asked between puffs. Her mother's eyes were red and swollen and the ashtray by her elbow had ten cigarette butts in it already.

Her mother had put out the cigarette and gone into the kitchen to make breakfast. Maya wanted to ask about her father, but was afraid of the answer. Two days later, after she had finished drinking her milk in the evening, her mother told her in a somber tone that her father wasn't coming back.

Maya had cried herself to sleep that night and from then on, immersed herself in every book she could find. Her father called, but it was only for two minutes and to ask her how she was doing. When he called next, her mother had picked up and she had screamed at him never to call again. Then she said something that had given her shivers.

"She's not your daughter! Don't you dare call again!"

As years passed, Maya assumed that her mother had said that only to cut all ties with her husband, but when she saw her with another man, her thoughts went where she could not stop them. Her mother remarried and she had a new husband, but Maya didn't have a father.

The new husband, as Maya called him in her mind, never cared for her. Six months later, following another heated argument, he left too. Her mother was back to smoking in the mornings and ignoring her.

When she turned sixteen, her mother married yet again. She was happy and Maya was too, seeing her like this. The new husband had a courteous relationship with her, but that was about it. Her mother was so deliriously happy that she started to ignore her completely.

Maya would come home from school with her problems, and her Mother wouldn't be there. She would bring home a certificate for winning an essay competition and her mother would be dressing up to go out. When Maya felt sick one day, her mother was out on a romantic weekend.

Maya would cry all night, wishing her mother was there to soothe her fever, but she would never even call.

College was when she had made new friends, and Maya finally found happiness. Her friends never made her feel lonely and Preeti especially had become more like a sister.

When she graduated with distinction, she ran home to find her mother crying and screaming that all men were cheats. Maya had gone into her room, closed the door and placed her graduation certificate on the table where it laid for two days before she picked it up and went off to look for a job.

The Gazette, immediately hired her after she produced two articles and Maya finally thought that life was getting better. She would go home and keep to herself while her mother took up drinking. Deep inside she longed to share the glorious first day she had, only to find her mother in a drunken stupor.

Maya decided that she didn't need to tell her mother anyway. She would go on living her life and excelling at her job. A year later, Maya received the promotion she was hoping for. She became an assistant editor and couldn't be happier.

"You're progressing fairly quickly," One of her coworkers remarked.

Maya had only smiled and went back to work. She was still writing articles while assigning stories to the other writers.

A walk one evening, inspired her to write an article that she thought would be worthy of an award. She worked on it day and night and when it was finished, she rushed out of her room to find her mother so that she too could see what a terrific writer she was.

A noise in her mother's bedroom directed her there, and when she opened the door, she saw her mother with another man. That had been it for her.

She screamed at her, venting all the frustrations and anger she had buried all these years. Her mother tried to interrupt and tell her that she was only talking to the man who was a lawyer, but in Maya's eyes, he was just another person who her mother was going to neglect her with.

Maya had stormed out of the house and walked down the streets aimlessly. She then went to Aksh's house who lived just a few kilometers from her.

Aksh welcomed her with a smile, but she could the tense expression on his face. His hair too had thinned. When he gave her a glass of water, Maya burst into tears.

Her friend put his arms around her and after she had managed to control her tears, she drank the water in the glass.

"Do you want to talk about it?" Aksh had asked.

"It's nothing I can't handle. I just don't want to go home," she had told him.

Aksh didn't persist. He let her sleep in the sofa that night and the next day asked her if she and the other friends could go on a get-together.

"I could use a break," He told her, rubbing his forehead where she saw more of his hair had fallen. "And it appears you could as well."

Maya had agreed. She had only one condition- that none of them would talk about their troubles. Her phone had buzzed with numerous texts from her mother, but she ignored them.

She called Preeti first who didn't pick up. After several tries, Maya just left a message, telling her about the plan. As the other friends were informed, Maya grew curious about Preeti and eventually realized that she too must be going through something. She guessed it was her boyfriend who Maya thought wasn't good for her friend anyway.

When Aksh found out that Preeti hadn't responded, he called her and was able to get through. The trip away from home was about to begin and Maya pushed aside her remorseful thoughts.

Everything was going smoothly, then of all her friends, Aksh had snapped and they had hit something. She raised her hand to support herself, but ended up hitting her head on the back of a seat.

Maya felt herself being thrust out of the car. At first she thought one of her friends had pulled her out. She imagined smelling smoke and thought she heard a cry.

Was the car in flames? Was everyone safe?

Her mind couldn't seem to process these thoughts without her wanting to throw up from the headache she was getting.

When she was able to open her eyes, she found herself lying in the middle of the road, staring at the starry night sky. Getting up, she checked herself and saw a gash on her left arm and a large bruise forming on her right leg.

She winced as she got up and putting a hand to her head, looked around. She was all alone on the road where the woods began. There was no car and none of her friends beside her.

"Hello?" she called. "Preeti? Aksh? Where are you?"

Limping down the road, she shivered when the fog started to settle all around her and envelope the woods.

"Help!" she screamed. "Where are all of you?"

The rustling of leaves caught her attention and she turned. Through the thick fog, she made out a figure walking in front of her. It looked like a woman and she guessed it must be Preeti.

"Preeti?" she called and went after her. An owl hooted and she jumped. Beneath the soles of her feet the dry leaves made a crackling sound, while the wind wailed in her ears.

"Preeti!" Maya called again. The woman in front of her continued to walk deeper into the woods and Maya stopped herself. The old man's words resounded in her ears—Don't go ahead!

She was already in the neck of the woods. Taking a deep breath, Maya called again, but the woman didn't turn. Realizing that the figure was only a figment of her imagination, Maya turned to go when she heard soft music playing.

Taking a few steps back, Maya saw the woman sitting under a tree and bringing her long hair to one side.

She started to plait it while singing and Maya felt her heart stop.

In the moonlight she realized it wasn't Preeti, but someone else. Someone who could perhaps help her.

She made her way soft-footed, feeling her heart thudding in her chest. Her mind screamed not to proceed, but the song... it was drawing her in. The words weren't coherent to her yet, but the music and the woman's soft voice was mesmerizing.

It was as if she were singing a lullaby. Maya came to where the woman was sitting and walked through the fog. The woman was dressed in a white dress and had long grey hair that she was slowly plaiting with every note she sang.

When Maya came to stand before her, the woman stopped singing and plaiting her hair. She raised her head and Maya felt her mouth drop open.

"Mom?"

Chapter Five

Rudra had been rejected in love twice.

When he was in seventh grade, he had fallen in love with Rashika, a girl with dark hair tied in a braid that fell to her waist. She had chocolate brown eyes, long lashes and a cute smile. The day he had asked her out for ice cream and she had accepted, he was certain that his love would last forever. They had spent a jovial afternoon scoffing down chocolate chip ice creams and talking about school and their classmates.

Rashika liked him, that much was certain. They went out after school every day; sometimes for walks along a nearby beach and sometimes for ice cream. They were teased by their classmates as lovers and not once did Rashika deny it. He immediately took it as her acceptance to be his formal girlfriend.

Then just before they went off to college, Rashika told him bluntly that they were never boyfriend-girlfriend and she had been going out with another guy as well.

Rudra had been heartbroken and was sure that he would never find and accept love again. He'd scolded himself for being so naive and promised that in college, he would only date girls but never get serious with them.

On the very first day, he had fallen head over heels, all over again. He had been waiting by the notice board, looking for his name and his assigned classes, when a girl an inch shorter than him, had stood beside him. She smelled like spring flowers and when they had looked at each other, he had felt a spark- something he had told himself at that time that he had never felt with Rashika.

She had smiled at him and looked over to find her name on the list. Like a true gentleman, he moved to the side to give her space and knew that she had found this gesture charming. Her cheeks turned pink and her eyes shied away from him. She wasn't looking at him but her finger traced the names on the sheet and stopped at her name- Preeti.

It had been an easy way for him to find out her name. As it turned out, she was in none of his classes, but with one of his friends- Dhiraj. He used this as an excuse to stand waiting in front of the class in the pretext of looking for Dhiraj while his eyes scanned the small crowd for her.

She had the most beautiful brown eyes he had ever seen and her dark hair was long and luxurious. She had the kind of charm that one found endearing and while she had walked into college alone, she had made tons of friends by the end of the semester.

Dhiraj found out about his feelings for Preeti and introduced them. The shy girl he had seen on the first day was no longer in front of him. Preeti had started talking to him as if they had always been friends. He wasn't sure that he wanted to be just her friend.

At nights, he would remind himself of the solemn promise he had made to himself in high school—to never fall in love again—but Preeti had invaded his mind and overpowered his resolve.

Every day he would go to college with a big smile on his face, and whenever she was absent he would sulk. Nothing felt nice without her. Through her, he met Maya who possessed the same effervescent personality found in Preeti. They became fast friends and one day when Preeti had not attended college, she had asked him straight up if he liked her friend.

Rudra admitted he did and Maya had decided to help him set up a romantic proposal. Unfortunately, what they had not known then was that on the days Preeti was not attending college, she was spending time with Abhi—a boy from a nearby college who had just asked her out.

On Valentine's Day, Rudra dressed up in a dark jacket and clean jeans, combed and gelled his hair and applied generous amounts of cologne. With a bouquet of red roses, he'd walked right up to Preeti, fell to his knees and told her he loved her.

Preeti had stared at him with her mouth agape and disappointment and surprise in her eyes. Then a smile appeared on her face, as she asked him if he was joking.

Rudra's heart shattered. He got up and told her that he had loved her ever since he had laid eyes on her, but she had taken his hands and told him politely that she was dating Abhi and they were getting serious.

Rudra was left humiliated and heartbroken. He cursed his heart for fooling him again and took a semester off to mend himself. Preeti texted him often, apologizing and asking if they could still be friends. He always replied with a yes, but deep inside, he couldn't bring himself to ever see her again.

Upon the insistence of his family to complete his education soon, he went back to college, maintained a distance from Preeti and concentrated on his studies. Preeti would ask him if they were still friends and he would make excuses about studying for a test.

When they graduated, Rudra was willing to stop ignoring Preeti and accept that she was in love with someone else. He didn't approve of Abhi when he saw him at the graduation ceremony, but he would never reveal that to Preeti or any of his friends.

After college, he went to work with his brother at a modeling agency where he proved his photography abilities. His brother handed him an assignment and that was when he met Mahi—an upcoming model.

Mahi was tall, had a dusky complexion and flawless skin. Her hair was silky and her smile was sensual. She walked up to him after the shoot was over and asked him out. Rudra couldn't say no.

They dated for several weeks and he could see that Mahi was becoming serious. Whether he was or wanted to—he couldn't decide. At nights, when he was alone with his thoughts, he kept thinking about Preeti and wishing that she had never met Abhi.

Mahi had told him all about her relationships; Rudra couldn't when he was never really in a serious relationship to begin with. However, Mahi had started to become suspicious and the day before he was to leave for his trip, she had gone through his phone and found pictures of Preeti.

They had a huge fight, with Mahi accusing him of cheating on her. He tried to tell her that Preeti was with someone else, but she had stopped him with one question:

"Are you still in love with her?"

The pause that had lasted for a few seconds was answer enough for Mahi. She had stormed out of his house and refused to take his calls.

When he met his friends, he had been distracted. When calling hadn't worked, he had started to text her, asking her to give him a chance to explain. She didn't respond until he sent her his fiftieth text. Then she had replied with: I NEVER WANT TO SPEAK TO YOU AGAIN! LEAVE ME ALONE!

In anger, he flung his phone on the dashboard, only to realize his friends had noticed his aggravation, especially Preeti who let out a tiny gasp.

The rest of the trip, he had spent in silence. He could see Preeti throw him curious glances from the rear view mirror and he had a hunch she knew that he had a girlfriend.

I wonder what she thinks about me being in a relationship...

He wanted to smack himself in the head for still thinking about Preeti after she had told him quite bluntly that she would never want to be in a relationship with him.

He had been distracted by these wandering thoughts when he saw a bright white light and then suddenly there was a feeling of being pushed and pulled at the same time, then a hard shove that caused his seat belt to break and throw him through the glass and hit something hard.

Looking down at his hands, his fingers trembled with the splash of blood. Blinking, he sat up. He could feel the minutes pass by, yet he could not stop himself from gaping at the blood on his hands. His blood.

When a thread of sense wound around him, he tore his eyes away from his hands and looked ahead. The car must be a mess, he thought. His friends... oh no... his friends...

"Preeti!" He yelled at the top of his lungs. A fit of coughing followed and a few droplets of blood sprayed out, but that didn't stop him from pulling himself up and staggering toward the road.

"Preeti! Where are you?" He stumbled, but dragged himself forward. Where was everyone? Where was the car? Where were his friends? Where was Preeti?

"Pre-"

"Rudra?" A woman's voice coming from behind, stopped him. Whipping his head around, he saw a woman standing by the tree. Was it her? Was it Preeti?

His mind couldn't make out anything but a dark figure. He wiped the blood out of his forehead and eyes and saw the woman walk into the forest.

"Stop! Preeti!" The voice hadn't belonged to Preeti, but he couldn't imagine who else it could be. Maya? No...

He pushed himself up, let out a hoarse cry and staggered after her. He stumbled on a branch and fell onto the dry leaves and twigs that covered the ground. A resounding snap was heard and then the sound of footsteps.

There was someone standing over him and when he looked up, he only saw a dark face. The woman kneeled and placed a gentle hand on his forehead.

"You're hurt," she said in a soft tone.

"You're not Preeti," he mumbled. His vision was clouding with darkness and he could feel something warm trickle down his forehead down to his shirt where it formed a thick pool that seeped through to his skin.

"No, I'm not." The woman's hand brushed his hair and patted it as if she were a mother.

"My friends... they were in the crash too... Preeti... they all must be hurt as well. We need help," He croaked. His hand traveled to his chest and he felt something sticking out.

It's my rib. I have a broken rib!

"You'll be fine," The woman told him, expressionlessly. She bent down and kissed his head. "I'm here to take care of you."

"Who are you?" he asked.

The woman put a cold bluish hand under his chin and raised it so that he could look up at her face. When he saw her face, Rudra screamed.

Chapter Six

*E*ver since Aksh was fifteen, he had wanted to be a doctor.

He had a normal childhood and an ideal family. His father was an accountant and his mother a housewife—both doted on their only son.

Aksh was a thin boy and his mother would often fret and fuss over him. He didn't mind his appearance; what he did care about was his popularity which day by day was declining. Puberty had struck him badly, turning his voice croaky and his face spotted with acne.

None of the girls showed the slightest interest in him and the boys wouldn't include him in any of the sports teams because of his lacking physique.

Aksh spent most of his teenage years in loneliness, but when he came home, his parents would treat him like the most popular boy in the school and at the end of the day, that was what mattered to him and he slept with a big smile on his face every night.

Everything was going in the usual manner, when a few days after his fifteenth birthday, Aksh's father had a car accident.

Aksh had been waiting with his mother for his father to arrive when the phone rang. His mother had picked up and as soon as a few words were exchanged, she had turned pale and her voice turned hollow

She had put down the phone with a tremble in her hands and had asked him to put on his shoes and call a taxi. Throughout the trip, he kept asking his mother what the matter was, but her ashen face didn't belie anything.

She clutched his hands in hers and when the taxi stopped in front of the hospital, Aksh remembered how his heart had sank and how every step inside had felt as if he were walking through a dense swamp.

His mother's face was impassive as she reached the reception and asked for her husband. They were directed to the ICU and Aksh had almost wailed when he saw his father wrapped in bandages. The only part visible was his face which was spotted with large bruises.

The doctor spoke to his mother who was frozen to the spot, but Aksh couldn't understand anything. His eyes wouldn't leave his father and he longed to go forward and embrace his father.

Then a warm hand had touched his shoulder and the doctor had given him a small comforting smile.

"He's going to make it."

Aksh had looked up at the doctor's face and seen worry in his eyes, but his smile and his touch had given him some hope.

The next few days had gone painstakingly slow. His mother would either be glued to the chair outside the ward or sitting by her husband's side, clutching his hand. Not once did he see his mother shed a tear.

He would wake up in the morning; have his maid give him breakfast, go to school then rush to the hospital once they were let out. There he would watch the doctors taking care of his father, while his mother picked on the sandwiches he brought for her.

One day, while he was distracting his mother from her grief by talking about a test he had aced, the alarm had gone off and the doctors had rushed to the ICU.

His mother had risen slowly, a hand clutched to her heart, while he pressed himself to the glass window.

His father was trembling violently and two nurses had to hold him down while the doctor injected him. Then there had been a loud stretching beep and Aksh saw the doctor tense.

Standing on his tiptoes, he saw the doctor do everything he could to revive his father and, when the nurse stepped away, he caught a glimpse of him lying absolutely still Aksh had felt his legs lose their strength and he staggered back. Behind him, his mother let out a moan, but Aksh kept staring at his father'schest.

The doctor was doing something, but Aksh could only see his father's chest lying still, and then he had seen a small movement.

It was gradual, but his father's chest started to heave and Aksh stepped back, relief washing over him. The doctor came out, informed them that the patient had suffered a setback but was doing fine now.

Aksh tore his eyes from his father and looked up at the man who had saved his life. The nurses too came out after a while, giving a reassuring smile to him before rushing off to attend another patient.

That day, Aksh had found his heroes. His father slowly recovered and shifted to the general ward. His mother appeared more relaxed while Aksh would spend his time with his textbook and watching the doctors and nurses take care of the patients.

When his father was well enough to come home, Aksh would sit with him every night and reveal his plans to become a doctor. His parents were happy and supported his decision all the way.

Aksh started to concentrate harder on his studies. He had no friends and no girls to talk to, but he had his books and his dreams.

He graduated from high school with excellent marks and had no trouble finding admission in a good college.

That's when his troubles had begun. Though his classmates regarded him as only a peer, it was the students from the college down the road that were heckling him.

Every day when he went home, he would have to go down the street where three boys would stand outside their college and make fun of him.

"Loser!"

"Four-eyes!"

He was only called names at first and Aksh found it easier to just ignore them, but when one of them slung mud at him, Aksh had started to lose his composure.

He was thin and weak while his tormentors were well-built and would beat him up easily if he ever revolted.

Things got worse when the three boys surrounded him one afternoon and shoved him hard until he stumbled and fell face first into sludge.

"He thinks he's better than us," One of them had said.

Aksh removed his glasses and answered meekly, "I haven't done anything to you. Leave me alone."

One of them had bent over and laughed in his face. Then he called to one of his friends and asked him to bring a nearby trashcan.

Aksh trembled with fear as the three drew closer, grabbing the filthiest and wettest garbage they could find.

"Leave him alone!" Someone had called.

Two boys and two girls had rushed over and stood before the bullies.

"Stay out of it Dhiraj!" The leader of the bullies had said.

Dhiraj had grabbed the collar of the bully and pushed him back. "Venting out your frustrations on an innocent just because your brother was denied admission in his college? You're pathetic, Sumit!"

The boys had exchanged rough words afterwards and the other boy had helped pick Aksh up.

"You okay?" He asked.

The two girls reached for tissues in their purses and handed it over to him.

"You could use the bathroom," One of them said.

Thanks," Aksh said, embarrassed by his deplorable state.

The girls led him to the bathroom and Aksh heard Dhiraj threaten Sumit to never bully him again.

"See you on the court," Sumit had said.

Aksh had wondered if Sumit was going to drag Dhiraj to criminal court, but he kept this ridiculous idea to himself and later found out that Sumit had been referring to the badminton court.

That one act of kindness from these four strangers had made him feel indebted to them. They didn't see it that way though, and that day, Aksh had made some friends.

They would meet up every day after their respective colleges closed for the day and Aksh told them why he wanted to be a doctor. His friends were supportive of him through all the grueling years he spent graduating from medical college and his internship.

The day when he finally became a doctor, Aksh was elated. All his hard work had paid off; his parents were proud and his friends were happy for him. Aksh thought his life couldn't get any better.

That was until one day, a face from the past stepped into the hospital he was working in. As he entered the ward, his heart had stopped upon seeing Sumit- the bully who had tormented him through college. Someone had beaten up Sumit pretty badly. His right cheek had a large purple bruise, his eye was swollen and his lip was cut and bleeding.

Reminding himself of the Hippocratic oath he walked inside, studying the charts the nurse had handed him.

"Well look who it is," Sumit taunted.

Aksh removed his stethoscope and was about to examine him, when Sumit stopped his hand. "I got beaten up here, on my face," he riled on. "Who the hell made you a doctor if you couldn't see and understand one simple thing?"

"I have to make sure there isn't any internal bleeding."

But Sumit kept annoying him. He teased him about paying his way into becoming a doctor and then refused to be treated by such an immature and incompetent doctor. The nurse had to step in and inform Sumit that there was no one else available to take his case, and so he had no choice.

"Bet they threw you out of all the important surgeries."

"I don't... I'm not..." Aksh was mortified to realize that he was so easily flustered by his nemesis' taunts.

"Get on with the treatment," The nurse advised him.

As Aksh looked over Sumit and tended to his cuts, Sumit kept making fun of him until something inside Aksh broke down. His anger surfaced from the depths he had buried it in. When the nurse handed him a prescription pad, he had paused. This was his chance...

One look at Sumit's chart had shown him that he was allergic to a well-known painkiller. His hands didn't falter as he wrote it down. At the last second, his conscience had made an appearance but it was too late. He was about to cancel the medication, when Sumit snatched it out of his hands.

"Were you this slow in writing your examinations too? Is that why it took you so long to become a doctor?" Sumit taunted.

Aksh clamped down on his conscience's voice and watched Sumit walk away with a painkiller he thought would help him.

That night Aksh had waited by the phone, half-expecting Sumit to call and scream at him about prescribing the medicine but chances were that he wouldn't know that the painkiller had been marketed under a different brand name.

His hands reached for the phone to call Sumit himself when the nurse had walked in.

"The patient you treated in the afternoon is back." Her voice had been solemn and Aksh's heart sank. He knew it was him.

He had expected to see Sumit in worse shape, with slight breathing problems and a rash; instead he was shown the corpse of his bully.

"He went into anaphylactic shock." He was told.

Aksh's hands had gone cold. What was worse was that Dhiraj had come to the hospital to get his hand bandaged and when he saw Sumit being taken to the morgue, his mouth had dropped open.

He met his friend's eyes across the room and Aksh had wondered if his friend had seen the guilt in his eyes. He knew. He didn't know how Dhiraj could possibly know, but he did. He was caught!

Dhiraj had walked out without another word and when they met for the trip he had organized to celebrate his success, he hadn't even looked at him. His guilt mounted into a bad mood that escalated when he met that crazy old man warning him of supernatural things that science couldn't prove.

Then he had been screaming, about what he didn't know, but there was a blinding light and the next thing he knew was that he was running through the dense forest.

When he came to his senses, he stopped, gasping for breath and falling to his knees. His mind reminded him that he had been running, though why he was doing that. He couldn't remember.

He looked down and saw a gash on his arm. He would have to do something about it before he bled out. Clutching a hand over his blue shirt sleeve that was rapidly staining with blood, he staggered through the path between trees, his mind dazed.

When he saw a house before him, he blinked in surprise. Was it real? What was it doing in the woods?

That was when he remembered that his friends were not with him. He looked all around but couldn't spot anyone else. He walked backwards, squinting in the darkness and realized that he had a scratch on the right lens of his glasses.

He was about to scream for help, when his back touched something. Holding his breath, he turned to see a girl with wild bushy hair covering part of her face. She was dressed in beige colored rags and there were streaks of dirt on her legs and arms—as if she hadn't bathed for several months.

"Who are you?" Aksh asked.

"Help," The girl said in a broken voice.

Aksh stooped and tried to see her features. Had he heard right. She needed help? "What?"

"Help me," The girl repeated.

Aksh used his hand to brush away the hair from her face and saw dark circles around the girl's eyes. "Who are you.? You look familiar."

The girl looked up with hollow dark eyes. "T-tina."

Aksh gasped. "Tina? Tina Sulekhna?"

The girl suddenly grinned, her face turning dark as her skin wrinkled. Her eyes changed color until they were grey and her mouth opened to reveal jagged teeth.

Before Aksh could react, she raised her hand and grabbed him by the throat. Dragging him close, she grinned wider. Aksh could smell something rancid on her breath like old meat or rotten eggs.

"Not anymore she's not." the girl cackled.

Chapter Seven

The first thing Preeti was aware of was a sharp pain in her arm on which her head was resting. Groaning, she opened one eye first, seeing the back of a seat, then she opened the other.

A small movement of her arm caused her to bite her lip to stifle a small scream as she raised herself. Her left arm felt sprained, her forehead warm and wet. Using her right hand, she tentatively touched the center of forehead and brought her hand down to see dark-red blood.

As if her brain had just registered she had been hurt, her forehead started to throb, sending prickles of pain down her sprained arm.

Preeti let out a moan and then looked all around the car. She saw her friends sitting in the front seat staring ahead, all of them crammed in one seat.

Preeti reached out a hand to touch Aksh's shoulder when they all turned around at once. Their eyes were white and their irises silver orbs. Bluish wrinkled skin was stretched over their faces and smeared with dark blood.

Preeti opened her mouth and let out a scream. In the next instant she was all alone. Her friends were no longer seated in front of her. She raised herself and saw the car empty.

"Wh-what?" Swallowing she used her right hand to fidget with the door handle. When the door opened, Preeti almost fell on her face. Using the door handle she stopped herself just in time. Her knees touched the cold damp road and she winced. Her whole body ached while her insides felt like fire.

Pulling herself up, she walked with unsteady feet to the front of the car and blinked. The car seemed to be in one piece. There was a small dent on the hood and when she inspected it closely, saw a scratch on one of the headlights. Other than that, she couldn't see any damage.

Resting her right hand on the hood, she looked all around her.

Where were her friends? Why had they left her alone?

She couldn't understand what was going on as her mind started to swim. Her knees buckled and she instinctively used her other hand to support herself. When her left hand touched the cold metal, she screamed in pain.

"Hey!" Someone called. "Are you fine?"

Preeti turned to see a couple standing below a tree. Fog was enveloping them and she could barely make out who had called out to her. The voice didn't seem familiar to her at all.

"Who's there?" She asked, walking with staggering steps toward them.

The man and woman turned around and walked into the woods. Preeti stood there, watching them. Her feet started to move in their direction when she screamed at herself to stop. They were people she didn't know and she was in the middle of the road in a strange place. What if they were dangerous criminals?

Preeti felt a shiver go through her as the couple disappeared into the thick fog. She went back to the car and turned on the ceiling light. The empty grey seats still made her nervous, but she ignored the clench in her stomach and proceeded to search for her cell phone. She found her purse pushed under the seat and grabbed it. Opening it, she rummaged through it and brought out her cellphone.

Her fingers were flitting over the keypad when she noticed the 'No Signal' on the corner of the screen. Preeti moved away from the car, with the phone in her hand and winced as her forehead throbbed. Taking another step back, she frowned when her phone still didn't catch a signal.

Muttering a curse under her breath, she walked back towards the car to search for her friends' phones. Chances were that she wouldn't find them, since they were obviously on their persons, but she had to try nevertheless.

She was about to bend to search in the car when the phone in her hand started to ring. Letting out a loud gasp, she dropped it and was about to pick it up when she heard more ringing. Peering into the car she saw four cellphones lying on the grey backseat with their screens lighting up. The ringing grew louder and louder until Preeti had to cover her ears.

For a second, Preeti was sure she had heard the shrill wail of a woman or t howl of a wolf—she wasn't sure. She turned away from the ringing and found herself facing a large tree. Putting a hand on the bark, she felt her fear rising. Wasn't she in the middle of the road?

Turning, she saw more trees behind her and thick fog sweeping the ground. Preeti walked back and found that somehow she had walked deep into the neck of the woods. There were trees all around her. A sweet woody smell permeated the air, then it grew denser until she started to feel nauseous.

The only sounds she heard were her breathing. She was alone in the dark and lost. The car was gone and so was her phone. She cursed herself for not picking it up.

"How did I get here?" she asked. Touching her throbbing forehead, she wondered if she had suffered a small episode of amnesia and just walked into the woods.

"Is anybody here?" she called out. "Guys? Aksh? Rudra? Maya?" She walked ahead slowly, trying not to give into her panic. "Dhiraj?"

Somewhere ahead she heard a rustling sound and wondered if perhaps it was the wind that had played with the leaves.

She saw a figure emerge from a large bush and run. Preeti watched, stunned, until her feet started to move in his direction. The dark figure pulled at another arm and Preeti saw a woman with long hair run with him.

"Stop!" Preeti called. "I need help!" she recognized the two as the ones who had been calling to her before.

To her astonishment, the couple did stop. They were holding each other's hands and looking at something in front of them.

With soft steps, Preeti inched closer. The peculiar couple was now turning to face each other and from up close, Preeti could see they had tears streaming down their eyes.

She came up behind them and saw that the couple looked to be about her age though their dresses appeared to be old. The man was dressed in a cream-colored striped shirt and khakis while the woman was wearing a short shirt over tights. Their clothes were pristine, despite them running through the dirt of the forest.

"Excuse me?" Preeti said in a small voice. She stepped closer until she was just a few inches away from them. It was only then that she noticed they were standing at the edge of the cliff.

Preeti sucked in a breath when she saw the ravine. From her view, she could only see darkness and no bottom. It then hit her as to what the couple intended to do.

Stepping back, she decided to walk away when the couple turned toward her. They glared at her with fiery red eyes, and their mouth curled into snarls.

"Leave us alone!" They screamed in unison. "No one can ever separate us! Not even in death!"

Preeti turned to run, when something grabbed her hair and she was pulled back. The next thing she knew was that couple had curled their long arms around her, until she couldn't move at all. She twisted and struggled in their grasp futilely, as their grip tightened making it impossible for her to breathe.

Then there was smell of burning wood and rotting meat and Preeti felt her chest tighten. She was suffocating and if she didn't release herself, she would die, but her limbs still wouldn't move.

"Let me go!" she tried to say in gasps. Dark clouds appeared in her vision and her forehead and arm screamed in agony.

"You are coming with us!" their voices merged into one booming monstrous roar and before Preeti could understand what was happening, the couple leapt and she felt the ground give way.

Preeti turned to see her falling into a dark empty pit, while the maniacal couple emitted shrill laughter. She closed her eyes, waiting for the impact that would kill her, while wishing she hadn't made the mistakes she had in her life.

Chapter Eight

"Keep moving," The gruff male voice instructed.

The cold circle of metal was still pressed against the back of his neck. Dhiraj complied with his mystery assailant, but his eyes darted around for an escape.

"Wh-where are we going?" He asked, turning his head. Before he could look behind, he was hit on his shoulder with a blow that he assumed was the butt of the gun.

"Walk straight"

Dhiraj muffled his cry of agony and did as he was told. He was surrounded by trees and little else. There was no one here to save him. When his hands felt for his phone in his pocket, his heart sank further.

A rough calloused hand grabbed him and shook his elbow.

"Hands above your head." There was a click and complied.

Of course his phone wasn't with him. He had it in his hands when the accident had occurred and he imagined it lying in a mangled mess.

The arrived near a small pit and Dhiraj let out a tiny whimper. No doubt this was to be his grave.

The man behind him kicked him in the legs, causing Dhiraj to fall down on his knees and let out a yelp.

"Search him."

The second those words were uttered; he heard the rustling of leaves, as three men emerged from behind the bushes carrying machine guns. Dhiraj felt the panic in his stomach mount.

One of the men came over and Dhiraj was about to look up, when he was slapped in the back of his head by his assailant.

"Keep your eyes down,"

From the glimpse he had managed, Dhiraj reckoned he wouldn't have identified the men anyway. Their faces were veiled by the darkness and shadows of the tall looming trees. While he kept his eyes down, he was only able to sense the rough pats of the man above him as he searched his back and chest before lowering his hands to check his pockets.

He brought out a wallet and tossed it to the man behind him.

"Are you a policeman?" The man behind him demanded.

"N-no." Dhiraj's throat tightened with fear.

The man behind him put his hand under his chin and turned it around roughly. "You are him."

Dhiraj blinked and then shut his eyes as a torch was shone over him.

"Sir, should we kill him?"

Dhiraj scrambled to his feet. "N-n-no p-please don't! I'll do anything you ask me to!"

The man lowered his torch and in the moonlight, Dhiraj saw the tall stout man give him a grin. He had straight hair that was combed to side and a long bushy mustache. He was dressed in a maroon shirt with a white tasseled scarf and black pants.

"Quiet!" he screamed. "You are not allowed to speak until I tell you too. Do you understand?"

"Y-yes..." Dhiraj nodded quickly.

"You do know who Sumit is, don't you?"

"Huh?"

One of the men pushed him in the back. "You weren't given permission to speak, and keep your eyes down."

Dhiraj immediately obeyed and shook his head, then nodded.

The man, who was apparently the leader, came over and tugged at his hair, pulling his head back. Dhiraj groaned and was rewarded with a slap on his mouth.

"?" He growled. "Did you know Sumit had a nefarious uncle?"

"I..." Dhiraj shook his head.

The man pushed him down on his knees again and slapped him again. "You were responsible for my nephew's, death weren't you!"

Dhiraj spat out blood and shook his head fervently.

"Do not lie to me!" The man said. "I'm a fugitive from the law. I've killed many people—younger and stronger than you."

"Please!" Dhiraj clasped his hands together. "Let me go."

"Did you kill him?"

"No, No it wasn't me!" Dhiraj begged.

"Give him the shovel!" He told the other man.

Dhiraj was made to clasp his hands around the shovel's handle.

"Now get up and start digging," He said.

"Please let me go!" Dhiraj implored, tears swimming in his eyes. "I didn't kill him. I swear I didn't."

"Then who did?" He screamed. "Give me a name!"

Dhiraj gulped, remembering that day in the hospital when he had come to get his hand looked at. He had seen Sumit's body being taken away to the morgue while Aksh had watched the whole scene with what he thought looked like culpability.

"Tell me who killed him or I'll blow your brains out." The cold metal was back against his temples.

Dhiraj palmed some dirt in his hands, turned and threw it in the eyes of his assaulter. The man let out a startled cry and Dhiraj picked himself up and ran as quickly as his feet would carry him.

He thanked his parents for making him run laps in the morning and building his stamina, or else he would not have had the endurance and agility to make his escape.

Shut up and run, he scolded himself. He couldn't believe his thoughts were going haywire as he ran. Trees dotted his path and he had to swerve around them to avoid being hit by the branches. Some of them were low and so he had to duck under them.

He ran and ran, sure that he had left the criminals way behind him. He still couldn't believe his rival Sumit had an uncle who was a criminal. No wonder; violence and bad tempers ran in the family.

He was jumping over a rock and passing a large bush, when he thought he heard a woman singing. That made him slow his speed, but not stop. He dismissed it as a trick from his delirious mind and ran ahead.

He was about to turn left when he saw three men blocking his path. In the moonlight, all he saw was their grim faces. A fourth came into view and Dhiraj skidded to a halt. It was them!

Dhiraj turned around and then back at him. He had been running straight, so how had these criminals made their way ahead of him?

A click made his heart stop.

"You shouldn't have escaped," The leader said and came forward. In the spot where the moon threw its light on the ground, forming a white luminescent circle, the man stepped forward. His face was purplish and he only had the whites of his eyes.

Four bullet holes had torn through his shirt and blood splattered his white scarf. He raised his arm and Dhiraj saw that the purplish mangy skin was peeling out, revealing bone beneath it.

The other three men also stepped forward and Dhiraj saw bullet holes on their chests as well. One of them had an oozing gash on his forehead while the other had an arm that was held together to the shoulder by a single ligament.

The third man appeared to be walking normally, yet he was missing his left leg.

Dhiraj stepped back, certain he was dreaming—*surely it was a nightmare!*

The leader grinned, revealing rotted teeth with a worm wriggling between the front teeth. "You'll pay for what you did."

Dhiraj heard a loud shot before he felt nothing.

Chapter Nine

*O*n closer inspection, Maya realized the woman wasn't her mother after all. Her mother looked younger than her age with no wrinkles on her face and just crow's feet near the corner of her eyes.

Her mother had dark thick wavy hair and wide eyes and a slim figure that was the envy of twenty year olds.

The woman sitting under the tree had long grey hair and a skin marred with wrinkles and a scar on her right cheek.

As her hands moved to comb her hair, Maya thought that that old woman's hair had perhaps increased in length by at least an inch. Or was it her imagination, she couldn't tell.

The old woman continued to sing softly, her voice melodic and soothing.

Maya gathered her thoughts and decided to go in search of her friends when she felt a cold hand grip her wrist. An icy shiver ran up to her shoulder when she turned.

"Come sit my child," The woman said in a voice as sweet as honey.

"I have to look for my friends," Maya replied. The woman had a kind face, she thought. Despite her many blemishes, the woman had warm brown eyes.

"You must be tired."

Maya knelt down in front of her, suddenly exhausted. "I am."

"Come lie down on my lap," The woman said.

I'm being hypnotized, Maya realized, but she did nothing to stop herself. Her body felt oddly calm and her mind sleepy. For once, after a long time, Maya felt like she had no problems at all.

The woman tapped her own lap and in Maya's mind, the white dress clad woman's lap was softer than any pillow. Maya turned sideways, pulling down her short skirt slightly.

The old woman stopped her hand. "There is nothing to worry about."

"There isn't anything to worry about," Maya repeated, laying her head on the old woman's lap. She was instantly reminded of the one summer she had spent at her grandmother's house when she was ten. Her grandmother too had made her sleep on her lap every night.

Maya breathed deeply, inhaling the sweet smell of jasmine and sandalwood.

"Close your eyes," The old woman instructed.

Maya didn't protest. She closed her eyes, relishing the tranquility washing over her. She felt the old woman's hand pat her gently. Her skin was cold, but her touch was leading her to a calm sleep.

The woman was singing again and with her eyes shut, Maya could hear the words.

"Sleep my sweet little child.
The full moon night has arrived.
Stars too have stunned the wild,
The beauty of the night
Has thus far strived."

Maya wasn't listening anymore. The strange lullaby was intoxicating her, turning her mind into a deep pool of water in which she dived willingly. She blinked sleepily, gazing at the woman's long grey hair moving towards her wrinkled feet in waves.

Beach waves, Maya thought absurdly.

When she blinked again, she was certain the woman's hair had grown at least an inch. Maya wanted to get up and inquire about it, but she was being lured into peaceful sleep and the temptation of that was too great for her to deny.

Taking one last deep breath, she closed her eyes, using the woman's soft voice to lull her deeper into sleep. She thought she would see only serene darkness, instead, she found herself in red-orange burning void. There was nothing above her and nothing under her feet.

The only thing she saw was a wall of orange smoke surrounding her.

There was no escape and no choice but to watch the images presented her on the screen of orange smoke.

"Like in the drive-in theatre Mom and Dad used to take me to when I was a child," She said in a numb voice.

She didn't see her father; only her mother. Her mother was young with thick black hair which she was combing in front of a mirror. She was humming to herself as she picked up a ruby bracelet and draped it over her wrist.

Her mother looked happy and carefree—in a flash that was gone.

She saw strange men in the translucent screen, throwing money at her mother and walking out the door. She in turn picked up the wads of money and screamed obscenities at them, or Maya thought she must have since the images were muted.

"What-?" She wanted to turn away and walk away from what she was seeing, but it was as if invisible hands were pulling on her until she could only stand in one spot.

"Let me go!" She screamed.

In the next instant, she saw her Mother running toward her, a sneer on her face and this time she heard the angry roar her Mother emitted as she charged.

Maya screamed, pulling at her invisible binds to no avail.

"Mom!" Maya screamed. "Don't!"

Her mother put her hands around her throat and squeezed. "I hate you!"

Maya felt the air grow thicker ad acrid. The smoke had morphed into giant flames and she felt her skin sizzling.

"It's all because of you!" Her mother screamed at her.

She could smell her breath—it was like rotten tomatoes burning. The breath was hot and the droplets of spit that sprayed out were acid.

"I didn't do anything." Maya was finding it hard to breathe.

"They left because of you! They didn't want to take care of you!"

"Mom!" Maya gasped.

The hands around her throat grew firmer and she started to cry and cough, but no air entered her lungs.

Dark clouds enveloped her vision and when she opened her eyes again, she saw the tall trees.

Then she realized she still couldn't breathe. Looking down, she found herself lying on the ground and over her body was the old woman, straddling her. She was pulling at her hair and Maya felt cold trembles rock her body when she saw that the old woman's long grey hair was curled around her throat.

She's using her hair to strangle me!

The old woman's melodic voice was no more. She emitted a shrill cry that turned Maya's blood cold.

The old woman pulled on both ends of her hair as her face turned gruesome. Her teeth were pointed and so was her tongue. Red glowing eyes burned into hers and as the darkness pulled her into unconsciousness, Maya was sure she had seen her very first demon.

Just before she succumbed to the empty darkness, Maya thought she heard rock music playing somewhere nearby.

Chapter Ten

*H*e heard his breathing first. It was slow and ragged, becoming louder in the black void he found himself in.

It's a dream, open your eyes! He told himself frantically.

Rudra obeyed and snapped his eyes open.

The darkness subsided and above him was a pale yellow ceiling. Bubbles were floating above him and he tilted his head, mystified. Raising one hand, he used his finger to pop one of them. A droplet of water stuck to his hand and he brought it closer to his eyes to inspect.

"I'm dreaming," He said aloud this time, still feeling traces of disorientation. .

He places both hands near his waist and felt a hard coolness. Turning he saw that he was lying on purple glittery tiles that illuminated whenever the light above touched its surface. He propped himself up, surprised by how painless he felt.

A hand to his chest didn't strike him with excruciating pain that should have been brought upon by the suffering of a broken rib. Looking down, he saw his blue striped shirt spotless—there was no blood or rips anywhere. His forehead wasn't oozing blood, either.

A bubble popped against his forehead and roused him from his daze.

Had the accident been a dream, or was this one?

It was then that he noticed that music was playing— an upbeat tempo that belonged to an electronic keyboard. He caught a movement from the side of his eye and turned to see a woman dressed in a red sparkly tank top and matching shorts. She had on sequined gloves and black long boots. The woman was swaying her hips in time to the music with her back towards him. Then she grabbed the pole beside her and twirled her right leg around it.

Rudra got up slowly, stumped by the vision before him. Empty white chairs occupied more than half the room and the lavender walls were decorated with streamers and fliers, though he couldn't make out what was written on them.

Rudra blinked. Was he in a club? Had he been drunk?

"I've been here before."

The woman in red was still swinging her hips with her leg still curled around the pole. Her dark straight hair swayed, brushing against her fair slim back.

Yes, he had been here before. Mahi had dropped him once to one of her male friend's bachelor party. She had wanted him to be open to new things, especially club scenes and he had been horrified that she had basically asked him to go to a strip club.

He grabbed one of the white cloth-chairs, gasping for breath by the rush of memories.

The woman turned around and he met her soft hazel eyes.

"You're not a monster," He blurted.

The woman put down her leg and laughed. Putting her arm around the pole, she stretched.

"We were in the woods... you were a monster," Rudra said, unable to help himself.

The woman said nothing and kept moving her body even though the music had long stopped.

She's slithering like a snake.

She kept staring at him with amusement in her eyes and then finally stopped. Walking seductively, she made her way to him with an unblinking gaze that sent cold shivers down his stomach.

"A monster?" She asked, raising an eyebrow. "Nothing else?"

Rudra stepped back and stumbled when his foot hit the chair's leg.

She put one long-fingered hand on his chest and Rudra stopped his breath.

"Shh! I won't hurt you."

Rudra let out a breath and swallowed. "What am I doing here? Where are my friends? Who are you?"

The woman gave a tinkling laugh.

Behind him he heard a chair move and turned to see that every chair in the room was occupied by middle-aged balding men in suits and ties.

He pulled back and felt the woman's hot arm around his chest.

"Let me go!" He screamed. The men around him roared with laughter, and he saw that they only had the whites of their eyes and hideous pointed toothy grins.

Rudra was sure his heart had stopped when the woman whipped him around and suddenly he felt his fear evaporating.

Hers was the kindest face he had ever seen with wide, brown, doe eyes; a small button nose and mouth. She reminded him of Preeti and Rudra felt his heart beating soundly again.

"Don't be afraid. You're safe here," She said kindly and pushed her long silky hair back.

Rudra thought how much her hair was like Preeti's.

"I'll answer your questions, all of them."

Rudra glanced behind him and saw that the room was empty once again.

The woman walked away to the other end of the room toward a grand piano. She flitted her hands over the keys and let out soft music.

Mesmerized by the way her long fingers played the keys, he walked ahead, unafraid.

"You play well." He was aware his voice sounded hollow.

She stopped playing and looked sad. "I can play a lot of musical instruments." She paused and scoffed. "Used to."

She resumed playing; humming to the melody her talented hands were creating.

Rudra stopped six feet away from her. "What happened to you?"

The woman sat down on the bench and looked thoughtful.

"My name was Nisha. I used to live in a tiny house with my parents and a sister and brother." Her hands never stopped running through the keys in synchronization.

"We were poor and one day a man appeared to me and offered a great opportunity to earn lots of money."

"This?" Rudra asked, waving his hands around.

Nisha nodded. "We needed that money. I started to perform here, changed my name to Rita and cleaned myself up."

The tune turned low and daunting. "The man who owned this club came to me one day with a scheme to seduce businessmen and cheat them out of their money."

Nisha stopped playing. There were tears in her eyes and her hands were clutching the side of the bench.

"Many were easily conned—except one," Nisha said, a tear rolling down her cheek.

"I told him I was pregnant with his child and needed the money for abortion," She continued, the pain apparent in her voice. "He kidnapped me, brought me here to the woods, where he raped and then killed me."

The silence in the room that followed was heavy. Rudra was compelled to say something before the fear clawed out his heart.

"You're dead? A- a ghost?"

Nisha smiled, looking up at him with sadness in his eyes and just like that Rudra knew.

He looked down at his clean shirt and uninjured body. "I'm dead too? I'm a ghost?"

In a flash, Nisha was right in front of him. "No. Not yet. There's still a chance for you to escape. But you and your friends must hurry!"

Chapter Eleven

The cracking sounds of bones resonated in the thick cold night air. Aksh watched the girl in front of him wriggle in her own skin. He was reminded of a snake shedding its skin—a sight he had not been able to forget when he had watched it on the science channel.

The girl who had been missing for two years and whose disappearance had been riddled with conspiracies, was in front of him struggling with a demon inside her.

Her bone was moving visibly in her body and her mouth opened for a scream, but he heard nothing.

"Help me!" She managed once, before her face morphed into that of a wolf.

Aksh stepped back, wanting to run away from the horrifying sight but too stumped to do anything else but watch her be tormented.

She collapsed to the ground, wriggling and fighting. Her arm raised, she was beckoning him, but he wouldn't move.

"I'm sorry," He mumbled and raised his foot to walk away when she let out a scream- a human one.

"You took a Hippocratic oath," She gasped.

"How do you—I can't!"

"Please," Tina begged, clutching her stomach. "She knows everything. She won't let me go!"

Then she rolled on her back and her eyes closed.

Aksh started to leave, rationalizing with himself that he had to find his friends, but he was reminded of Sumit in a flash and how he had neglected his oath for his animosity.

He glanced over at the girl lying still on the ground. The pain had clearly exhausted her. Kneeling down, he tentatively placed a finger on her wrist.

When she didn't flinch, he grew bold and placed another finger to check her pulse.

He felt the pulsating vein under her almost translucent skin and used his forefinger and thumb to pull at her eyelid.

He was aware of the cold tickling sensation in the pit of his stomach, yet he knew he had to ignore his fear. He had been trained to work in extreme pressure and now was not the time to let his mentors down.

Besides, he told himself, he should imagine and focus on the adulation he would receive when he brought back the girl whose mysterious disappearance had shocked the city.

With this in mind, he drew courage within himself and put both his arms under her body. When he picked her up, he was surprised to find that she barely weighed anything and he was reminded of the one time he had carried a sack of hay when he had gone to visit his extended family at the farm. There had been a scarecrow standing in the middle of the fields and, though the painted face was supposed to evoke fear, Aksh thought it had looked less menacing compared to Tina's alter ego.

She's possessed, he reminded himself. He had to be careful not to awaken the demon inside her.

"Where do I take you?" He asked, looking at her purple face. He was aware that her skin was rapidly heating up.

Her eyes fluttered and she opened her mouth. Aksh almost dropped her when she spoke.

"There..." She used one frail hand to point and Aksh followed her tired gaze to a small structure between two trees.

"What is that?"

But Tina had lost consciousness again and her skin grew hotter.

Pulling in all his energy, he huffed over to where she had gestured and stopped when he saw a small cottage in the dark.

He took one step forward, when the lights suddenly came on. There were lanterns hanging by the door and on a string from the roof. A lone window was open and he peered inside to see a small wooden cupboard and a single cot. He climbed up the two steps and kicked open the door.

Pausing with bated breath, he looked around the small space, seeing a wooden chair in the corner near a messy cot that must have served as her bed.

He took her to the cot and lay her down. Panting, he surveyed the rest of the room, noticing two more doors at the back.

He turned back to Tina and placed his hand on her forehead. The skin was hot to the touch and Aksh hissed and pulled back.

He had to do something to bring her fever down.

Staring at the two doors near the end of the room, he rose slowly. It was too quiet except for the soft moans Tina made as she twisted in her bed.

"You'll be fine," He told her. Walking to the doors, he was aware that his pulse was racing and that a bead of sweat had rolled down the side of his face.

Taking a deep breath, he walked five paces before he exhaled. He pushed open the door and found a tiny kitchen inside—or what was left of it.

The cabinet doors were hanging by the last hinge and the small cupboards seemed to be fragile enough to disintegrate by the smallest breeze. The floors were covered in dust, broken shards of pottery and straw which Aksh assumed had been part of a broom once.

When he stepped inside there was a loud crunching sound as he stepped on a tiny piece of wood that immediately turned to dust.

Aksh coughed as the thick musty air entered his lungs. This room hadn't been ventilated in years and he knew before he even searched, that he wouldn't find food or water. He opened up a tin with a sticky lid and found the remains of unrecognizable grains. The few remaining pots that were intact had no water in them—not that he had expected to find any in the first place.

He opened the cabinets at the bottom and jumped when the door crashed to the floor. More dust flew out and Aksh coughed harder. He peered in the darkness and saw a few tins. Removing them, he saw they were food tins from at least twenty years ago. One of the brand names he recognized was of a company that closed down a decade ago.

He got up and walked out, keeping an eye on Tina as he made his way to the other room.

She was still gasping and writhing, but he didn't see any signs of consciousness. He had to work fast if he wanted to avoid coming face to face with the demon possessing her.

The next door had to be opened with more force. Turning sideways, he pushed against it with his shoulder. When the door wouldn't budge, he chided himself for not going to the gym more often, even though Dhiraj had advised him many times.

At his fifth try, the door moved a little and made a groaning noise.

Behind him, Tina let out a cry. He turned, his hand still on the door handle, and expected to see her right behind him reaching for his throat.

But Tina was still squirming in her bed. No doubt the cry had been due to her spiking temperatures. He pushed open the door and almost fell inside the dark room. Grabbing a lit lantern from the nearby shelf, he walked into the small room and slapped a hand over his nose when the stench hit him.

He whirled and gagged, clutching his stomach as the only thing that came out was a thin string of saliva. He raised the lantern higher and saw a small hole in the ground, a rusted mug on the side and a large rusted metal bucket in the corner of the room.

He deduced this small room had once been a bathroom. He rushed out, still with a hand clamped around his mouth and nose, hoping he hadn't inhaled any toxins.

Closing the door, he gasped for breath. There was no water and since there was no waste matter anywhere, Aksh realized with horror that Tina hadn't eaten anything or excreted any waste for who knew how long.

He went over to her and thought that if he tested her, he wouldn't find a single morsel of food in her stomach.

Perhaps she ate animals, he told himself. There was still a chance that she would go out and feed on small animals that inhabited the woods.

Surveying the tiny room, he realized something else. Despite the cottage being in shambles, he had yet to see any vermin inside the house. There should have been flies or mosquitoes at least, he thought.

This wasn't comforting to him at all. If Tina hadn't reminded him of his oaths, he would have walked out right now.

No, he would help her. If she got healthier then she may be able to fight the demon who had a hold on her. He walked toward the window on the other side of the room, determined to do everything he could to help her. There was a tree branch sticking inside through the window that had large leaves. It had been raining a few hours ago and some of the water droplets still clung to the leaves. He started to pluck them out, intending to spray the droplets on Tina's hot forehead. Then he would go out in search of food or help, whichever opportunity came first.

There was a loud creak on the floorboards and he jumped. Turning, he saw the bed empty and the torn stained sheets on the floor.

He straightened, his heart pounding in his chest.

"T-Tina?" His voice was hardly a whisper.

The room was completely empty. The lantern in his hand went off and he dropped it. It rolled over and hit the legs of the bed where it rocked back and forth.

Aksh swallowed, looking at the ajar front door and wondering if Tina had walked out while he had been distracted. In her condition, she probably hadn't gotten very far.

He stepped forward when he saw a hand stick out from under the cot and grab the lantern.

Aksh almost screamed. He moved sideways, his hands skimming over the rough wood of the large cupboard. He had to get out, now!

Moving slowly, he stuck his back to the wall, and then the cupboard. As long as his back was to a surface, he ran little risk of being attacked from behind.

Another lantern flickered off and Aksh felt his harnessed scream clutch his throat. He heard soft laughter coming from under the bed.

Aksh put his hands on the sides of the cupboard. Just a few more steps and he would be outside.

The lantern rolled out of the bed again and he saw the glass had been broken on the side.

Aksh moved toward the door when the cupboard door creaked open. He froze, hearing his own heart pound in his ear. His eyes were fixated on the bed. He had to move fast and avoid being grabbed by the demon.

The cupboard door let out another long creak and Aksh turned his head slowly.

One of the cupboard doors was open and he saw a foot emerge.

He looked at the bed again, from where he still heard laughter, and then the cupboard.

Backing away slowly, he heard more creaking but not from the door. Bluish, swollen feet were now clearly visible from under the door of the cupboard.

He was a mere five feet from the door. Without another thought, Aksh sprang to his feet and ran when the front door slammed shut with such force that the walls rumbled.

"No!" He yelled. He tried prying open the door, but it wouldn't budge.

Behind him he heard more creaking on the wooden floorboards. Someone was behind him.

Cold sweat trickled down the back of his neck. It was only simple voluntary curiosity that made him turn.

When he saw two women in white, with glowing eyes standing behind him, Aksh screamed as loud as his lungs would allow.

The two women tilted their heads and grinned as Aksh's blood ran cold.

"Who are you?" He screamed, panic and terror clawing at his throat.

"Welcome to our house," The two women said in unison.

Chapter Twelve

*H*er first thought when she was falling was that she was going to die. The two monsters on her side still had her in their grasp and they were whispering something in her ear that she couldn't register.

Her next thought was that time must have slowed down for her because there was still that suspenseful wait for making impact with something hard that would crush all her bones.

"Don't come back!" The whisper loudened and Preeti snapped her eyes open.

There was only blackness around her. She could still feel the arms of her captors singeing her skin, but she couldn't see their grotesque faces.

There was nothing beneath her feet either and, for a few minutes, she felt herself floating in a stagnant medium.

Then, without warning she was pulled down again. She was falling, faster than before.

I'm going to die! I'm going to die!

She looked up and saw a face peering through the dark squishy wall. She raised her palm and touched before her, feeling the black jelly wobble between her fingers. Instantly she was reminded of a dream she had once where she had fallen down an elevator shaft.

I'm in my nightmare!

As she fell, she saw a smudge of light that was someone's face.

Abhi, she recognized instinctively. The man she had loved once had now become part of her never-ending nightmare where there was no redemption and no escape.

Her flailing hands tried to grab onto something; even the black squishy material that posed as a wall around her, but her fingers wouldn't grasp anything.

"Don't come back into the woods!" The woman screeched in her ear.

Preeti let out her own scream, subconsciously aware that there were other sounds around her. A wail of a wild animal, the hypnotizing melody of a song and the thump and creak that was unrecognizable.

Preeti felt a whoosh of air and fell hard on something cool and metallic. But she didn't stay there for long. She rolled down a small slope and toppled onto a cold wet surface.

"Aaahowww." Preeti could only cry. She clutched her arm and writhed on the ground. Opening her eyes she saw blood all over her skin.

She got up, with tears streaming down her face and a scream still in her throat.

Twin lights came on and Preeti crawled away in fright and then blinked when her brain registered that she was staring at a vehicle—a SUV—the one she and her friends had been traveling in before...

"Before what? What happened?" She asked aloud and received no answer.

Getting up with a hand still clutched on her arm to stop the bleeding, she then walked to the side of the car, hoping like crazy that her friends were inside.

When she saw the side doors ajar and no one inside, her heart sank and she burst into loud sobs.

She was in the middle of the road, all alone and no idea what was going on.

Her phone!

Before, when she had her phone in her hands, something bizarre had happened and she had dropped it in the car.

She got in and started to feel for her phone on the carpeted floor.

Her panic rose when her hands didn't feel anything solid. She remembered how she had seen her friends' phones in the car as well, but she realized now that had just been a cruel and confusing trick played on her by the spirits or demons of whatever they were.

She straightened, caught her breath and looked out the window to see a movement in the trees. Preeti gasped when the two figures she had encountered before, emerged from the trees. They were holding hands and staring in her direction with their blank white eyes and ink-blue faces. Their white gowns, swayed in the wind.

Preeti put a hand on her mouth to stop herself from screaming.

Just then a phone rang and Preeti pushed herself back so suddenly that she almost fell out. She saw her cellphone lighting up on the floor she had just checked. Closing the car door, she quickly locked all of the doors, trying not to look out at the two figures standing at the apex of the woods.

She picked up the phone and saw Abhi's name flashing.

"Hello?" She said picking up. "Abhi? I'm... I need help!" The tears were running down her face and her voice was shaking with fear.

When she didn't hear his voice, she wiped her tears and cleared her throat.

"Abhi? Please. I need help. My friends... we were in an accident."

"You bitch!" Abhi screamed at her. "I hope you die in the woods!"

The phone dropped from her hands and landed on the floor with a thud.

Preeti let out a sob, staring at her phone. With trembling lips and hands, she picked it up again and saw the screen still on, displaying a 'No Signal' sign.

Had it been real? Preeti stared at the phone, expecting it to start ringing again when she heard a knock on the window.

She looked up to see the two faces staring at her. Preeti screamed as the woman's coarse brownish-grey hair was brushed from her face to reveal a blue veiny face. The white glowing eyes seemed to be pulling her in while her long curly fingers tapped on the glass.

Preeti pulled herself further into the corner of the seat as the faces of the couple tilted, watching her with unblinking eyes.

"Go away!" Preeti sobbed. "Leave me alone!"

She brought her knees up and put her arms around them, then put her head down and kept screaming until her lungs felt hot and her breaths felt weighed down.

The tapping on the glass continued and Preeti was sure she would go crazy if it didn't stop soon.

"Help!" Preeti had looked up and saw that the two ghosts were gone. The tapping too had stopped and she put her legs down, taking deep breaths as she did so.

She crawled to the window on the other side and peered out. All she saw was the empty road and the swaying of trees on the other side of the road.

She let out a small sound when she saw the ghost couple walk hand in hand back into the woods.

They were gazing at each other as if nothing and no one else mattered.

Preeti leaned back in her seat, relieved for a few seconds before she was struck with her dilemma again. Her phone wasn't working, her friends had disappeared and she had no idea how to get out of this place.

She looked ahead to see that the key wasn't in the ignition and wasn't surprised. This eerie place was a trap. Nothing was real and she would have to find a way to escape without encountering the ghost couple again. She looked out the window at the woods and saw no one there. Looking down at the wet road, she saw wet mud smeared on the surface.

She was about to pull back when her eyes noticed something else.

In the smears of the mud, she just about made footprints- several of them.

Unlocking the door, she breathed deeply before she opened it and stepped out. Her hand still clutched the door handle as a safety measure when she bent down to study the foot prints.

She followed the prints and saw them entering the woods.

Do ghosts leave footprints? She wondered.

Gulping, she took another step forward and looked towards the woods. Still no movement and still no ghosts.

She knelt and saw there were five pairs of footprints of people who had walked in a horizontal line towards the woods.

She placed one foot next to them and saw that the size and shape of her boots matched the prints. Next to it were those of heavy shoes, and then ones that belonged to sports shoes. She could just make out the brand of sports shoes that Dhiraj always wore.

Her hands left the door handle and she walked in a line, with her hand grazing over the cold metal surface of the car. Somehow feeling something under her hand made her feel safe.

At the end of the prints she saw the shape of a heeled footprint that she guessed belonged to Maya.

"We all walked into the woods?" She said in a daze. "Together?"

Her stomach clenched and Preeti fought hard not to vomit. Cold fear clutched at her throat as she saw the footprints leading to the woods and disappear beyond the trees where the ghosts had been standing.

If they had been together, why hadn't she seen any of them?

"Don't come back!" The ghosts' warning resounded in her ears and she leaned back on the car.

She had no intention of going back into the woods, but her friends... They were somewhere inside—lost and confused like she had been when she was inside. What if they were in trouble and needed her help?

Preeti put a hand on the side of her face and started to cry. She was scared, cold and alone with no idea what to do.

"What do I do?" She kept asking herself.

"I have to help them," She said with determination. There was nothing she could do here.

She took a step forward when the ghost couple reemerged. They tilted their heads, warning her with their lifeless eyes and menacing snarls.

"I have to," She said, realizing that her fear was diminishing with her unwavering resolve.

The couple turned around and walked back.

Preeti bit back on her sobs and clenched her hands. She took another step forward, expecting something terrible to happen. She looked back at the car, wishing she could just hide in there, but that wouldn't yield anything. She would still be here and her friends would still be missing.

Another step forward and the wind howled in her ears. Swallowing, she walked to the part where the road ended and the muddy path to the woods began.

"I have to do this," She said and took her first step into the woods.

Chapter Thirteen

There was a sound of a shovel being inserted into the ground and then dirt being tossed aside. It repeated again, over and over.

Dhiraj felt something land on his face, but he was unable to brush it off. He was aware his hands were by his sides, but for some reason he felt immobilized.

The sound of metal coming in contact with stiff mud was heard again. And then he felt something cold and dry land on his skin. Some of it even entered his nostrils, but again, he found himself paralyzed by something invisible.

At least open your eyes, he told himself.

His eyelids seemed glued shut and panic started to rise up his throat, hindering his breathing.

It was a nightmare that he couldn't wake himself from nor control his movements—and that was far worse than the horror that was beyond his closed eyelids.

Dhiraj started to gather all his energy, something he had trained himself to do just before he would see the finish line when he was racing against his father.

He would save up all his energy for those last few feet when his body would come in contact with the ribbon tied between two trees in the park.

Taking a deep breath and just about managing to clench his hands, he snapped his eyes open and saw the starry night sky above him.

There were a few wispy clouds floating in the inky sky but otherwise the full moon was clearly visible.

It was a peaceful, cold night and the breeze was refreshing rather than harsh.

Then he heard the sound of the shovel again and he pulled himself back to reality.

"Throw his body in here." He heard a hoarse commanding voice.

Dhiraj sat up and saw the criminals gather before a large tree just ten feet away from him. He touched his face and saw small clumps of dirt on his hand. Gazing up, he guessed that the breeze must have tossed some of the dirt on his face.

"Yes, sir." He heard one of the men say.

His body and mind became fully energized when he heard those words. He pushed himself back by his heels until his back was against the tree trunk.

The expectation of being dragged into the grave was growing within him until he was sure his heart would give out from sheer terror.

He couldn't keep his eyes away from the men as they stepped away from the grave and walked to the side. From behind a tree, they dragged an elongated cloth bundle that Dhiraj could at first not comprehend.

His vision was blurring from his heart pounding in his chest. He rubbed his eyes and felt wetness on his fingers. When he blinked and watched the men, he saw them carry the bundle by the knots on both ends and head back to the grave.

Dhiraj's eyes wouldn't leave the cloth bundle. It was a bluish-grey bed-sheet, with red flowers at the bottom, large enough to wrap a body in.

He blinked again, his fear subsiding when his mind registered that they weren't going to throw him in the grave.

Then terror crept back into his chest when he realized that those weren't red flower patterns on the bed-sheet but blood stains. It wasn't a bundle of clothes, he realized. It was a corpse wrapped in bedsheets!

He clamped a hand on his mouth to stop himself from screaming. The men were oblivious to his ordeal and went about their activities that seemed habitual to them. They swung the wrapped corpse over the grave then threw it inside.

Dhiraj heard a loud thump and he pushed himself back even more causing his back to be squished against the tree trunk. He had to move- he had to escape- but his legs felt numb.

Putting both his hands on his side, he picked himself up and moved to the side. Then sitting back again, he pushed himself further away, though his eyes were fixated on the five men standing around the tree. Two of them were shoveling earth back in the hole they had made.

He feared that once they were done with whoever's body they were disposing off, they would turn to him and-

Bury you alive!

This thought tore into the blanket of fear that was paralyzing him. He was up on his feet, his hands trembling with the adrenaline rushing through his body. Turning, he ran as fast as he could.

He was jolted when the image of the men standing before him returned. He had been running before too. His feet slowed but he didn't stop. His escape had been hindered when the men had appeared out of nowhere with grotesque faces. Then one of the—the leader had pointed a gun at him and—

Dhiraj stumbled and fell to the ground, clutching a hand to his chest where he thought he had felt the bullet pierce his skin.

He removed his hand and saw that his hand was covered in blood. Dhiraj put both hands on the ground, bent his head and vomited.

When it was over, he heaved, his mind reminding him that he didn't feel any pain in his chest. He touched his wound again and found that indeed there was no pain at all- only the blood.

"Where is he?" He heard the gruff voice of the leader.

Dhiraj scrambled to his feet, almost slipped over his own pool of vomit, then grabbed a branch to steady himself.

He started running again, even though he knew that the men would catch up to him like before. But he had to try. He just had to!

He turned his head and saw no one was chasing him yet. Pausing, he jogged on one spot, watching behind him, expecting the men to pursue him with weapons.

When there still wasn't any sign of them, he started running again and ran straight into someone. The force with which he hit someone's muscled chest, propelled him back and he fell on his back with a thud.

He howled in agony and writhed on the ground. He was caught!

A face appeared above him, but it was not one of them. His face was black and static, and his eyes glowing red. Dhiraj was certain it was just dark clouds forming on his vision before he would become unconscious, but when the apparition spoke, his heart turned into ice.

"You're not leaving so soon, are you?"

Dhiraj raised his neck, to see the figure standing before him. The static clouds were gradually taking shape until it took form of someone he was familiar with.

When he made out the form of the figure, Dhiraj let out a gasp.

"Sumit?"

His nemesis from his college days, gave a wide toothed grin, then in an instant, he had pounced and grabbed his leg.

Dhiraj screamed, certain Sumit's spirit had come to seek vengeance and would complete his task by ripping out his throat. Instead, the apparition caught hold of his right leg and started to drag him through the trees.

Chapter Fourteen

She wasn't breathing—not properly at least. The air would enter her windpipe but form a lump in her lungs that would slowly spread only seconds later. Another lump of air burned in her lungs before supplying her clenched body with oxygen. Her stomach was stiff and her limbs were numb.

When more air entered through her slightly open mouth, it didn't enter her lungs; rather it lodged in her throat where it constricted her muscles.

Maya opened her eyes and started to cough and fresh air entered her lungs. She could breathe again, but only barely.

Rolling over to her side, with her head raised, she was attacked by another bout of coughing that hurt her throat and chest.

Between coughs, she took in big gulps of air and felt her muscles relax and invigorate.

A hand patted her on her back and Maya stiffened. She looked down and saw the hem of a white chiffon dress. She turned to see the old woman look down upon her with concern.

Maya let out a small scream and dragged herself away. The old woman didn't seem perturbed by her reaction; instead she turned away and picked up her wide comb. Gathering her hair with one hand, she started to comb with the other while singing softly again.

In the moonlight, her tendrils looked like silver threads and Maya found herself being mesmerized by her long hair. It took her several seconds to register that the old woman had used her silver long hair to strangle her. And her face had turned...

In a stupor, she stared at the old woman whose face looked kind in the soft light of the moon.

"You tried to kill me." The words had left her mouth before she could stop herself.

The woman's hand paused as she combed her hair and so did her humming. She had heard her, yet when she resumed combing her hair, Maya realized the woman was ignoring her.

She pushed herself away from her, watching for any change in expression. The old woman had begun singing again, her voice so soft and comforting, as if she were singing a lullaby to a child.

Maya's eyelids grew heavier and she fought hard to not be drawn back in. A voice was awakening in her mind, telling her about going back to the old woman and fall asleep in her lap. She would never have her mother's love, but she could have this—a dreamless night's sleep free from all her troubles. The voice egged her on, telling her to stop thinking of ever escaping these woods.

"Don't go," The wind whispered in her ear.

"No," Maya told herself and then again, firmly.

This was all a mirage of lies, a trick to hold her back.

She forced herself to remember how grotesque the old woman's face had become and how she had tried to strangle her with her silvery hair.

Her limbs gathered up all her energy and made her stand up. She had to run as fast as she could, but something was still holding her back.

The old woman seemed not to have noticed her predicament or her movements since she had veiled the side of her face with her own hair.

Maya stepped back as soft-footed as she could manage. She cursed her heels and wished she had worn something more practical like sneakers. Raising one leg, she used her hands to unstrap her heels. Her fingers deftly unbuckled and pulled off the shoe and she repeated this with the other.

With her heels in her hands, she gazed at the woman who remained oblivious of her movements and her plans to escape.

She took another step back, wincing as the soles of her feet scraped against a thorn. Taking a deep breath, she whirled and began running when she heard a voice.

"Don't leave me." The voice was familiar and Maya immediately stopped in her tracks.

She looked at the old woman and saw her with despair in her eyes.

"Please don't leave me here alone." The old woman begged.

Maya blinked at the old woman whose voice was now that of her mother's. For a fleeting second her face had morphed into her mother's as well.

She raised up her hand, beckoning her and Maya could do nothing but stare with utter disbelief.

"You're not my mother," She managed through numb lips. The energy had been zapped out of her limbs again and she was standing only because she was incapable of any other movement.

"No, but I can give you a mother's love," The old woman said sadly. "I used to have children, two of them. A son and a daughter. I loved them so much."

"Wh-what happened to them?" Maya asked.

"They wanted to leave me." Her tone had changed though it still sounded like her mother's voice. She turned so that she was now standing face to face with her. "So I killed them."

Maya felt a cold shiver run down her chest to her stomach. The woman's eyes were no longer kind. It had darkened into a well of madness and a wide grin appeared on her face.

Maya gasped and stepped back, but still couldn't make herself escape this place.

The old woman raised one pointed finger up at the sky. "Until I bring their souls back with me. They won't let me in."

"Who won't let you in?"

"They." The old woman tilted her head, her silver hair swaying as the cold breeze of the night brushed against them.

"But I can't find them." The old woman put both hands on her head and then straightened when her eyes fixed on her. "You're here."

"I'm not your daughter," Maya replied, finding her voice.

The old woman appeared dejected. "I know. But then how do I leave this place?"

The old woman waved her hand around their surroundings. "I don't want to be here any longer."

"Please don't kill me!" Maya sobbed. "Please..."

The old woman gave a kind smile. She stepped closer and put one of her taloned hand on her head, smoothing he hair.

"It's not you. I thought you were. It's one of your friends."

"What?" Maya asked, rattled by her words. She wanted to pull away but was afraid she may anger the mad woman.

"One of your friends will die tonight," She continued, speaking to her as if she were soothing a crying child. "It's not you."

"Who's going to die, and how do you know? Please don't kill them!" Maya rambled.

The old woman turned away, her silver hair swayed in the gentle breeze.

"Someone will die tonight."

Maya saw the woman stretch out her arm. "It's a message rushing through my veins. One of them will meet their demise tonight."

"I have to find my friends," Maya said, more to herself.

The old woman stiffened. "I can feel it now. They are close."

"What? Who?" Maya wanted to grab the woman and shake her until she revealed more, but the image of being strangled by silver hair returned and she paused.

"The one who's going to die," The old woman said, her voice devoid of emotion. She dropped her shoulders and bent her legs. When she turned with her clawed hands before her, Maya was reminded of a wild animal getting ready to charge and pounce on its victim.

The old woman's face morphed into a demon's. Her purplish skin looked wrinkled and stretched, while her eyes had turned into a fiery red glow. She opened her mouth and saw pointed needles instead of teeth.

Maya fell on the ground at the sight of such a demonic person. He heart turned cold and she held her breath when the creature before her opened her mouth.

Maya uttered a shrill scream and found herself being swept back by an invisible force. She struck a tree and hit her back on a rock, but was too frightened to feel the pain or the wetness of blood pouring down her back.

Her eyes searched for the demonic creature and found her walking with hoofed feet towards a grove.

"Don't kill..." Maya tried to say, but the creature didn't hear her.

With the last of her strength, Maya opened her mouth and screamed.

"Run! She's coming after you! She'll kill you!"

The demonic creature turned its head to look at her and then gave a low hoarse chuckle before going in search of its victim.

Chapter Fifteen

Rudra felt a harsh jolt and then something small and cold fall on top of his head. He looked up, putting his palms out, expecting drops of rain. Instead, he saw drops of blood fall onto his fingers and stream down to his palm.

His mouth opened to scream when all of a sudden he found himself standing in front of a large birch tree. He blinked and then looked down at his hands again only to see water splash in his open palms. Looking up he saw pinkish rain clouds above him, parting just a little bit to allow a lone star peek through.

More rain fell and he felt a cold shiver run down his spine.

Rudra turned, finding himself surrounded by thorny hedges and vines twirled around the large tree.

He put a hand to his forehead. Had he been dreaming it all?

The row of hedges—had he imagined them to be chairs and tables at a nightclub? The pole where he had seen Nisha dance around, had that only been a tree?

He looked down at himself and saw a large splotch of blood on his shirt. He touched his ribs gingerly, wincing at the expectation of feeling excruciating pain, but when his touch didn't yield any pain, he grew even more confused.

A scratching sound caught his attention and he followed it to the large tree where he saw someone crouching by the roots poking through the firm ground. Through the blanket of torrents, he saw that it was a woman with long dark hair, dressed in red.

Rudra rushed to her and put his hand on her clammy bare shoulder.

"Nisha?"

The woman turned but, Rudra could feel his heart stop. Instead of the alluring face of the woman he had seen moments ago, he found himself staring at the grotesque face of a blackened creature with a snout and a ribbon of pink tongue. Her skin was dotted with brown spots and green streaks that looked like mold. But what was far worse was the malodor.

Rudra doubled over and gagged, clutching his stomach as the stench grew bolder.

"Leave me alone!" The creature warned.

"This isn't you!" Rudra managed to say while trying to keep his nausea down. "Nisha... you were telling me something about my friends."

"My baby!" She howled and resumed scratching at the ground with her clawed fingers. The nails were sharp and yellow and when they struck a rock, he heard a screech that made him feel faint.

Putting his hands to his ears, he staggered towards her. "Nisha... you don't have a baby."

The creature would not listen to him. She dug with her nails as fast as she could and Rudra could just about make out white bone in the small hole.

Straightening, he realized what she was doing. "You were buried here."

"He killed my baby!" She wailed.

As disgusted as he was by her appearance and smell, Rudra went to her and put his arm around her slimy shoulder. "He was never born." The cold rain was coming down harder, making it harder to breathe as it fell on his head. He wiped his face and saw Nisha crying.

Taking deep breaths, he put his other arm around her and brought her close to him. Nisha cried in his arms and after a while, Rudra was aware that her skin no longer felt slimy and the stench too had lessened. Looking down at her, he saw her resume her human appearance.

She clutched the front of his shirt in her now human fingers and slowly her sobs turned into sniffles. He kept patting her back and contemplated going further under the tree to shelter themselves from the pouring rain.

Nisha stiffened in his arms suddenly and raised her head. Though she had turned into her human form, her nose turned pointed and her nostrils flared.

She took a deep breath and flattened her palms on his chest, then pushed.

"Oh..." Her eyes grew frightened as she took another deep breath.

"What's wrong?" He asked. Nisha ignored him and pulled away.

She got on her feet and turned all around her in a circle, sniffing at every turn.

"She's here," She said, her voice so soft that Rudra couldn't hear her over the sound of rain drops splattering on the rocks around the tree.

"Nisha? What's wrong?" He asked, getting up.

"The foreteller of death." Her voice was still barely audible, but Rudra caught the fear etched in her tone.

Nisha backed away, her eyes darting from one spot to another.

Rudra caught her by the shoulders and shook her. "Who? Who are you afraid of?"

"She's the one who lives here, in the woods," Nisha explained. "If she screams then that means..."

Suddenly she put her hands over her ears and bent over as if she were in dire pain.

"Nisha!" Rudra tried to grab her again but she was writhing and when he came closer, she pushed him away with such force that he was thrown against the large tree.

When he recovered, he clutched at his right arm and winced. He pulled himself to a sitting position and looked for Nisha. She had been right in front of him, but now there was no trace of her and he started to feel panic rise to his chest.

"Nisha!" He called, trying to get up on his feet, then stumbled as his leg screamed in agony. Clutching his leg, he supported himself with a protruding tree branch and straightened.

"Nisha, where are you?"

He received no answer and was reminded by how silent the woods were, except for the rain that was now slowing down. Ever since he had come here, it had been only Nisha and him—no birds, crickets or wild animals.

It was so quiet that he was sure that he would go crazy if he didn't find his only companion in the woods.

Clutching the tree branch still to support himself, he realized he had no idea what to do. Nisha had clearly heard something or someone, but who?

The rain slowed down further but he remained under the shelter of the tree, deciding his next plan of action. He felt a drop of warm liquid at the back of his neck and jumped. With his other hand, he used it to wipe away the droplet and was stunned when he brought his hand forward.

His breath caught in his throat as he saw that it was blood that was smeared on his fingers.

It was then that he was aware that his other hand was no longer clutching the rough surface of wood but something wet and smooth and when he traced his hands down he felt something rough like a broken plate.

Rudra turned his head around and gasped. Above him was the corpse of a woman hanging by the neck. He staggered back and saw to his horror, more corpses hanging from the tree branches. There were young men and women hanging by their necks and their faces were blackened.

Rudra wanted to scream but his chest had tightened too much to let even a breath in.

More droplets fell on him and he saw that they were all blood. He stared at the corpses and saw blood streaming down from their hands and feet.

Rudra forced his feet to move further back but when he saw the corpses move, his heart skipped a beat.

All of a sudden the corpses snapped their eyes open and turned their heads to watch him. Rudra could hear the clicking sounds of their eyes as they blinked and the creaking of their necks.

Rudra put his hands on his head and screamed, certain that he had gone crazy or was about to. He was still screaming while he was walking backwards, unable to tear his eyes away from the glowing whites of their eyes. Their limbs moved furiously and he imagined them tearing themselves from their binds and pouncing on him.

Rudra let out another panicked scream when one of the corpses fell on the ground.

Everything was still for a moment. The quietness of the woods had returned and with it the eerie sensation that he was not alone.

Then he heard a shrill woman's scream.

Chapter Sixteen

The two women started to walk around the small room, sorting out items only visible to them. Aksh saw one of them bend down to pick an invisible object and put it on top of a shelf that was hanging by rusted nails. The other woman closed the cupboard from which she had emerged and then opened it again, making hand gestures as if she were folding clothes and then stacking them in the shelves inside.

He watched the two women continue their absurd household chores and felt some of his fear lessening and replaced by curiosity.

The two women looked like twins. They had the same length of bushy brown hair, almond-shaped eyes, small pointed nose and thin lips. They were dressed the same too, in pristine white flowing night gowns. He looked down and swallowed through the lump lodged in his throat. Their feet were blackish, streaked with what looked like wet mud and turned backwards.

There were horror stories he had read as a child about witches who could be identified by their feet, which was always turned backwards and had spent many nights terrified by the dark tales, until his childish imagination had been confronted by his adult logic. Witches with feet turned backwards, did not exist.

Yet here he was, in the presence of two of them. One of the women walked over to the kitchen and brought out a broom—an unbroken one that looked new. Aksh looked around the room and let out a small gasp when he saw the interiors had changed. There were paintings of women dancing by the lake, hanging on the wall. Striped blue cotton curtains hanging by the windows and a plant on the sill. The bed beside it was no longer broken, but covered in a blue flower patterned sheets. There were two pillows and a cushion in between them with the same pattern.

The cracks on the walls had disappeared and he saw a bench next to the wall that was adorned with a red striped sheet with tassels. The cupboard was clean and as one of the women finished her invisible chore, he saw clean clothes folded properly and organized inside.

All women's clothes, Aksh noticed.

The room now looked comfortable, as if it had been lovingly taken care of. The two women continued dusting imaginary dirt from the floor, oblivious to him for the time being at least.

Then one of them dropped her broom suddenly and walked into the kitchen. Aksh clutched the chair in the corner, surprised that although it looked newly polished, his hand felt the roughness of wood and he winced when a splinter pierced his skin.

He heard the clang of steel utensils being moved around and grew even more frightened. There had been no utensils in the kitchen when he had surveyed it and definitely no food. Yet the delicious aroma of rice permeated the air.

The other woman carried both brooms into the kitchen and then entered the other room where he saw steel buckets and soaps.

"I'll join you soon," She said in an affable manner, without looking at him.

Aksh eyed the exit again, contemplating trying to escape again. What if the door didn't open and his struggle with the locks caught the women's attention?

He had to try nevertheless.

Creeping forward, he kept his eyes at the doors of the two rooms from where he heard sounds of cooking in one and the gush of water running through the other.

His hand had just clasped around the handle when he heard the woman call him.

"Dinner is served." She sounded jovial as if he were one of their usual guests.

He turned and stuck his back to the door. The other woman emerged from the bathroom with a towel in her hands. There was water dripping from it but not from her person.

"Sit." She smiled.

They have normal eyes, Aksh thought. Though their skin was still blackish-blue.

"Where is Tina?" He asked, no longer sure of whether she had escaped or kidnapped by these women again.

"I'll set the table," The other twin said. She hung her towel on an invisible hook and went into the kitchen where he heard more rummaging and sounds of utensils being tossed around.

"What have you done with her?" He persisted. His hands were still clasped on the door handle, trying to pry it open without letting them catch him.

The woman's smile dropped and her eyes grew angry. She lowered her head and glared at him with predatory eyes.

The other twin reemerged with steel plates and an unnerving smile.

"Sit," She instructed with unsmiling eyes.

Aksh had no choice but to comply.

He took a step forward and a small round dining table appeared right before him. The twins pulled out their chairs, sat and turned their plates face up. Aksh pulled out his own chair, lasciviously eyeing the array of dishes laid out before him. There was rice, vegetables, baked breads and fruits. All of it smelled delicious and his stomach grumbled with hunger. He sat down, turning over his own plate.

One of the twins handed him a bowl of steamed vegetables and he took it from her without a fuss and served himself. When he set the bowl down, he saw the twins staring at him.

"You are our guest. Please, eat first," They both said.

Aksh raised his spoon and paused. Everything about this was making little sense to him. He had been in the kitchen and there had been no food of utensils or any means of cooking. He couldn't imagine where the food must have come from and wondered if it was a mirage. This whole thing seemed like a nightmare from which he would never awake.

Aksh glanced sideways and still didn't find any sign of Tina.

"Go on," They both said again, their voices awakening terror in him.

He swallowed and put down his spoon, aware that what he felt in his hands didn't feel like steel, but something rougher and scaly.

"Why don't you both tell me something about yourselves," He said with a smile, hoping to sound pleasant. Maybe, he hoped, if he befriended them, they would let him go and even tell him where Tina was.

The twins looked at each other and their smiles fell. He was sure he had seen uncertainty in their eyes, but he couldn't be sure.

Then they turned back and he saw only dry amusement in their eyes.

"Why don't you tell us about yourself? Guests first," The one on the left said. The right woman poked her twin playfully.

"He's a doctor. Right, Aksh?"

They knew his name but at this point he was no longer surprised by the strangeness of the situation.

"Yes," He replied. He wouldn't let them make him nervous and so he wasn't going to elaborate on anything.

Just single syllables, he told himself.

The twins seemed copious to his plan. They both leaned forward, their crossed arms on the table.

"We hear that you killed someone," They said together.

Aksh swallowed, but made sure not to drop his gaze even though his heart was beating wildly. Maybe like wild animals, they too would sense fear and attack him.

If he was sure about the food and water before him, he would have taken a sip of water to stall, but though the water in the steel glass looked clear, he could smell the stench of sewage reeking from it.

"No." That was all he would say.

"That's not what we heard." Their voices together was too inhuman. "What was his name again?"

Aksh grabbed the edge of the table, looking away and knowing he had lost in keeping his cool.

"Your turn," He said with confidence he didn't feel. "What are you both doing here in the woods?"

The twins looked each other with nervousness again but turned back to him with peeved expressions.

"This is our house."

"How old are you?"

The twins were getting angrier but they were too stubborn to let him see how much he was affecting them.

"Eighteen." Their voices was a rush of wind.

Keep going, he urged himself. Their change in demeanor was perhaps a way to defeat them because their uncertainty was surfacing into their faces. He was sure they were afraid of something but he couldn't imagine what it was about asking them these questions that was frightening them.

"Did you both run away from home? Where are your parents?" He asked in a steady voice.

"Our parents wanted to separate us by marrying us off," They said. "We had to run away and come live in the woods."

"How many years have you been living here?" He asked, keeping his gaze steady as well.

The girls looked up into space as if calculating something and then nodded. "Fifty years."

They opened their mouths to what he thought was to question him when he blurted another.

"What did you do with Tina? Where is she?"

The twins looked sad all of a sudden. "We were killed in this house. There was a don who had come to bury the body of his victims. He saw us and wanted to take advantage of us. We had to kill ourselves before he found us."

Aksh leaned back in his chair, stunned by the revelation.

"Our souls were trapped in the house for decades. Then Tina stumbled upon our cottage and when she entered, she couldn't play our game, so we punished her."

"You possessed her," Aksh said. For a minute he was sympathizing with the twins but when they revealed how they had taken control of Tina's body just because she lost a game, he went back to his earlier impression of them—these girls were psychotic.

"Where is she now?"

"She's here, right in this room."

Aksh looked all around him and slowly, the room started to take on its earlier worn out appearance. The walls turned grey and grew larger cracks than there had been before. Most of the furniture disappeared except for the broken cot and the cupboard. He looked down at the table and saw rotting food on the plate and brown murky water in his glass. Some of the lanterns went out too and he grabbed his own knee to stop himself from letting out a scream when he saw the spoon had just been a dead earthworm.

He heard a creak coming from the cupboard and turned, his breath caught. The girls were grinning at him and then the left one got up and went to the cupboard.

"Here she is," She said in a sweet melodic voice. She opened the cupboard door and let out a moan.

He had thought the girl had been folding invisible clothes and stacking them in the cupboard. Instead, it had been Tina's body that they had folded into the middle shelf. Tina was unconscious or dead, he couldn't tell. Her skin was blackish and there were veins sticking out of her face. By the way her legs were folded under her, he wondered if all her bones had been broken to be fit into that narrow shelf. Then his eyes moved up and he saw another girl's body stuffed into the top shelf and the rotting remains of two squished bodies in the bottom one. He stared at the two ribcages decaying and resisted the urge to cover his nose as the stench reached his nostrils.

The other twin joined her and they watched him with maniacal smiles.

"Now it's your turn to play," They said in one eerie voice.

"Guess our names and we will let you go."

Chapter Seventeen

She was walking for two minutes now, voluntarily into the woods. Preeti was tempted to turn back and walk to the car that seemed like the only real thing in her nightmare, but what would she do then. There was no way to get off the road and her friends were lost somewhere.

"Oh," She said in a small voice when she spotted the ghostly couple, standing under a tree, holding hands and watching her with a quiet warning. She was surprised to discover she wasn't even a tiny bit afraid of them. Deep inside she felt they didn't want to harm her, but perhaps that was a trickery of the mind as well.

She passed them, looking straight ahead at the maze of trees around her. Where would she find her friends in the darkness? She wondered if they were at least together.

When she saw the luminescent judgmental eyes of the couple again, she did jump. They were on her left, ten feet away, staring at her with eerie quietness.

"I'm not afraid of you," She said in a soft yet firm voice. "Go away!"

When she said that she was reminded of some of the myths she had read online once about how to get rid of ghosts in the house. In that article it had been mentioned that one must use a firm tone and command the ghosts to leave this place.

Preeti walked diligently ahead and when she didn't see the couple again, she grew hopeful that her ordering them to leave had worked.

She stopped near a tree, pausing to collect her thoughts. There were trees and shrubs everywhere, blocking her view of the stretch of woods. There had to be an easier way to search for her friends. Calling them was one of the solutions but the drawback was that there was a chance that the ghostly couple were not the only spirits wandering the woods. What if there were demons...?

Preeti shuddered realizing something she should have before. The woods were strangely quiet except the occasional whoosh of the wind through the tree branches. Apart from that, there were no hoots of owls or other birds, cries of wild animals or even the sound of crickets.

If a tree fell in the woods, would anyone hear it?

That had been a riddle she had been asked in school and the one she had answered no, because no one would be there to hear it. Now, standing in the middle of the woods, she amused herself by thinking that yes, she was here all alone to hear it.

A cold drop of liquid plopped on her head and ran down the back of her neck, chilling her. She used her hand to wipe it off and saw in the light of the moon that it was only water.

Gazing up, she saw droplets of water streaming down the large leaves of the tree, then falling. All she could see above were the tops of the trees and a small tear of the night sky. She looked down at her hands and wondered where the light was even coming from. Was it even the moon? Was it that bright?

A drop fell on her outstretched hands and she let out a surprised gasp. The droplet wasn't transparent but thick and red.

She looked up and saw drops of blood streaming down the leaves and stepped back in fear. Her back bumped against the trunk of a tree and she heard a sudden creaking sound above her.

She turned her neck slowly and screamed when she saw a pair of legs hanging. Looking up, she saw the body of a man with a noose around his neck. When she stepped back, his eyes suddenly opened and stared at her with glowing red eyes.

Preeti let out another scream and turned on her heels and ran. Behind her she heard more creaks and when she turned to look, she saw more bodies hanging from the tree. She felt a chill run through her at the sight and tripped over a protruding tree root.

Someone grabbed her shoulder and Preeti let out a scream that rumbled through her chest.

"Leave me!" She cried. "Let me go!"

She didn't see the face but whoever it was, grabbed her shoulders and shook her. He was saying something but Preeti couldn't hear it over her own screaming.

Finally, she felt a hand clamp down on her mouth.

"Preeti!" She heard.

She looked up and saw Rudra looking down at her. Her breath immediately slowed down to a normal pace and she pushed his hand away.

"Rudra?" She pushed herself into his arm and broke into sobs.

Rudra was stroking her back and saying something but she couldn't hear him over her own sobs. She was so relieved to have finally found someone and held onto him as she trembled.

"I was all alone and then the next minute I was in the woods and then these two... This couple... spirits, I don't know what, grabbed me and threw me off a cliff and I was back in the middle of the road. "

"Shh!" Rudra said. "It's okay. You're okay now."

But Preeti couldn't stop blubbering. "I was all alone and came back in and there was no sound and..."

"Wait, what?" Rudra took her face in his hands, wiping away her tears. "You came back into the woods? On purpose?"

Preeti took deep breaths to calm her stressed nerves. "Yes. They told me not to but I had to find you guys."

"There's a way out?" Rudra looked relieved all of a sudden and smiled at her. "How did you get out? Where is the exit? I've been roaming these woods for what feels like forever. Nisha said I had to find and help you guys."

"Nisha?" Preeti pulled back from him. "Your girlfriend?"

"What? No!" Rudra looked mortified. "She's a... Creature... A ghost of some kind." He shook himself. "Anyway she was helping me as well. Then she disappeared and I was all alone." His eyes softened as he wiped away another tear from her face. "But now I found you."

Preeti smiled at him and embraced him. "I was so scared. There's a tree back there, where..."

"There are corpses hanging," Rudra finished. "I know."

"We have to find the others," She said.

Rudra got up and helped her up. "I haven't seen anyone else. I thought I heard a shrill scream—a woman's—but in these woods nothing seems real."

"Oh?"

Rudra absently touched his stomach and Preeti saw a large stain of reddish-brown.

"Is that blood?" She asked, shocked.

"It was," Rudra answered. "I woke up here and had broken ribs... from the accident. Then Nisha found me and I was... Not hurt anymore."

"Who is she?"

"I'll tell you later. First tell me, from where did you get out?"

"What about the others?" She asked. The rain had stopped again and there were no sounds except for theirs, but she was glad that at least she wasn't alone.

"We'll get back on the road and call for help." Rudra was already walking.

"Wait! Nothing works." Preeti grabbed his hand. "The car is intact but doesn't move. The phones are fine but I couldn't place a call. That's why I came back here."

"There has to be a way," Rudra said. "Nisha said we were in some kind of purgatory and we still have a chance to escape from this. That must be it. You know how to get out from here."

"It didn't work Rudra," Preeti replied. Rudra was so excited at the prospect of leaving that he wasn't even listening to her. She wondered about the things he had seen and could understand his desire to escape, but what he didn't realize was that there was none. It was all a nightmarish trap that required a miracle to get out of.

"There is a way out," Rudra kept saying, as if trying to convince himself that things were going to be okay.

"We should look for the others," Preeti said in a meek voice.

Rudra looked at her and he must have seen how worried and scared she looked. He gave a tiny smile and nodded. "Okay. We'll look for the others but if we don't find them in half an hour, we'll go through the exit and find a way to help them outside the woods."

Preeti looked down at her watch. "Is yours working?" She asked. Her watch was stuck on two-fifty am.

Rudra looked at his watch and frowned. He tapped at the dial and shook his head. "No it stopped."

Preeti peeked over and put her wrist next to his. "Same time."

Rudra looked at the two watches but didn't say anything. "We'll find a way out of this. I promise."

Preeti felt so relieved at his words that she had tears in her eyes. "I know."

Rudra took her hand and they walked forward.

Chapter Eighteen

"Don't kill me!" Dhiraj screamed. "Let me go!"

Sumit's ghost had his long wispy fingers, coiled around his ankle and dragged him through a path between trees that was blanketed with thorns and pebbles. His back was being scratched and he sensed blood streaming down and wet his shirt as well as the waistband of his jeans. But what was frightening him was that although he could see Sumit tugging at his foot, he couldn't feel his touch.

Dhiraj saw the root of a banyan tree hanging and grabbed it.

"Please let me..."

Sumit turned with such ferocity that Dhiraj's breath was taken away.

He used his other wispy hand and put a finger to his lips.

"Shhhh." The voice emitted through his parted lips, sounded more like the hiss of a snake getting ready to strike with its venomous bite.

He felt something cold slithering in his hand and looked down to see a python climbing up his arm.

Dhiraj screamed and let go of his grip. Above him, Sumit let out a low chuckle and started to drag him by his leg again. Dhiraj scrambled to grab at anything, but his hands slipped over the soft earth. Then suddenly he felt something curl around his wrist. He screamed when he saw a skeletal hand shoot up from the ground and grab him. Another decayed hand shot up and grabbed his other wrist.

Sumit whipped around and growled. More hands shot up from the ground and Dhiraj heard the drone of inhumane cries. He felt more hands scratch against this back and legs and couldn't decide whether being held down by rotten hands was better than Sumit dragging him to a terrible fate.

The hands then started to pull him into the ground and Dhiraj screamed in terror.

"Help!" His mind was devoid of any other word but that.

Sumit took pleasure in his fright and let out a short demonic laugh. He reached down with his wispy hands grabbing his throat, and. Dhiraj found himself airborne as Sumit raised his arms.

"You're mine." The voice was not Sumit's, but deeper and ominous. He had heard something like that in the horror movies he had watched as a child where the devil had possessed such a terrifying tone.

"I'm sorry!" Dhiraj screeched. His heart was palpitating and his chest felt cold. He kicked with his legs but they went right through Sumit's wispy frame. "I didn't kill you, it wasn't me!"

Sumit's face grew amused and he tilted his head, his eyes turning white. Then he dropped him to the ground and bent his black flaming head.

"I'm going to drag you to hell," Sumit promised and let out a low chuckle. "You'll burn there with me."

His teeth became sharp and smeared with blood, while his jaw grew pointed.

Dhiraj clasped his hands together and bowed his head. "Please forgive me," He implored. "I don't want to die."

Sumit found only amusement in his pleas. "How do you know you're not already dead?"

Dhiraj looked up in shock, feeling the coolness of his own tears on his flushed skin. "What?"

"You were in an accident." Sumit reminded, straightening. "Welcome to your hell!"

Dhiraj started to quiver uncontrollably as it hit him. "B-but I survived. I d-didn't d-die!"

Sumit put his misty hand under his chin, as if coddling a small child. "Does this all look real to you? You're as good as dead."

Dhiraj pushed himself back with his hands. Then he realized what Sumit said. "I'm as good as dead?" He swallowed. "That means I'm not. Not yet, anyway."

Sumit looked peeved and his eyes grew fiery. "You will die tonight!"

"You're going to kill me?" Dhiraj sobbed.

Sumit smiled, his eyes returning to their original whiteness. This was exactly the effect he had desired from him. "We'll see won't we? Or maybe..."

Dhiraj saw a movement behind the trees and then four dark figures step out and head towards them.

"Maybe I'll let my uncle do it," Sumit finished and the four figures slowly became visible.

Dhiraj was certain his heart had stopped when the goons he had escaped from, made their appearance. The leader put his arm around Sumit in a brief hug.

"It's terrible that you had to join us in this way, nephew," He said. "But I promise, we will avenge your death."

"I didn't kill him!" Dhiraj screamed. "Please let me go!"

The demonic ghosts all started to laugh heartily, while Dhiraj cried, certain he was going mad, which in this case would be a blessing. At least then he wouldn't feel the pain of whatever these creatures were going to inflict on him.

The five figures suddenly stopped laughing and their faces grew grim. They appeared to be listening to something he couldn't hear.

"What was that?" Sumit asked and Dhiraj was sure he had heard terror in his voice. His mind couldn't grasp that these terrifying ghosts could be afraid of anything.

"We need to go. Now!" The uncle said. "Grab him!"

"No!" Dhiraj tried to fight off the smoky hands to no avail. They coiled around his wrist and started to drag him when Sumit let out a loud painful moan. Behind him, the uncle and his followers dropped to their knees, putting their hands over their ears.

Sumit too let go of him and fell to the ground beside him, howling in pain. Dhiraj saw his chance, scrambled to his feet and ran. He dodged the trees in his path and went under low branches. The only sounds he heard were of his heartbeat and his feet coming in contact with the gravelly ground. Turning his head, he could still make out Sumit, writhing in pain from a sound only the ghosts could hear. He turned straight and skidded to a complete halt when he saw a woman with long silver hair up ahead. She was dressed in white and standing sideways with her head bowed. Dhiraj panted, wondering if he should approach her when he felt something warm plop on the back of his neck. He looked up and another warm droplet fell on his face. He wiped at it with his hands and saw red streaks on his fingers.

He opened his mouth in surprise and then heard the creak of bones. Looking up, he saw the old woman turn her head. Her hands turned into sharp claws and her feet transformed into hooves. She no longer appeared human but half a beast. She looked at him and he saw her wrinkled skin was stretched over her face and she had red eyes.

Instead of a nose she had a snout and her mouth opened to reveal pointed needles and a snake-like tongue.

Then she let out a shrill scream and Dhiraj understood why the ghosts had been afraid.

Chapter Nineteen

Maya was wandering the forest aimlessly, waiting to hear at least one lone sound—especially the voices of her friends. But so far, apart from her own footsteps and whimpering, there was dead silence. She had worn her heels again and silently cursed them for not being able to carry her faster through these dreaded woods.

She saw a small space between two trees and wiped away her tears. Walking toward it, she decided that the best thing to do now was to go to sleep and hope that when she woke up in the morning, everything would make sense and she would find a way out of this place.

Yes, the sun's rays would dispel all the blackness of the woods and show her a path that would either lead her to her friends or get her back to the main road.

She got on her knees and peered inside the small space that looked like an alcove. It smelled dank and of rotted meat, but was otherwise empty. She crawled in and huddled inside, drawing her knees close to her chest. Wrapping her arms around them, she began to weep, wishing she wasn't all alone. Her foot struck something in the ground and she saw something sticking out. Using two fingers, she picked up the object and brought it close to her eyes.

In the dark all she could make out was that it was a cylindrical object that felt as tough as a...

The bone dropped from her fingers and she let out a cry. Using her heels, she kicked the bone away and began to cry again.

She hated this—being all alone and scared in the dark and wished she had her mother with her. Not that it would have made any difference, she thought wryly. Her mother wouldn't magically start caring for her just because she wanted her to.

For a second, Maya couldn't believe she missed the loving touch of the fiendish woman. It was the first time she had ever felt the touch of love and she shook herself from the absurdity of those thoughts.

Was she that desperate for a mother's love? The answer was always yes.

She wondered if her mother was even concerned about her daughter's whereabouts. She was probably out with another man, glad that her meddlesome daughter was out of the way.

She heard plinking sounds on the rock outside her little cave and saw that it had begun raining. In seconds it began to fall harder, forming puddles everywhere. She nestled inside, shivering as the cold wind blanketed her. It was getting so chilly that she wished she had worn something warm, instead of this ridiculous short skirt.

Some of the rainwater streamed inside and Maya noticed that it wasn't clear or even muddy. Rather it appeared thick and frothy, as the force of rain falling struck it. With tentative fingers, she touched the surface of the liquid and retracted her hand quickly when she felt the warm stickiness instead of the coldness of the ice water.

She moaned when her fingers showed her blood. Maya burst out crying, pushing herself back but finding there was no more space. Her back touched the cold wall of the arched space and she let out a frustrated cry.

"Help me!" She screamed. "Please get me out of here! Please!"

Her panic clutched mercilessly at her heart, making it harder for her to breathe. She fell sideways, still clutching her knees and cried when she felt the warm blood wet her face.

Maya tried to splash it away from her with one hand, but the blood rain kept coming down faster until she was sure she would drown in the blood puddle.

She crawled out, still crying and one of her heels got stuck in the wet bloody mud. Maya tried to pull away, but felt her left foot going deeper. She used her hands to raise her leg, but the imbalance caused her right foot to sink into the mud.

Standing still, she realized to her horror that she was slowly sinking.

This isn't mud! Her mind was screaming like a mad person and Maya could do nothing to shut it. The blood rain soaked into her clothes and streamed down her leg, making the surface beneath, even wetter and mushy.

Scream, she told herself but she had to shut even that logical voice. There was no one here to hear her.

A low growl sent a chill down her spine and she stiffened, certain that it was just her imagination. The blood rain was blanketing whatever was making that sound, but Maya knew there was a beast lurking nearby.

She held her breath, praying silently that it just be a trick of her tired mind.

It was then that she saw the red glowing eyes just ten feet away from her. Panic rushed through her veins and she started to struggle in the quicksand, only causing her to sink deeper.

The rain lessened considerably and she saw a dark beast step forward from the shadows of the trees. Her first impression of it being a mongrel was quickly dismissed when the beast advanced. It was four feet tall with black fur and silver streaks. Its snout was long and phosphorescent, and a mouth that revealed small knives for teeth. But what sent terror straight into Maya's heart were the flaming eyes of the beast that seemed to show her the depths of hell.

Maya tried to shake herself from these ominous thoughts and chided herself for imagining things. There was a possibility after all, that it was just an illusion.

Then the demonic creature stepped onto the quicksand and Maya let out a small cry. The beast's paws didn't sink and he walked easily over the surface, drawing closer to her, inch by inch.

"No..." Maya whined, trying to writhe away from the wet slimy grip of the quicksand.

The beast let out a grunt and Maya knew that regardless of what the old woman had told her, she was going to die tonight.

The rain was no longer blood, but clear warm water that did nothing to ease the terror she felt. She twisted and turned, to no avail, when suddenly her foot slipped out and she lost her balance.

Her arms flailing, she could do nothing as she fell backwards. Warm wetness swallowed her upper body and she started to suffocate as the quicksand splashed all over her. Above her, the beast pounced and she saw him jump over her.

Maya let out one final cry before she was engulfed in the slime.

Chapter Twenty

Rudra was telling her about his experiences in the woods and a girl he had met—Nisha, but Preeti was too distracted to pay full attention to his narration.

He was holding her hand as they walked and even helped her over a fallen tree that was blocking their path. She saw no obstacles and didn't even feel the cold. The rain was gone leaving behind a chill in the air and small puddles which Rudra navigated them around.

She didn't care how eerie the forest was or how quiet—just that she was no longer alone.

Her boyfriend Abhi had held her hands many times, but not once had she felt safe like she did just now. She knew that it wasn't the appropriate time to think about her relationships, but she wished she had never been with Abhi. Watching Rudra taking care of her right now, she thought back to the time he had proposed her and she had said no. If only she could go back in time, she would kick herself for rejecting his proposal, because now it was too late... Rudra was with someone else. He loved someone else and he cared about some girl whose name she didn't even want to know.

Tears sprang to her eyes and that was when Rudra turned.

"Hey, are you okay?" He asked.

Preeti blinked back her tears and feigned a small smile. "Yes."

"Where was the cliff?" He asked, dropping her hand.

Preeti felt disappointment but there was nothing she could say, could she? There was only so much she could ask from him as a friend.

"We need to find the others," She told him.

"I think we should revisit my idea. We could call for help."

Preeti shook her head. "Don't you think I tried? Nothing works. It's all like a weird illusion. Things are there, intact, but you can't do anything. I mean we were all in an accident and the car...it was there without a scratch."

She was finding it hard to breathe as panic weighed on her chest.

Rudra put a hand on her shoulder. "Breathe."

Preeti did exactly that and felt some of her composure returning. "You said that girl...Nisha, said that there was still a chance for your friends. Maybe, we all have to escape together."

"Maybe... but..."

"Trust me," Preeti said. "There is nothing we could do even if we were out of these woods."

"I trust you," He said, without blinking.

"We have to find them."

"How? Calling their names isn't helping."

Preeti looked all around her, seeing nothing but trees and bushes. Looking back, she half expected to see the tree with the hanging corpses behind her. When she didn't see it, she took another calming breath.

"How did we find each other?" She asked.

"I was there..." Rudra pointed behind them. "Near that tree where..."

"Yeah," Preeti interrupted, not wanting to hear words that would trigger a terrible memory. She wanted to forget those blank faces with white glowing eyes.

"And then you appeared," He said, looking thoughtful. "At first I couldn't see you properly because it was raining and thought it was Nisha. Then when I heard your voice, you can't imagine how relieved I was to have found you."

Preeti smiled at him, despite the circumstances surrounding them. "Me too." She said softly.

Rudra turned away quickly then, as if trying to hide something. He put a hand to his forehead and rubbed. "So that's how we find the others? Hoping we cross their paths by chance?"

"Maybe," She replied sullenly.

"We'll have to walk every inch of these woods," He said, frustrated. "And how do we know we didn't already? I've been walking around here for god knows how long."

"I followed a couple—they were ghosts. They led me to the cliff."

"Wait!" Rudra said, turning back to her. "Do you not know the way to the cliffs that could get us out?"

Preeti looked up far ahead and tried to remember the first time she had come in here. There were trees and more trees. She had been following the couple so keenly that she hadn't really noticed anything that stuck out and would bring her back to that same path.

"I don't know," She said. "We could go back. The couple was there near the entrance of the forest and they kept warning me to not enter."

Rudra threw up his hands in frustration and sat down on a tree stump. He dropped his head dejectedly and Preeti knelt beside him.

We'll be okay. There has to be a way out and find our friends," She said.

Rudra looked annoyed and said nothing. There was that silence again she hated, and one that sent fear running through her veins.

"We have to try." She decided that if he wouldn't speak, then she would. Anything was better than the frightening silence.

Rudra picked up a sharp rock and stood. He walked to a tree and started hitting the trunk with the pointed edge of the rock.

Some of the wood chipped off under his ministrations and Rudra backed up. "There. Now we'll know we're not going around in circles."

Preeti was following quietly behind him, lost in her thoughts no doubt. He walked over to another tree and chipped at the bark. He wished he had chalk or paint with him that would make his job easier. In the dim of the moonlight, the chipped bark wasn't that visible from afar, but something was better than nothing. He resumed walking, making sure he heard Preeti's footsteps behind him.

He walked up to another tree and chipped it, wishing he could think of a way to escape from these woods. So far he had seen no sign of his friends. He wanted to call out their names, but from what he had experienced, and so did Preeti, chances were they would attract some creature. Still, it was a better solution than walking aimlessly in the forest hoping they would chance upon their friends.

When he began walking and didn't hear Preeti behind him, he turned and saw that she was no longer with him.

"Preeti?" He panicked and was about to run in search of her when he saw he staring at a tree and its branches. He came to her and saw that her eyes looked glazed, as if she were in a trance. Her mouth was slightly open and she stood completely still.

Rudra put his hand on her shoulder and shook her. "Preeti?"

She turned slowly toward him. "I thought I heard someone call my name," She said in a numb voice.

Rudra looked up at the tree and saw a dark figure sitting on the branches. He clutched Preeti's shoulder and blinked. The figure disappeared instantly, leaving him wondering if perhaps he had imagined it all.

"There's no one here," He said, hoping his voice didn't belie the fright he felt.

"The voice was familiar. I thought it was one of them..." Preeti trailed off, looking dazed.

"You can't wander off like that," Rudra told her. He took her hand and led her away from the tree. "We have to stick together."

"Taking a chance are we?" A voice seemed to come out of nowhere. .

Rudra turned. "What?"

Preeti shrugged. "Hmm?"

"Did you hear that?"

Preeti looked scared. "No," She said in a tiny voice.

Rudra resumed walking, squeezing Preeti's hand.

"Now that Mahi isn't here, you have your chance with Preeti." The deep voice was now a whisper.

Rudra stopped, looking all around him. The voice was closer to him and for a second he had thought that it was his inner voice.

"What's wrong?" Preeti asked in a scared voice.

"Nothing," Rudra said. Preeti was already rattled by whatever was happening around here. He had to make sure not to scare her even more.

"Why search for your friends when you can spend your time wooing the love of your life," the voice said, again.

Rudra tried not responding to it or reacting, in case he frightened Preeti.

He felt a tug on his hand and saw her looking confused. "Aren't you going to mark the trees?"

"Yeah." He walked over to the nearest one and without letting go of her hand, he chipped the bark.

"This is the most time you can spend with her. Why go back home?"

The voice was annoying him to no end. Yet he thought it was better to ignore it. He felt a warm brush against his arm and turned, seeing no one except Preeti.

"What's going on?" She asked.

He had to tell her before he went mad. "I think..."

"Shhh!" The voice spoke up again. "If you tell her, I'll not make any of your wishes come true."

"What?" He asked.

"I didn't say anything," Preeti said with wide, frightened eyes.

"I can make her love you," The invisible being said. "She'll never leave your side."

The promise was enticing. He looked at Preeti, the girl he was so much in love with that he had regretted every moment he wasn't with her. But wasn't she with someone else?

"I'll make her boyfriend disappear." He was promised. "She'll only belong to you."

"Rudra, what's wrong?" Preeti asked.

"Just speak to me in your mind and I'll answer," The voice said.

"Nothing." He smiled at her reassuringly and began walking.

"Do we have a deal?"

Rudra squeezed Preeti's hand without knowing he had. He could have her and they could live happily ever after. The offer of everlasting love was too good to pass.

"We have a deal," He muttered.

"Did you say something?" Preeti asked.

Rudra smiled. "No."
"Then do exactly as I say," The invisible being said.

Chapter Twenty-One

"How could I possibly guess your names?" Aksh asked, unable to take his eyes away from the rotting flesh in the bottom shelf. Tina's body was still lying limp and until he checked her pulse he couldn't determine if she was still alive or not.

The twins were laughing as if he had just cracked a joke. They spoke again, in one voice that was evil and robotic. "It's the rule." They chuckled. "If you guess our names then we can't possess you. If you don't then we get another home and can walk out of this house."

Aksh looked out the window and saw the leafless branches and the gloom of the night. He would do anything to get out of these woods and this house but the task presented to him was impossible. They were already referring to his body as their 'home' and it terrified him more than anything ever had.

The twins were smiling at him, watching... waiting....

"How do I... I can't just... guess..."

"Didn't you say he was a doctor?" One of the twins asked the other.

The other tilted her head and put a finger on her lips, pretending to look thoughtful. "Hmm... He's supposed to be smart."

"I can't do this."

"Then you give up?" They asked.

Aksh's eyes darted around the room, looking for any words written anywhere. There were no pictures and no names that could provide him with a clue. He tried to remember if he had seen anything on the outside wall of the house, but at that time he had been distracted. He had been carrying Tina in his arms and thinking about the adulation he was going to receive when he brought her to her millionaire parents.

"I think he's giving us permission to enter him," One said.

"Looks like it." The other agreed. They took a step toward him and he backed away, almost knocking away a small table in the corner. He grabbed it with both hands, but the vase on it wobbled. Steadying it with his hands, he looked up to see the twins staring at him with impassive expressions.

"I need a hint," Aksh blurted. "It's only fair, otherwise you both are cheaters!"

The twins' faces contorted into a grimace and they let out a shriek. "We're not cheaters!"

Their screams were so forceful that Aksh found himself being propelled back and fall to the floor. He had never felt such fear and wished he had his friends with him. Dhiraj for one would try to protect him the way he had done all those years ago in college. He wondered what nightmare Dhiraj was battling and then chided himself for still being such a coward. He was a doctor now, about to settle down and he still hadn't found the courage to defend himself. Then how could he possibly defend his family?

Mustering up enough courage, he clenched his fists and cried. "Then let me go!"

The twins drew closer and bent, so that their faces were close to him. He could smell rotting eggs and burnt wood and up close he saw maggots squirm in their hair and necks.

"We are not going to let you go!"

Their words were acidic and Aksh nodded. "Then give me a clue," He said, pulling his chin up. His pulse was racing and he could hear his own heartbeat. He was certain that his face and ears must be bright red by now.

The twins straightened and looked at each other. "That seems fair, doesn't it?" Their voices together were still eerie to him and he wished they would stop speaking in a monotone.

While the twins seemed to be having a muted conversation with each other, he eyed the closed front door and estimated his much time it would take for him to reach it and flee this house. Then he estimated how much time it would take for the twins to catch him and punish him for trying to escape.

However, once he was out of the house, the twins could not follow him because they needed a vessel to travel out of the house that was keeping them like prisoners.

"We've reached a decision," They said and Aksh almost jumped out of his skin, scared that maybe they had read his thoughts.

The twins were smiling pleasantly as if they were going to speak in his favor. "The hint is this," They started together, then only one in the left continued.

"You know how twins are often named in rhyming words?"

The other nodded in agreement. "Yes, like Tina—Reena, Sita—Gita, etc?"

Aksh tried not to let his gaze return to the front door and decided to agree with whatever they would say.

"Well... our names are not like that."

"No, not at all. Our names don't rhyme at all."

Aksh swallowed. "Okay. Er... what else?"

The twins looked at each other, frowning. "We decided on one hint and we gave it to you."

"That's not a hint!" Aksh argued. "If your names rhymed I would have had some chance guess it. Now it could be anything in the world. There are so many names..."

"Shhh!" They said. "That is all you get."

Aksh swallowed. "I'll need at least a day..."

The twins snorted. "There are no days here," They said, looking at him as if he were crazy. "In the woods there's only a large stretch of time."

Aksh checked his watch and found it frozen on two-fifty a.m.

"But we'll give you some time to figure it out," One said.

"Yes, we're fair. While we clean up the dishes, you'll have ample time to think."

Both twins floated to the kitchen and Aksh let out a breath he wasn't aware he was holding. He kept his eyes on the twins as they threw the empty dishes and utensils into the sink. From his view he could see them opening taps and let the water run in the sink. He had checked those very faucets and knew there was no water running in them. Standing on tiptoes he saw rusted water spurt and the twins reach for a scrubber that had worms squirming in it. This didn't seem to faze the twins who attended to their chores as if they were still alive and all this was real.

Was it not?

When he had entered the house had been in shambles, but now with all the furniture intact and the fresh paint on walls, he wondered which one had been the illusion. He shook his head and sidestepped toward the door. The twins were singing in the kitchen as they cleaned. Their backs were toward him and he thought that if he was silent enough, he could make a break for it. He was now only inches away from the door. Just a few more steps and he would open it and rush out.

His eyes fell on Tina who was still stuffed into the shelf. The desire to survive this rather than come back as a hero was stronger. Giving her a silent apology, he placed his hands on the door handle and pulled. Turning, he was about to step forward when he came face to face with a brick wall. His hands felt the bricks but his mind was not ready to accept that his only escape was sealed. He pushed at the bricks certain that, like everything else, this too was a trick of his mind. But when the wall wouldn't budge, he felt his heart sink. Despair clung to his heart and he fought the tears that came to his eyes. He wanted to crumble to the floor and weep in frustration, but that would only amuse his hosts. Closing the door, he turned back and saw the twins were still singing. They hadn't noticed him, and for now that was a good thing. If they found out he had tried to escape, who knew what pain they would inflict on him.

He returned to the chair he had been sitting on and pulled it back. Paper... he would need a pen and some sheets to write down every possible name and then submit it to them. He would get their names wrong and then they would enter his body and after a while when they got bored, they would stuff him into one of the shelves.

"I have to try," He told himself, starting to cry.

The twins were oblivious to his inner struggles and kept singing their jovial song, drawing his attention to it. It was an unusual song, not from the movies or any of the lullabies he had heard as a child.

> *"No one will guess our name,*
> *For it isn't at all the same.*
> *He will get it all wrong,*
> *And then we will become strong.*
> *He'll never guess our true demeanor,*
> *Or that our names are Antara and Meena."*

Aksh could actually feel his heart stop. Had they just given out their names? He pushed back the chair and crept to the kitchen door. If the twins had any indication of him being behind them, they didn't show it.

They sang their song again except this time one twin sang one line, the other the next one. Aksh pushed his head further in, unable to believe they had just revealed their names. A smile spread on his lips and relief washed over him. He was going to be saved!

He opened his mouth to call them, when a small frail hand clamped over his mouth. He whipped around with wide eyes and saw Tina standing behind him, shaking her head. Aksh put a hand over hers, pulling it down. Her tiny frame was swaying and her skin was feverish; she could fall any second and the twins would hear her and heavens knew how they would react.

Taking her hand in his and putting his arm around her tiny waist, he led her to the bed and made her sit.

"You're alive," He said. "Don't worry, I'll get you out of here. I've learned their names! Now they have to let me go."

"No!" Tina gasped, her voice a hoarse whisper. "Don't say those names. It's a trick. Don't..." Tina fell on the bed and writhed as no doubt her fever spiked. "They're... they're tricking you..."

Aksh stood and felt a feathery touch on his shoulder.

"Are you ready?" The twins said.

Aksh cringed at their voices and turned slowly to far their ferocious faces and wicked smiles. He had to think fast.

"I'm ready."

"Good," They said. "Tell us our names."

"First..." Aksh put up his hands. "I have a condition!"

Chapter Twenty-Two

"Don't! Please don't kill me!" Dhiraj shrieked. The creature advanced toward him and he could smell the stench of rotten flesh, even from fifteen feet away.

He tried pushing himself back with his feet, but his limbs had become numb with fear. All around him there was nothing but the empty silence of the woods. He almost wished that Sumit's ghost was with him. After the creature had made an appearance, all the ghosts had crumbled to the ground and disappeared. They were frightened of it and this thought sent fresh panic to his chest.

In a few strides, the creature had crossed the distance and was now standing above him as he writhed on the ground. The creature's silver hair swayed as it walked on its heavy legs. In the moonlight, the entire lower body looked like it belonged to a horse while her claws looked like that of a vulture's. Her head was human, but grotesque—as if her skin was melted and then swirled together. Her long silver hair made him wonder if she was a woman.

The creature emitted another shrill sound and hot acidic saliva dripped onto the side of his neck.

"Let me go!" He screamed.

The creature seemed to be amused at his predicament and tilted its head. Before his eyes, he saw the silver hair lengthen until it reached to the hooves. Then it started to wrap around his feet and leg.

"What are you doing?"

The creature's tongue lashed out and lapped at his face. It felt hot and sticky. When the spiky tongue wormed into one of his nostrils, he cringed.

Looking down, he saw his upper legs were completely wrapped by silver hair and making its way further up. When it twirled around his waist, he screamed again, muttering please to dead ears. He was being cocooned with silver hair and he was unable to squirm away from the grasp.

When it curled around his neck and tightened, Dhiraj felt his breathing constricted and dark clouds entered his vision. The coarse hair wrapped around his mouth and then over his head, leaving his eyes free to see the horror in front of him. The creature pulled him closer and hissed.

"Now sleep."

The command was hypnotizing and his eyes grew heavier. He fought to remain conscious, but his whole body had given up trying to escape. Eventually his mind gave in with the realization he was going to die anyway tonight. If this creature hadn't arrived, Sumit and his uncle's ghost would have overpowered him.

His last thought, before he was swooped away into darkness, was that at least he hadn't died in the hands of his enemy's

***

The sun felt nice and warm on his skin and when he opened his eyes, he saw a sight he had been secretly pining for. Part of the sky was lighting up with yellows and oranges while the other was a magnificent blue with white streaks of clouds. Then he heard a divine sound—the chirping of birds and the flapping of their wings, as they flew from one tree to another.

Dhiraj rubbed his eyes and swung his legs over from his bed. The sight before him was to behold. Green trees, leaves appearing golden as the sunlight teased it and the sounds of water gushing somewhere afar. He couldn't see a water body from his position, but he was sure it was out there somewhere.

A pat on his back shook him from his trance. "Ready to go, Champ?"

He turned his head to see his father standing behind him. Dressed in white shorts and matching polo T-shirt, he looked ready for his morning jog. Coming before him, he began jogging on the spot, his grey curly hair bouncing on his head. He plucked a headband from the pocket of his shorts and wore it, tucking away every grey strand from his forehead.

Dhiraj looked down at his father's pristine white shoes and socks and his own dirt-smeared ones. How did his father always manage to look so... clean?

"Time is running out, Son," He said. "Come on."

Dhiraj didn't give another thought and stood. "Okay, Dad. I'm ready."

He started slow first, navigating himself carefully through the trees while his father ran uninterrupted and at a faster pace.

Dhiraj smiled. When he was younger, his father would beat him in their little race every time. In his adolescent years he had well managed to gather enough energy to beat his father, but after seeing the forlorn look on his face every time he did beat him, he had no choice but to lose intentionally just so he could see the triumphant smile in his father's face.

"You're losing," His father called.

"I wasn't aware we were running." He grinned and quickened his pace. He didn't really care about winning, but running felt good. He enjoyed the wind rushing past his ears making a whooshing sound and the way he felt a rush of excitement as he jumped over the obstacles in his path.

The trees were now a blur as he ran and when he looked up ahead, he saw his father was still quite ahead of him.

"You can't imagine how proud I am of you," His father was saying. "You qualifying for the finals has made your mom and me so happy."

Dhiraj smiled and looked down at his wrist wrapped in a white wrist band. He dare not tell his father about his injury... not yet...

Then he caught a movement in the blur of trees and skidded to a halt with such force that he could feel his feet squeeze in the front of his shoes.

It was surprisingly quiet in the middle of the woods. The birds were no longer singing their melodic songs and the wind had stilled. The blue sky was hidden behind the cluster of trees.

"Dad?" From the corner of his eye he spotted movement and turned, seeing no one. The only sounds now came from his own heart, pounding in his chest. Looking up ahead, his father was just a speck of white in the distance. Dhiraj started running again, as fast as he could.

"Dad!" He called. "Wait up." But the speck of white continued to move further away.

Then he saw someone come from behind a tree and jog past him. Dhiraj turned, his feet still moving, certain that all he had seen was a hallucination of his sleepy mind.

But what he saw wasn't an illusion. It was a boy, his age, dressed in dark blue track pants and a scarlet shirt. He turned as well and Dhiraj recognized him.

"Sumit?"

His nemesis smiled with rotting teeth and right before Dhiraj's eyes, his skin started to chip away and float in the stillness of the wind.

Then there was a gust of wind, pushing him back and Dhiraj found himself on his back and staring at a white ceiling with brightly lit tube-lights. The floor under him was linoleum and smelled like alcohol. Pulling himself up, he saw white walls and a flurry of activity in the room ahead.

Using the wall for support, he stood and walked slowly on the floor, hearing the squeaking sounds of his shoes as it made contact with the floor.

Amongst the crowd of people, his eyes went over to a short man with glasses standing in front of an ICU with a chart in his hands. A man came over to him and started yelling at the doctor while a stretcher was brought forward with a black body bag on it.

"You killed him!" The man screamed at the doctor, who had an impassive expression on his face.

Dhiraj blinked and found himself in a ward with a single bed in which Sumit was sitting. He was saying something to the doctor and when the voices became clearer he heard abuses spit out from Sumit's mouth.

The doctor was apparently trying to ignore him, but the way he was clenching his jaw and the tight grip on the pen as he wrote, Dhiraj could see the doctor lose patience.

The doctor turned to him then and he froze.

"I don't know what I'm doing here," He explained.

The man adjusted his long white coat and badge, then smiled. There was nothing kind about the smile, rather it felt evil and secretive.

He drew closer and whispered. "Now's our chance to make him pay."

Dhiraj looked down at the clip-on badge and saw Dr. Aksh printed on it.

"Aksh! Buddy! It's you!" Dhiraj felt relief wash over him.

Aksh seemed unperturbed by his excitement. He lowered his voice even more and Dhiraj had to bring himself closer. Aksh smelled of antiseptic and cough medicine.

"We shouldn't let go of this opportunity," He said.

"What are you talking about?"

Aksh grinned. "I have an idea on how we can kill him. No one will suspect us. I'll be accused of negligence but I can..." He picked up his chart and tore a sheet. "There. Now I can tell them that I never knew about his allergies."

Dhiraj gasped and in the next instant, he was back in the woods, but found himself standing on a tree branch. He swallowed and looked down to see a woman sitting right below and combing her incredibly long silver hair. She was dressed in a white dress that came up to her feet.

"Help!" Dhiraj called in a throaty gasp. That was when he realized that there was something strung around his neck. He clawed at it and managed to pluck out a strand of silver hair.

The woman looked up and let out a small cry. She had lines etched on her skin and milky eyes. Her lips were a pale pink and her teeth though yellow, were intact and pointed.

"Help me!" He gasped again.

The old woman stood and let her wrinkled hand curl around her silver hair. Then she yanked and Dhiraj was thrown to the ground, landing on the arm with his injured wrist. He screamed and writhed on the rough terrain as raw prickly pain swept over him.

Before he could clutch at his arm, something wrapped around his leg and dragged him forward.

The old woman used her hair to tug again and Dhiraj started to claw at his bind. He followed it and saw that the old woman had been using her long hair to hold him down.

"Let go of me!" He screamed.

The old woman gave him a toothy smile. Her milky white eyes turned glowing red and her face morphed into an animal's. Her white dress shriveled as did her body and he saw her legs turn into that of a horse's.

"It wasn't you," She said.

"What?"

The old woman looked disappointed and transformed back into her human form. "It's not you either. Perhaps it is him."

"I have no idea..."

"Shhh..." The old woman said, putting a pointy finger on her dry lips. "It's not you, but that doesn't mean you're innocent."

Before Dhiraj could utter another word, she whipped around, her white dress fluttering behind her. "I'll leave you to be punished now." She cackled and then vanished before his eyes.

There was complete silence again, getting thicker and thicker. Dhiraj rubbed his arm as the pain waned. He was all alone again, in the darkness.

There was a sound of a twig snapping under someone's feet and Dhiraj felt his heart grow cold.

"There you are," He heard Sumit's voice.

Dhiraj turned to see Sumit and his uncle emerge from behind the trees. They were followed by four other men and Dhiraj readied himself to run. He got up and was about to run, when Sumit came before him and put a hand on his chest.

"You're not going anywhere," He said. "We're not going to leave anything incomplete."

Chapter Twenty-Three

*T*he slime entered her mouth and nostrils, while the blanket of quicksand became heavier on her chest.

I'm dying....

Every little movement made her sink further and she had stopped breathing completely. Maya struck a hand through, feeling the cold night air, before that sensation too subsided as her arm sank.

There was no point struggling anymore.

I'm dying... I can't do anything about it.

At least she wasn't being mauled to death by that dark beast. This was a far easier death.

She heard a low growl and her heartbeat that had been slowing down, knocked in her chest.

Maya heard a loud bark and felt her slowly sinking hand, yanked hard until her head was jolted up. Then a flurry of white grabbed her by the front of her soaked blouse and threw her back.

Maya could see nothing much except blurry brown lines, but she could feel the thick hot breath of something near her throat before a powerful force propelled her backwards.

She let out a cry as she landed on a grassy patch.

I'm alive, I'm alive!

Then she opened her mouth and vomited all the wet sand she had consumed. Her breath came in a rush, overpowering her and making her feel dizzy. Supporting herself with her hands, she bowed her head and vomited again and again until her stomach clenched tight.

Then she rolled on her back and took long deep breaths while she wiped at her face with her hands. If she hasn't been where she was, she would have been mortified to let wet mud touch her soft skin. She hated the idea of mud baths and facials even though they were supposed to be beneficial in exfoliating the skin.

To her astonishment, she broke into loud sobs that trembled through her whole body. She had just survived a terrible ordeal and she was thinking of beauty treatments? This made her laugh and she clutched her stomach as every snicker made it cramp.

A loud growl tore into her mind ramblings and she sat up even though her muscles ached from the loss of oxygen they had suffered.

Sitting up, she had to wipe at her eyes some more to see a large creature with glowing orange eyes standing before her. Her first thought when she saw the bright white fur was that she was looking at a horse, but when she heard the low ominous growl again, her skin broke into goosebumps.

The creature was too large to be a wolf and he had too many pointed teeth to fit into that tiny mouth. She was reminded of shark teeth she had seen on a nature channel once.

With one hand, she dragged herself back. The creature stood still, watching her with its eyes that had fiery depths. She could feel herself being hypnotized by them, imagining that was what hell's eternal fire must look like.

Then she heard a ferocious roar and felt the hair on the back of her neck stand.

Turning to her right, she saw the black beast advance toward her with blood red eyes cutting the darkness of the night.

She was trapped! How could she have believed she was safe in this nightmare?

She huddled closer to a tree as the black beast crept towards her, emitting loud breathing sounds.

The white beast gave a roar of its own and Maya shrieked as it charged forward. When it leapt, Maya covered her face and cowered near the roots of the tree.

When she didn't feel the dreaded bite of the monsters, she peeked through two fingers and saw the two beasts rolling on the ground and snapping at the air with their sharp teeth. The black beast struggled fiercely, but the white beast was stronger and in minutes had the other pinned on the ground.

Maya expected to see the beast tear open throats, instead the white beast opened its mouth wide and let out a burst of air that seemed to subdue the black beast. There was more growling and it appeared that the beasts were conversing with each other through their growls.

Maya removed her hands from her face and watched the white beast leap off from its counterpart.

The black beast got up dejectedly and with its head bowed, followed the white beast away from her.

Maya couldn't believe the spectacle she had just experienced. The two large beasts were walking further away from her, sparing her life.

"I'm alive?" She said through numb trembling lips.

"They weren't going to kill you," A woman's voice spoke.

Maya gasped when the old woman made an appearance from behind a hedge.

Her mouth went dry as the old woman walked up to her carrying her silver hair like a drape behind her. Despite the murky ground, her silver hair remained untouched from all dirt as did her dress and feet.

"Don't kill me," She implored.

The old woman looked at her with pity. "I said I wouldn't kill you, child."

She sat down next to her and ran her fingers through the tangles of her hair. Maya wanted to pull herself away, but she knew better than to enrage a woman that could transform into a hideous and terrifying beast.

"Unless you come with me," The old woman said. "I see you as my child and if you come with me, I can find a place in heaven."

"You want me to kill myself?" Maya asked, aghast. The old woman gave her the kindest maternal smile, she had never seen on her own mother's face.

"I won't ask you to," She said. "Look how messy your hair is. Come, let me plait it."

"I don't like my hair plaited!" Maya blurted and bit down her lip. She had to be careful around this woman.

The old woman gave a small tinkling laugh. "It will bring forward your beautiful face. Now, turn a little."

Maya wasn't given a chance to comply. The old woman used her surprising strength to pick her up and turn her.

"There." The old woman brought out her comb and started combing Maya's hair. From the side, she could see all the slimy sand drip off her hair.

"Why didn't the beasts kill me?" She asked carefully.

"They're the beasts of the forest," The old woman replied. "The black one is malicious and evil. It only kills. The white beast makes sure that the black one doesn't kill innocents."

"Oh."

"That's why I won't kill you," The old woman said. "Even though you remind me of my children and it would be easier to claim my place in heaven for making amends to the terrible mistake I made."

"You said one of my friends was going to..." Maya took a deep breath. "Are you going to kill them?"

"Child," She replied in a kind consoling voice. "I don't decide who dies. I can feel who will and I must kill them as replacements for my children."

"Are my friends here?" The old woman had stopped combing and was parting her hair in three equal parts.

"Of course. Where else would they be?"

"Why haven't I seen them yet?" Maya asked, pushing herself forward so that she wouldn't have to feel the cold touch of the old woman as she plaited her hair.

"You'll see them when you're ready to." The old woman reached the end of her hair and Maya heard her plucking something. There were three pops before the woman resumed making her hair.

"Let me put flowers in your hair."

"No, don't! I" Maya cried out and then berated herself for acting like a child—the old woman's child.

"You look so pretty," The old woman said and put her plait on the side.

Maya peered into the old woman's eyes. They were like emeralds and she found herself trying to remember if they had been a different color before.

"Please let me and my friends go." Maya sniveled.

The old woman got up and caressed her head lovingly. Another gesture her own mother had never bestowed on her.

"Someone is going to die. I don't decide it. I just do what the wind tells me to do," She said in a honeyed voice.

Then the woman had gone and Maya blinked, turning all around her.

Had it been a dream?

She looked at her plait and stared at the flowers on her hair. They were brown and smelled putrid.

"Are these flowers?" She said to herself and then gasped when she saw them move. Worms!

The big fat worms squirmed in the knots of her hair and Maya jumped up and shook her plait until some of them flew out. One thick worm squirmed against her scalp. Using her fingers as forks, she pulled at it and tossed it away.

Then she let herself fall to the ground and let out a frustrated cry. She wanted to scream but the last thing she wanted was to attract the beasts back to her.

"What do I do?" She said, throwing up her hands. "I don't know what to do!"

She had to save her friends; the answer came to her loud and clear. There had to be a way to find them and get out of this godforsaken place.

"There has to be a way," She whispered.

Chapter Twenty-Four

The path through the forest was endless and the further Preeti looked, the more she felt discouraged. There were trees, hedges, ferns and rocks. Apart from that, there were no sounds to be heard except the weighing silence.

Rudra was walking a few steps ahead from her, apparently lost in his own thoughts. He had left behind quite a few trees unmarked and she had to make up for his absent-mindedness. She picked up a rock and started chipping away at the bark. A little dust flew out, but she had barely caused a dent in the wood. She sighed, feeling defeated and then her eyes fell on a vine lying by her feet. She picked it up and tugged, feeling the tautness of the green vine. She tied the vine around the trunk and pushed the rock under it. This would be her sign that they had passed this way.

She saw a few more vines lying on the ground and bent over to gather them. Rudra kept walking, oblivious to her activities and when she looked up, she felt fear dawn on her when she saw how far he had walked away from her.

"Rudra!" she screamed. "Rudra!"

He turned the second time and she saw the blank look on his face. Then it was replaced by confusion and fear. He made his way to her and smiled. "I don't know what happened."

Preeti handed him some of the vines and collected some more. "I was thinking we should use these as markings."

A vine twirled around her ankle and tugged suddenly. Preeti gasped and using her fingers broke it easily. "What the hell!"

"You probably stepped on a bunch of vines and got tangled," He said. His tone was listless, his eyes blank again.

"No, I was careful!"

"It's the forest and the darkness. You're letting your imagination run away with you."

"What?" Preeti asked in disbelief. "You saw what happened."

"I didn't see anything," Rudra said defensively. He appeared annoyed at her for complaining and she decided she might as well keep quiet rather than argue with the only person present at the moment - and to think she had started to think twice about Rudra. He was obviously distracted thinking about being in the arms of his lovely girlfriend.

"Let's move forward," She said angrily.

Rudra caught her hand and frowned. "I'm sorry. I just don't feel like myself."

"Neither do I," Preeti said. "Once we get out of this, everything will be okay. You promised we'll get out of this, remember?"

Rudra smiled and he looked like his old self again. "I did. Now let's walk. You're not tired I hope."

"Strangely, no," Preeti said, carrying the vines in her hands awkwardly. She wished she had large pockets or a bag to carry them. "I'm neither hungry nor thirsty either."

"Same here," Rudra said. "I don't mind sleeping though. I don't want to sit, I want to sleep. That's weird, right?"

Preeti walked over to a tree and tied a vine around it. "No, I get it. All I can think about is that when I get out of here, I want to find a nice bed and sleep on it forever."

"Not forever!" Rudra said, horrified. "Just for a day or something."

She laughed. "Yes, a day. Maybe two!"

Rudra helped her find a small rock to hang on the vine so that it looked like the tree was wearing a necklace. "Now we'll know for sure that we made these markings."

"My idea!" Preeti bragged. "So how long do you think it'll be before we find the others?"

He stopped suddenly, as if he was struck. The blank look on his face returned and he looked pale. "We have to go back," His voice sounded hollow.

"Are you okay?" She asked. "We are not going back. Only ahead to find the others."

"I have to find Nisha,"

"Why?"

He twirled on his feet and began walking back. "I have to find her."

"Rudra!" Preeti ran behind him. Suddenly he was walking at an alarmingly quick pace. "Stop!"

"The tree. She has to hang by the tree," He said.

"What are you talking about? What has come over you?"

"That's the only way I can repay." Rudra stopped so suddenly that she tripped on her own feet and fell hard on the ground.

"Repay?" She spat out the sand that had entered her mouth. "You're not making any sense."

"The tree. That's where she belongs," He said, deadpan.

Getting up, she stood before him. Rudra not only looked pale, but his skin was slowly turning blue. His lips turned dry and the skin of his face started to wrinkle.

"Rudra?" she asked in a soft voice. He stared at her with eyes devoid of any emotion, and then bent over and vomited all over her shoes.

Preeti screamed when she saw the blood spewing from his mouth and backed away only to trip again. She looked up and saw Rudra straighten then collapse on the ground beside her. His eyes were wide and his nostrils red and flared. His mouth was still open and a trickle of blood dripped on the ground.

She crawled over him and shook him. "Rudra! Rudra! Wake up! Please, get up!" She burst into tears when he didn't respond. "Don't leave me alone...."

She placed her hands on his chest and felt for his heartbeat. When she didn't feel it, her stomach clenched and she let out a loud scream.

"No! Rudra, please....don't die...don't..." She grabbed his cold blue hands and rubbed them, trying to bring him warmth. When he still didn't move, she shook him again. "Rudra, please!" She put her head on her chest and wept.

There was that nothingness again. This time it wasn't only the woods but Rudra's chest. There was no heartbeat, no sounds of his breathing. She had lost him, forever.

Collapsing into tears, she felt her own heart grow heavier. "I love you," She whispered. "Please don't leave me alone."

A cold firm hand grasped her wrist and she let out a shriek. She looked up to see Rudra staring at the small patch of night sky visible through the trees. Then he turned to her and smiled.

"Why are you crying?" he asked. "What happened?"

***

*H*e wasn't aware he had been sleeping. When he woke up, he found himself lying on the coarse ground with Preeti crying over him. Her tears had soaked through his shirt and her hands were clenched tight around his wrist.

Despite not wanting to lose her touch, Rudra let out a moan and tugged at her hands. Preeti understood and let go of him, apologizing profusely.

"You're alive!" she cried though a smile of relief spread on her face.

"I don't understand," He replied truthfully and sat up. "Were we sleeping?"

"No," Preeti said, wiping her face with both hands. "You just collapsed. Before that you threw up a lot of blood. A *lot* of blood."

Rudra blinked and then looked around him. He expected to see a puddle of blood beside him as per Preeti's statement, but he saw nothing but dry crumpled leaves and pebbles.

Not even animal droppings....

"I don't remember anything like that."

"You were talking about Nisha. The girl you met when you came in the forest; do you remember her." Preeti looked frightened and he wished he could console her, but he needed to know what had happened. "You said we had to go back and take Nisha to a tree. Then you vomited and died. I couldn't feel your heartbeat!"

Rudra swirled a tongue around his mouth, wetting it. His throat felt parched and even though there was nothing but his own spit to swallow, he did just that.

"I'm so thirsty all of a sudden," He said. "My throat...hurts..."

"Oh." Preeti moved away, helping him up. "I didn't see any lake or river."

"I'm so hungry... ravenous..." He felt his stomach throb mercilessly and keeled over when a cluster of cramps took over his body.

"Rudra!" Preeti screamed. "I don't know what to do!"

Then just like that, the pain vanished and he straightened, feeling a burst of energy along with the voice that had concealed itself.

"Now you know what I can do," It spoke in his mind. "If you don't comply with my demands, I can do far worse. I can make you kill Preeti with your own bare hands."

Rudra swallowed as his thirst diminished, so did his hunger. He didn't know Nisha as long as he did Preeti, but he felt he had a special connection with the former. Poor Nisha; it wasn't her fault that she had been cursed to roam these woods.

Then he remembered what was going on. He had been talking to Preeti when suddenly the voice had asked him to do a favor wherein he had to find Nisha and hang her by the tree. He had instantly refused; Nisha was his friend—even though their friendship was peculiar. The voice had threatened him and then he could feel unusual symptoms blanketing over him. At first his limbs had felt numb, even though their mobility wasn't affected. Then his own voice in his mind had been muted. Before he knew it, the strange voice had taken leadership of his body and soul.

Preeti had then said something that had snapped him out of his delirium and he had felt a surge of love fighting off the numb black feeling. That emotion had lost the fight as soon as he recalled his argument with his girlfriend Mahi. She had asked him if he had feelings for Preeti and though he had said nothing, he had to admit to himself that Preeti was with someone else; in love with someone else.

Everything had been a blur after that.

"Rudra?" Preeti was shaking his arm, but he hadn't felt a thing.

"Yeah, I'm fine!" he snapped at her. Preeti looked hurt, but backed away. "Let's find Nisha!"

"Why?"

"Because I said so!" Rudra then recalled something else. When he had been lying on the ground, hadn't Preeti said something? Something that had brought him to his senses.

"You said something," He said. "I can't remember what."

"What? When?" Preeti asked. "I was just asking why we need to find Nisha."

"You said something when I was asleep or unconscious or dead, whatever it was," Rudra said. "What was it?"

She frowned not understanding what he wanted to know. She pushed her hair back and shrugged. "I was scared you were dying."

He looked into her wide brown eyes and thought how beautiful she looked even in insufficient light. Her hair shimmered and her skin felt soft and he knew that when he touched it, he would never want to stop holding her in his arms.

"Why are you looking at me like that?" She asked, looking nervous.

"Never mind," He said, scolding himself for being unable to stop himself from loving her.

"I can make her boyfriend go away!" The eerie voice spoke. The more he listened to it, the more Rudra was convinced it belonged to an imp and he pictured a small beast-like creature with horns and dancing gleefully at being able to blackmail people and make them do ridiculous things.

"I just want her to be happy," He said inwardly. "If she's happy with Abhi, then I'm okay with that."

"See how beautiful she looks in the moonlight? Imagine seeing her every day and holding her and touching her and loving her. A pretty tempting offer, isn't it?"

Rudra pressed his lips together, trying to suppress a scream. The temptation was undeniably great. To know that Preeti would reciprocate his love forever was making him giddy with happiness. So what if it was a bit of magic that would create that love for him. Everything was fair in love and war and if he had to play a few tricks, or in this case do an imp a favor, he should just submit himself to it.

"You look pale," Preeti said. "You were all blue before. Maybe you should rest while I go find you some water to drink."

"I'm not thirsty anymore," He said, holding her hand.

She looked at him curiously but didn't say anything.

"Then, let's go find Nisha," The impish voice said.

"Wait," Rudra said. Then he turned and smiled at her. "Let me sit here for a while."

Nodding, she went over to a tree to tie a vine around it.

"I need proof you'll keep your end of the deal," Rudra told the voice in his head. "You may back away after I deliver Nisha. I need some collateral."

"I don't lie. I keep my promises." The voice sounded angry, but Rudra persisted.

"I don't know you therefore don't trust you."

The voice stayed quiet for a few minutes and then spoke so suddenly that Rudra jumped from his sitting position. "What do you want, as an advance?"

"Show me you can make Preeti love me," He replied. Preeti was tying the vine around a small rock. After she was done, she walked back to him, with a small smile on her face.

"Make her kiss me," He said, boldly.

He heard a disgruntled sound and then the impish voice replied with a sigh. "Fine."

Rudra heard a loud snap and then a whooshing sound in his ears. Preeti was standing right in front of him, a confused expression on her face. Then that was gone and replaced with a widening smile and soft eyes.

Rudra put a finger under her chin and drew her closer until their lips were just a breath away. Preeti gave him an encouraging smile and closed her eyes. Her lips touched his, delicately, and he felt a shiver run through him. He'd desired this very moment for years, and finally here it was.

Preeti pressed her lips harder, parting his lips so that she could deepen the kiss. Rudra let his hand fall on her shoulder and then her waist, pulling her even closer until their bodies were crushed together. He could distinctively hear her heartbeat and thought it was the most magnificent sound he'd ever heard.

There was a loud snap again and the voice spoke in his head with such suddenness, that Rudra felt disoriented.

"All right, that's enough."

Preeti pushed him away, a confused and angry look on her face. Then she raised her hand and slapped him hard.

The spell was broken and Rudra stared at her as she got up and regarded him with disgust, as if he had just betrayed her.

"Preeti…"

"I don't know what the hell happened here, but…" She was blushing and Rudra felt his guilt rising. He was using her after all, and taking advantage of the situation. Perhaps he shouldn't have.

"Now imagine, Preeti never waking up from her love spell," The impish voice said. "The spell will last forever. Even after death."

"I…"

"We had a deal!" the voice said. "You have two seconds to decide. If you don't I'll have you strangle her!"

"Wait…."

"One!"

"What do you want with Nisha? Why her?" He asked, his panic rising. Standing in front of him, Preeti was screaming at him, but he heard nothing except for the impish voice and his own heartbeat resonating throughout his body.

"Two!"

"Okay!" Rudra screamed out loud. "I'll do it!"

"Do what?" Preeti asked.

Rudra got up and grabbed her arms, close to tears. "Nothing!" he sobbed. "Just…help me find Nisha."

Chapter Twenty-Five

The twins shared an expressionless look with each other. Aksh had read somewhere that twins shared a telepathic bond in which sometimes one of them would automatically know what the other was thinking. There were also reportedly cases wherein twins claimed that they felt each other's pain, even though they were far apart, and didn't know of the other's injury.

There was no scientific proof to back their theories, but as he watched the two girls in front of him exchange vicious looks and raise eyebrows as if they were engaged in a heated silent discussion, he wondered if all those theories were true; or if it only worked if they were ghosts.

"*You* have a condition?" The girl on the right asked.

"What makes you think you are in a position to make demands?" The other said.

"It's not a demand," Aksh said, pushing up his glasses. He could feel a bead of sweat running down the side of his head, but he didn't make any attempt to wipe it off. At the moment, he could only feel fear rushing through his body, cramping his muscles and hindering his breathing until all he could manage was loud gasps.

"Let me take Tina with me," He said. "After I guess your names."

The twins chortled. "You can't take her with you."

"Yes, she belongs to us."

Aksh swallowed and threw Tina a look who had fallen unconscious again. "Then...then let me examine her." He thought quickly. "I'm a doctor. I can't see a sick person and not do anything. I have to make sure she's okay."

"Later," They said. "First tell us our names."

Aksh wiped the sweat from his brow and put his hands on his hips, hoping he looked intimidating even though he had a small frame. "No, now," He replied. "She may not have much time to live if I don't help her."

"Fine, go ahead," One of them said. The other twin slapped her arm and raised an eyebrow. The former shrugged and gave her a sly smile.

"I'll need some cold water," he said. "Oh, and those leaves." He pointed behind them. "I'll need them crushed into a paste."

"Those leaves?"

"Why would we do that?" The twins asked, looking at him as if he had gone mad. "What makes you think we'll help."

"Er…it's my condition. Then I'll guess your names," Aksh said, certain they weren't going to relent and badger him until he revealed their names.

They let out a puff of breath and turned around to go into the kitchen. The second they entered the other room, Aksh fell to his knees and shook Tina.

"Tina, Tina!" He said in a low voice. "Wake up. Tell me what you were going to say."

Her eyes flickered, but she was too weak to get up or even move. She let out a moan and Aksh was relieved to know that she hadn't died yet.

"Look, we don't have much time," He said. Turning, he saw the twins mumbling as they plucked the leaves from the tree branch that protruded through the kitchen window. Those leaves had no healing properties whatsoever and he could hardly identify them in the dim light. He could only hope the twins would be distracted enough not to notice that he had tricked them to buy himself some time.

Tina's eyes flickered open and she stared at him with hollow eyes. Her lips were chapped and her skin looked like it would chip away with a small breath of air. "Don't," she said in a raspy voice. "That's how they got me."

It was taking Tina every ounce of strength to talk and he hated at not being able to genuinely help her. Tina was far too gone to make it out of the woods, much less this house which was her prison. But he *could* help himself.

"How?" He asked. From the kitchen, he heard pounding and more heated mutterings. The twins were obviously irritated with their task.

"Their names…" Tina coughed. "Their names, when said together is…."

"Is what?" Aksh asked, shaking her as she kept slipping into a faint.

"In another language, it means you're giving them permission to enter you." Tina managed, gasping for air.

Aksh said their names in his mind. Antara- Meena. Which language was these words in that gave an entity permission to enter a mortal's body?

"Are you sure?"

"L-l-latin." Tina moaned.

"I know of some words, their names are not…." Aksh stopped himself. No, but if their names were spoken in a different way, they could sound like Latin, or even Romanian.

Intra me….

It was a trick. They had used names similar to those in another language as a guise.

Those devious little minxes!

"How do I get out of here?" Aksh asked, shaking Tina from her dazed state. "Tell me how to escape."

"You…can't," Tina said and her head fell sideways.

Aksh collapsed on the floor. Behind him the twins were calling him.

"We're almost done," They said in a cheerful tone. "Get ready to guess our names."

Aksh felt his heart plunge to his stomach. There was no escape from this nightmare. There was nothing he could do. All was lost! He would die and no one would even find his corpse because the twins would be using it to prance around the woods, luring hapless victims to their house and make them play games which they had no chance of winning.

"Here you go!" One of them said, handing him over a bowl of greenish-brown paste, while the other gave him a glass of water.

Aksh looked at them and took the items he was handed, quietly. He looked at Tina's pallid face and saw her skin turning blue.

"She's dying," He said.

"Then save her."

"She needs to be in a hospital," He said, putting down the bowl and glass

"There's no hospital here." The twins were speaking together again in that terrifying monotone that made his skin crawl.

"Then she's as good as dead."

"Oh well, at least we have you."

"I haven't guessed your names yet," He said, knowing he was doomed. There was no way out of here and he kept imagining having his corpse found by another sucker who would enter these woods—someone who wouldn't be able to escape either.

Aksh wondered if there ever would be a day when the loop would be broken and someone found find his rotting corpse or skeleton and cremate him, so he could find peace.

"You can't enter me until I guess your names," He said, desperately. "That's the deal we made."

"Then tell us," They said.

Aksh looked at Tina and then back at the twins— then at the front door and then the window. Eventually his gaze rested on the wooden cupboard which was destined to be his tomb.

"Times up," They said gleefully.

"You said there was no such thing as time in the woods," Aksh said.

"Answer us now!" They growled, their faces turning ferocious. Aksh stumbled back with fright and fell onto the cot which creaked under the weight of two bodies. He turned to see Tina lying with her eyes closed, her chest not rising anymore.

I'm sorry.

He turned back to the twins, knowing he had failed and that he was trapped. There was only one option left for him. He had to take a shot at running to the front door and escaping, even though there was a chance the twins would overpower him.

Taking a deep breath, he had turned sideways when there was a loud rap on the door.

"It's her," One of the twins said, her face changing from ferocity to fright. The other looked at her in disbelief. There was another knock, and her face reflected her twin's.

Aksh couldn't make sense of anything as they stepped back. He'd his chance to flee, but now he was too frightened to make a move. He'd thought these two were the ones to fear, but if they were scared of someone else then that meant there was something beyond the door that was even more terrifying.

Glancing at Tina's still body, he decided he deserved whatever was going to happen next.

"Why is she here?" One of them whispered.

"The bringer of death on our doorstep?"

"Aren't y-you b-both already dead?" Aksh intervened.

The twins looked at him with wide dark eyes and frowns on their faces. "Shut up!" They said.

The knocking continued and the twins retreated further and started putting out the lanterns. Aksh was torn between the decision to still make a run for it, or hide. He considered going into the kitchen and jumping out the window and had taken a step forward when the twins floated toward him and put their hands on his chest.

"Don't move," They whispered.

"What's going on?" He replied.

"It's her…Shantarani…or rather her ghost," They explained. "Every time she's seen, someone dies; or in our case, our souls could be sucked into a dark void from which we would never be able to free ourselves."

"W-why is s-she here?" Aksh tried to keep the fright out of his voice but failed. His heart pounded in his ears and he knew he would have to take deep calming breaths, but at the moment it was all he could do not to scream.

"We saw her before we were killed by the don," they said in one voice. "She was roaming in a circle around our house and we shooed her away. Then at the stroke of midnight, the don came over and threatened us. We had no choice but to kill ourselves before he could harm us."

Aksh looked at their sad faces and found himself sympathizing with their circumstances, even though he had to remind himself that these girls wanted to possess him and uses his body as a puppet.

"Maybe she's here for Tina," He said.

"Maybe…but we can't take that chance and open the door."

Aksh eyed the kitchen window once again and decided that at least he did have an escape. Whoever was on the other side of the door wouldn't see him if he escaped out the back and the twins' souls were cursed to remain in this house.

Aksh took a step to the side when he saw the twins stare at the door with wide eyes. They were clasping each other's hands and whispering words of comfort. Another long stride got him halfway across the room. Just ten more steps and he would be near the window.

Tip-toeing, he was in the kitchen and he kept his eyes firmly on the twins, who had their backs towards him. He put his hands on the sill and lifted himself up on the kitchen counter. Putting one leg out, he held his breath, making sure they hadn't caught his movements.

He was about to move his other leg when he felt a tug on it. Turning, he saw an old woman with silver billowing hair staring at him with a wide wicked grin on her face. Her long hands had talons and were curled around his ankle.

"There you are, my son," She said happily. "I've come to bring you home."

Chapter Twenty-Six

With a flick of his hand, Sumit had Dhiraj thrown on the ground and engulfed in a new terror. Sumit's wispy hands turned into smoky ribbons and swirled around Dhiraj's ankles. With one hand, his nemesis was dragging him through the long-winding path of the forest, which was clear of trees.

His back was scratched as Sumit chose rough terrain to drag him through, but all Dhiraj could do was scream whatever words popped into his head. Struggling was futile, as the demonic ghost possessed surprising strength which Sumit, when he was alive, hadn't.

Suddenly Sumit stopped and Dhiraj screamed even louder. This was it—now would be the time when Sumit would avenge his death.

"Ready to play?" The words were barely out of the ghost's mouth when the starry night sky above him, parted like clouds and revealed bright blue sky. He was no longer lying on a patch of pebbles and twigs and thorns, but soft fragrant grass.

"Let's go in." Sumit was telling him.

Dhiraj got up; his stomach in knots and his back screaming with pain. Before him was the badminton stadium where he was going to play the finals. The white building was decorated with banners, announcing the thrilling match between him and…

"I'm playing against you?" He asked in terror.

Sumit smiled, no longer in a black wispy form but his human one. He was dressed in a grey t-shirt and white shorts with black stripes. On his feet were white socks and shoes, free from dirt. Sumit ran his fingers through his hair and stretched his arms.

"Of course," He said, bending to touch his own feet.

Dhiraj pushed himself away when he thought Sumit was going to grab him again. Sumit snickered and gave him a hand.

"Come on, I'm not about to leave anything incomplete."

Dhiraj took the hand and got up, dusting the seat of his jeans. "How did we come here?"

"Asking too many questions," Sumit scoffed. "Don't tell me you're nervous; afraid I'll beat you?"

Just let me just go," Dhiraj pleaded. "I'll do anything…

"Play the match. If you win, then I'll let you go," Sumit said, and out of nowhere a badminton racket appeared in his hands. "Lose however, and you pay with your life." He smiled then, showing his pointed teeth stained red.

Dhiraj swallowed. "I've hurt my wrist. I was playing a backhand shot and accidentally…."

"Oh stop acting like a child." Sumit scoffed and adjusted the strings of his racket.

"I don't have my gear."

"It'll be inside." Sumit turned back to look at him and Dhiraj saw that his eyes had become hollow. They were just pits of blackness that had black smoke coming out of them. Sumit grabbed his wrist and pulled him inside the stadium, breaking the hypnotizing gaze of the hollow sockets.

Dhiraj followed Sumit through dark corridors, hearing the bustle from the area ahead. This was the moment he had been waiting for—when he would play the finals that would launch his sports career. He could imagine his parents sitting in the front row, applauding him for every point he scored while his opponent paced restlessly, wiping the sweat from his face as he tried to guess what shot he would have to face. He knew he had it in him to win; even after he had injured his wrist, he felt he could still try.

"Ready?" Sumit asked.

Dhiraj blinked and then when he looked down, he saw he was wearing his white shoes with blue laces and white thick socks. He was dressed in his club's colors—red with a black stripe cutting diagonally. In his hand, he found his trusty badminton racket—the one he had bought after saving for months. The racket felt light and sturdy in his hands and...real.

There was a flash of light on his face and he put up his hand to shield his eyes.

"And now, let me call upon the finalists—Sumit and Dhiraj!" The announcer said. Thousands of people appeared on the stands and threw up their hands to cheer. People screamed his name and he could see many of them holding posters of him. Right in the front, he spotted his parents talking amongst themselves while clapping.

"This isn't real," He said to himself.

"Maybe it is, maybe it isn't," Sumit said and picking up his bag, walked over to the court.

The referee beckoned him and Dhiraj complied, watching his parents looking straight ahead. He couldn't tell if they were an illusion or if they really were there.

"Heads or tails?" He was asked.

"Uh..." Dhiraj saw his parents turn their heads to look at him, their eyes displaying no emotion. The spectators all seemed to be looking at him and this made him nervous. "T....heads."

The coin was tossed and Dhiraj followed it as it flipped in the air and landed on the outstretched palm of the referee who then clasped a hand over it.

This isn't real.

"Heads it is."

Dhiraj smiled as he saw Sumit's surly expression. From here on, he hoped Sumit would only meet with failures. He grinned and walked over to the court to stand in the corner. The shuttlecock was tossed to him and he put his left leg forward and exercised his arm.

The arena had grown silent. All that he heard was the whoosh of air as he struck the shuttlecock with his racket. Sumit stood knees slightly bent, awaiting his move.

Dhiraj turned and saw that every spectator had their eyes on him. He swallowed and turned his concentration to the game.

He struck the shuttlecock and watched it fly in the air. Sumit lunged forward and struck at it before it could hit the ground. Dhiraj quickly countered. They rallied for several minutes before the shuttlecock plonked to the ground on Sumit's side.

"Yes!" Dhiraj cheered.

Sumit's face darkened and he mumbled obscenities. Dhiraj scoffed; Sumit was a sore loser.

"Your serve," The umpire told him.

Dhiraj glanced at the scoreboard and saw a point under his name while the zero looked satisfying under Sumit's. As his opponent readied himself Dhiraj served from the right. Sumit missed the shot and slammed his racket down, covering his face with his hands, letting out a scream.

Dhiraj pumped his fist. His parents sat quietly, staring at him.

No, they're staring into me.

He tore himself away from the strange spectators and took the shuttlecock in his hands again when the umpire passed it to him. Nineteen more points and he would win the game—then he could go home.

Sumit picked up his racket and twirled it in his hands. He stood diagonally, bent slightly over and glaring at him. Dhiraj could feel the heat of his eyes from his position and looked away. He had to focus if he wanted to win. Sumit wasn't one to keep promises, but at the moment this was his only chance.

A quick scan around the arena showed him no doors through which he could make a hasty exit. His eyes fell on the stands again where it was eerily quiet and every hollow eye was on him. It seemed that the people were disappointed that he was winning—even his parents.

Dhiraj swallowed and using his racket, tapped the bottom of the shuttlecock and watched it fly over the net. Sumit jumped and slammed the shuttlecock hard, causing it to fly to his end and disintegrate.

"Point to Sumit." He heard.

Dhiraj stared at the patch on the court where the shuttlecock had been and saw a dark burn. His mouth went dry, and when he looked up he saw Sumit teasing him with his eyes. He was up to something!

Sumit served and Dhiraj couldn't return it. The shuttlecock bounced off his racket and hit the ground.

The digital board made a clicking sound and Dhiraj saw that they were now tied. His parents sat gazing at him. They wore no other expression and it was unnerving him.

Sumit served again and scored another point. Dhiraj hadn't even realized that the shot was being made as he continued to stare at his parents. He dropped his racket and walked over to them. Falling to his knees, he took their hands in his.

"Mom? Dad?"

"Hey, come back and play!" Sumit yelled.

"Is it really you?" Dhiraj asked.

His parents didn't move a muscle. All Dhiraj could feel in his hands was a burning sensation and he pulled his hands back. Stepping away from them, he could see the wisps of black smoke rising from their bodies and then they were gone.

Dhiraj stared at the empty bench where his parents had been and realized that the spectators—all of them—were smoke too.

"Nothing is real," He said.

"The game is, and you're losing!" Sumit whispered in his ear.

Dhiraj turned to see his opponent standing right behind him, grinning. Black wispy smoke rose from his head as well and made him look even more frightening.

"Play!" Sumit roared. His mouth opened wide and he emitted a burst of air that had Dhiraj propelling backward and hit his back on the empty benches.

"I don't want to!"

Sumit advanced toward him and Dhiraj covered his head, certain that he was going to be hit. i. Instead, he found himself being dragged back to the court.

"Play with me!"

Dhiraj sniveled and reached for his discarded racket. He saw Sumit's shoes walking away from his as he took his position on the other side.

"Get the hell up!"

Feeling every muscle tremble in his body, Dhiraj nevertheless forced himself up and raised his racket. Sumit served and the shuttlecock smacked against the net.

"Shit!" He screamed and threw his racket at the net. The racket bounced back and landed with a clatter on the ground.

Dhiraj wiped at his tears and took the shuttlecock from the umpire. "Your serve."

Dhiraj nodded. He was about to play his shot, when he saw Sumit still cursing and clenching at the racket like he was trying to squeeze the life out of it. Then it hit him-the reason why Sumit had never progressed this far was because of his rage issues. He remembered hearing the coach once berate Sumit for being too impulsive and irritable.

Sumit had walked away in a huff but not before he had heard him curse the coach. Dhiraj smiled inwardly. He now knew how to beat Sumit!

Chapter Twenty-Seven

"Where do I start?" Maya was talking to herself out loud, but she thought she rather hear herself talk than the constant nothingness. Even the breeze had slowed down enough to not cause the trees to sway and the leaves to make rustling sounds.

"Speaking of trees..." She stood before one and looked up. The only reason she hadn't been screaming her friends' names was because she was afraid the beasts would return. Though the white wolf-like creature meant no harm, the black one was ominous and unpredictable and if he heard her and came back, she didn't think she could protect herself.

"If I climb up this tree, I could see the rest of the forest and my friends."

But when was the last time she had climbed a tree?

"Never. Well I'll have to now." She removed her heels and then frowned. These were designer heels and she didn't want to leave them behind, but she couldn't carry them in her hands either.

Removing her scarf, she tied it around the straps of her shoes and then tied the scarf around her waist.

"There." She looked at the tree and let out a breath. Her hands touched the rough bark and then she looked up at the closest branch that she would have to use to climb up.

"That's not too low," She said, pushing back her hair that was still in a plait.

Using her finger, she poked at the center of the plait to unravel it. How she hated tying her hair in plaits, but for a second when that old woman had been tying her hair and talking to her with such tenderness she hadn't mind anything. She had received a mother's love from a creature of the forest!

Maya let out a sigh. "I'm pathetic."

She put up a foot on the trunk and felt something smooth under her heel.

Looking down, she saw a vine tied around the trunk with a rock hanging in the middle.

"Like a necklace." She took the rock in her hand and brushed a thumb over it. This definitely didn't look like one of nature's surprises. Vines didn't tie themselves around trees in a knot and they definitely didn't have a rock hanging from them like a pendant.

"Someone did this—used it as a marking perhaps? But for what?"

Maya dropped it and standing on her tiptoes, grabbed the branch. Then she hauled herself up and scraped her knee against the wood.

"Damn it!" She grabbed another branch and climbed. Every time she pulled herself up she felt the slap of her shoes against her back, and though it was uncomfortable, somehow having her shoes with her made her feel safe.

She reached another branch and stopped, taking large deep breaths. "This is so *not* easy."

Looking down, she saw she was about fifteen feet up. There were still more distance she must cover if she wanted a better view.

"Come on, Maya! Let's do this!" With renewed energy, she clambered up, ignoring the scrapes on her legs and arms. She found a thick branch near the top and swung a leg over, as if she were sitting atop a saddle.

Maya was now quite high up—not enough to see the entire area of the forest, but safe enough not to be mauled by strange creatures.

Gathering up enough air in her lungs, she opened her mouth and called out.

"Aksh! Dhiraj! Preeti! Rudra!" She inhaled deeply and looked all around her. Not a leaf had stirred nor had she heard any human voices respond to her calls.

She screamed her friends' names again and felt an ache in her throat.

"Where the hell are you guys?"

She leaned her back against the trunk, making sure she had her hands tightly grasped around the thick branch she was sitting on.

"This is pointless," She said, feeling tears pricking her eyes. "I can't find anyone!"

A twig snapped and she gasped. She checked the branch she was seated on and felt no cracks. Holding her breath, she listened for more sounds—half expecting to hear the branch snap and throw her off the tree.

"Why are we looking for her?" She heard a girl's voice... Preeti's voice!

Looking down, she saw Preeti and Rudra walking by her tree.

Maya felt her heart leap with joy. She almost slipped off the branch as she scrambled off it and then paused.

"Rudra! Preeti!"

Her screams apparently went unheard, because they didn't stop.

Rudra was walking with long strides while Preeti was trying hard to catch up with him.

"Will you speak to me?" She was saying.

Maya dropped herself onto a lower branch and screamed for them, but her friends still didn't show any indication that they had heard her.

Very carefully, Maya jumped off the lowest branch and landed on her knees. Letting out a groan, she winced again when her heels dug into her back.

"Guys! Wait up!"

Her friends were walking further away and Maya chased after them, barefoot. She caught up with them and was running right next to them, but her friends didn't notice her presence. Preeti looked intense as she spoke to Rudra who was looking straight ahead, determined to find whatever he was looking for.

Then Preeti grabbed his arm and made him turn to her.

"What the hell is wrong with you?"

Maya stepped forward and found herself being bounced back by an invisible force. She tried again and found she was unable to take another step toward her friends. She stretched her arms and felt a wall shielding her from them. She traced it by walking ahead and felt the firmness of the wall. She tried kicking it, and let out a cry when she hurt herself.

"No!" She wailed. "No!"

This couldn't be happening to her, she thought. Her friends were only five feet away and she couldn't go to them.

"Preeti! Look here! Look at me!"

But Preeti didn't, rather she was yelling at Rudra.

"Why do we need to find Nisha?" She heard her say.

Rudra remained motionless, a stoic expression on his face that was so unlike his usually genial self.

"Rudr..." His name caught in her throat when she noticed something on his shoulder. She had been so excited to see her friends, that she hadn't noticed that they were not alone.

Sitting on Rudra's shoulder was a silhouette of a person with horns in his head and a pointed upturned cone for legs. When he turned his head, she saw red glowing eyes and Maya uttered a gasp and stepped back instinctively.

It's not a silhouette, she thought with fear rising up her throat. It's a creature—a ghost.

"Oh no!" The black ghost lowered his head and whispered something in Rudra's ear making her friend even more stoic in his expressions.

She saw Rudra clench his hands and scream at Preeti who looked stung and dejected as he berated her for something.

"Rudra! No!" Maya screeched. "There's something on your shoulder!"

She saw him grab Preeti's wrist and drag her behind him.

"Preeti!" Maya collapsed into tears and fell on the ground. The heels poked her back and she untied her scarf and flung it away.

"Listen to me! Hear my voice!" She sobbed.

She heard the crunching of dry leaves behind her and held her breath.

What was that?

A shrill cry erupted from somewhere behind her and Maya felt a shiver run through her. Rudra and Preeti were far ahead now, so the sounds were definitely not coming from those two. Whoever it was, had to be somewhere nearer.

"Please don't come back! Please don't come back you horrible creatures!"

She considered climbing up a tree again to save herself from the creatures who must have returned to maul and devour her, when she noticed a human figure through the leaves.

It was a girl, no older than her, dressed in a red sequin tank top and matching shorts. She had one knee-high red sparkly boots that Maya thought couldn't be comfortable walking on the rough path.

The girl's long hair shielded her face and she appeared to be wailing.

Maya followed her and watched the girl drag herself to a tree and collapse on the ground. She covered her face with her hands and sobbed loudly.

Maya came over to her, guessing that the girl too must have gotten lost just like her. She bent her knees and tried to get a peek of the girl's face.

"Hey!" She said softly. "Are you lost? Like me?"

The girl appeared not to have heard her and pulled up her knees while sobbing harder.

Maya sat down beside her and put a hand on the girl's shoulder. Her skin felt cold and wet and strangely bumpy.

"Hey!" She said, patting her.

The girl looked up and for a second Maya thought her face had looked like a beast's with a large snout and bumps on her scaly skin.

Then that illusion was gone and she looked like a normal girl with wide brown eyes, small nose and full red lips.

"Are you okay?" Maya asked.

The girl's lips trembled as she looked at her and then she put her arms around her waist. "I'm so scared!" She cried.

Maya was taken aback when the girl hugged her and almost pushed her away. The girl's skin felt slimy and she could feel the unpleasant sensation through her clothes.

"I thought that if I did a good deed, I would get to leave the forest but I can't seem to get out of here!" The girl was half screaming and half sobbing. Maya considered telling the girl to quiet down in case the black beast returned but the girl was inconsolable.

"I told him how he could save his friends and then when I saw him again, he was looking for me and he wants to take me back to the tree." She cried.

"Who? What tree?"

The girl grabbed Maya's clothes, tight in her fists, sobbing so loud that it was starting to resemble the howl of an animal.

It started to drizzle then and Maya looked up at the perpetual night sky and saw that unlike last time, the droplets were clear water. She put her hand on the girl's skin and saw it change color. She rubbed her eyes and saw the girl's skin turn greenish-brown and rougher.

"I can't go back!" The girl continued to cry. "I escaped from there after I died. If I go back I'll never be able to escape from it again and I'll never get to leave!"

The girl pulled back to reveal a grotesque beast-like face and large pointed teeth. Maya let out a scream and stumbled back. "Get away from me!" She turned and was about to run, when she felt a hand grab her ankle.

"You're one of them!" She cried in a hoarse voice. "One of his friends?"

Maya kicked at her hand, but the girl beast held on tight.

"Rudra! Rudra's friend, right?" The beast morphed back into the girl and Maya let out a moan. "Answer me!"

"Yes!" Maya cried. "I'm Maya! Let me go!"

"I'm not going to hurt you," She said, wiping her tears. Her clawed hands turned into human hands with large red painted nails.

"How do you know him?"

"I was the one who found him after the accident," She explained. "I'm going to let go of your foot, but promise me you won't leave me alone."

Maya swallowed and then nodded.

The girl let go of her foot, watching her carefully. Maya considered making a run for it anyway, then seeing the sincerity on her face, she only pushed herself back a few inches.

"Who are you?" She asked wondering if she should instead ask what she was.

"My name is Nisha," The girl said, putting her hands on her knees and saying nothing else.

"Nisha?" Maya remembered Rudra saying her name and that he had to take her back to the tree. And then she thought back to the monster sitting on her friend's shoulder and whispering. "I saw Rudra and Preeti right now and they were looking for you."

"I saw them too," Nisha replied. "When I heard Rudra wanted to take me back to the tree, I ran away from there."

"Why would he want to take you back to the tree?"

"After I was murdered, I woke up to find myself hanging by the neck on that tree," Nisha explained.

The rain was falling harder now and every droplet that landed on Nisha turned her skin translucent. Maya tore her eyes away from her skin and focused on what the girl was saying.

"It took me a long time to free myself from the binds. There were so many others..." Nisha sniffed. "Then there was a voice in my head that told me that I could leave the forest and the gateway to hell if I helped someone."

"The tree? It's a gateway to hell?"

"I suppose... All I know is that the longer one stays hanged on the tree, the better that chances are that the soul is transported to hell. It's like purgatory except you get to decide if you want to seek redemption or let your soul be condemned."

"So someone wants you in hell?" Maya asked.

Nisha nodded. "I tried to help Rudra, but I failed!" She cried.

Maya put a shivering hand on Nisha's shoulder. "Hey, it's all going to be okay. Rudra has something evil attached to him. Once he gets rid of it, he will be his normal self again."

"There's something attached to him?" Nisha asked, still crying.

"Yes, a black shadowy thing," Maya explained.

"So he didn't turn against me on his own?" Nisha looked so pitiful that Maya felt her heart melt.

"No. Didn't you see that black thing sitting on his shoulder?"

Nisha shook her head and then her eyes widened. "Did it have horns and glowing eyes? Did he have no legs?"

"Yes, why?"

Nisha gasped. "Oh... Oh no! That's not just any ghost, it's a jinn."

"A jinn?" Maya shook her head and let out a breath. "They are not real."

"Forget everything you know and think," Nisha said. "All the monsters you read in your story books are real."

"Okay." Maya let that information settle in. "So what does a jinn do?"

"He makes deals. He'll offer a wish to a person and in return he'll ask for an evil favor," Nisha said.

"Okay, we know that the jinn wants you."

"But what did Rudra ask for in return?" Nisha asked.

"I don't know..." Maya said. Then she remembered the day Rudra had proposed to Preeti in college, in front of everyone. "He wants her."

"Who?"

"Preeti!" Maya slapped her forehead. "What Rudra doesn't know is that Preeti isn't in a relationship with Abhi anymore."

Nisha looked at her in confusion.

Maya shook herself. "Abhi was cheating on Preeti. I saw that rascal with another girl. I knew even though Preeti didn't tell me, but Rudra doesn't!"

"Are you sure?"

"If there's one person Rudra loves more than anything in the world—it's Preeti."

"So what do we do now?"

"We'll have to find a way to let Rudra know he's being tricked," Maya said. "And we'll have to act fast!"

Chapter Twenty-Eight

"*P*lease let me go!"

Aksh's pleas fell to deaf ears. The old woman had dragged him out the window and held him by the throat, launching him in midair. Then taking a long sniff, she seemed satisfied and then bringing him down, started to drag him all the while clutching his throat.

The old woman's hand had short fur on her palms and the side of her nails felt like blades against his throat. Her grip was tight yet not squeezing, so he was still able to breathe.

"Please!" He cried again, feeling the heels of his feet hit a rock. He hissed but the old woman ignored him and walked smoothly. When Aksh lowered his eyes he saw that the hem of the woman's long white dress barely touched the ground.

She's floating, his mind screamed in panic.

Aksh put his hands over her furry ones and tried to pry them off, but he was no match for her abominable strength.

Then she stopped and pushing him at arm's length, growled at him. Her face changed before his eyes, becoming more wrinkly and ferocious. Her eyes burned with utter hatred and her mouth was twisted in a snarl.

Then she was using something silvery white to tie around his neck and the next thing he knew, he was being hauled up by his neck.

Aksh pushed two fingers between his throat and whatever the old woman was using to strangle him, and took large deep breaths.

When he was pulled higher, he looked down to see a trail of thick silver ribbon attached to the old woman's head.

It's her hair! She's using her hair as a noose!

He dangled his feet, trying to find something to support them on and found a thin branch. Whirling his head, he saw a large tree behind him.

"Why are you doing this to me?" He screamed.

The old woman cackled. "I've been searching for you," She said in a raspy voice. "It took me a long while, but I finally have you in my grasp."

"Please, not me!" Aksh tried swinging to a thicker branch, but the old woman's hair was taut and restricted his movements. He tried to tear the bind around his throat, but all he managed to do was break a single strand.

"Ouch! You're hurting me!" The old woman said, though her tone was teasing.

"I-I won't h-hurt you anymore. Don't kill me!"

"Child, it is you that I've been assigned to kill," She said. The whispers of the forest told me that your soul must be plucked from your body and harnessed. Your soul will give the forest more power."

"Why me?" He cried. "Take anyone else's. Take ... the twins' souls. They live in that house back there."

"They already belong to the forest. Their power drew you to them. After they were going to be done playing with your body, they were going to submit your soul to the tree."

Aksh began to sob. This wasn't now be bad imagined his death to be. He had hoped for a life of a revered surgeon and remembered for his skills eons later. He had only begun his life as a doctor and now all that was being taken away from him- all his hard work and all the nights he had spent studying... all that was going down the drain.

"Tina! Take her! Please!" He cried in desperation.

The old woman scoffed. "She isn't even alive." She waved off as if he had uttered something ludicrous.

"What?"

"She died a long time ago but her soul refuses to give up and keeps entering her body." She explained. "Since she's dead, her soul can't adhere to her body for more than a couple of minutes."

"She spoke to me," He said.

"She also hasn't eaten or drunk anything in years." The old woman laughed. "You're a doctor—a human being cannot survive without food or water, remember?"

"I was talking to a dead person," Aksh said, his hands turning cold and numb.

"You're talking to a dead person now," She said. "I died years ago too. I was given a task to find redemption by taking a soul back with me for judgement and submit it to the tree to become even more powerful."

Aksh curled his foot and supported himself on the thick branch. He tried pushing away her hair from his neck, but it wouldn't budge.

"I can smell you—you're the one whose soul must be released," She said.

"My friends!" Aksh cried, managing to break a white strand, though the woman barely winced. "Are they in the forest too?"

The old woman's face grew grave. "Yes." She looked watchful as if wondering what he was going to suggest next.

"I-it could be one of them!"

The old woman raised her eyebrow. "Are you telling me I had made a mistake in my task?"

"I...."

"Because, here's the truth, Aksh." His name from her mouth felt poisonous and he hoped she would never repeat it again. "I don't make mistakes. It is you that must be taken. Five of you entered the forest; one of you doesn't get to leave."

"Please! Take one of them!" He cried. Tears streamed down to his shirt and wetted it, making the cloth clutch uncomfortably on his skin. Everything was starting to feel heavier on his chest as his breathing was hindered.

"One of them?" The old woman narrowed her dark swirling eyes. She tapped a finger on her scaly lips. "Who exactly do you have in mind?"

Aksh inhaled deeply. "Pick one yourself! But please let me go!"

"Who are you willing to sacrifice instead of yourself?" The old woman asked and with a small tug, brought him down.

Aksh saw the old woman gazing deep into his eyes, searching his mind for answers.

"I met your friend Dhiraj," The old woman said. "It wasn't him, so I let him go."

"He's safe," He said to himself.

The old woman made a face. "He has his own monsters to deal with. Now tell me, which one of your friends are you willing to sacrifice in your place?"

"I can do that?" Aksh asked, hope rising in his chest.

"Maybe. Tell me which one of your friends?"

Aksh thought back to his college days when he was friendless and being bullied by Sumit. At that time, it had been Dhiraj who had stepped up for him. It had been Rudra who had instilled him in the group and it had been Preeti who had picked his calls in the middle of the night when he had been too nervous to sit for his exams.

"Maya," He said.

"Maya?" The old woman's face grew stern and her eyes became darker. "Why her?" She growled.

Aksh swallowed, making sure his fingers were still pushing her hair away from his throat. "She was always moody and never a great friend to me. She was such a snob and only cared about the clothes she wore. Take her!"

"Just because she wouldn't speak to you?" The old woman's tone sharpened.

"I don't think she even liked me," Aksh said. "She would barely look at me and was never there when I wanted her. Whenever I was nervous about my medical career, it was Preeti who encouraged me. Whenever I had bully problems, Rudra and Dhiraj stepped up for me. Maya, she never did anything for me."

"Hmm." The old woman seemed to consider his statements sincerely. "And what exactly have you done for *your* friends?"

"What?" Even though the old woman's voice was calm, her face was still twisted in a snarl. She was up to something and he had to be careful.

"All you've told me so far is what the others have done for you. What have you done for them when they needed someone to stand by them?"

"I... uh..."

The old woman smiled. "You don't have an answer do you?"

She shook her head in dismay. "While you were busy judging Maya, you were unaware of all the troubles she was going through."

Aksh thought back to all the times he had spent with his friends and remembered thinking how properly and fashionably Maya was always dressed. She also rarely smiled and participated in conversations with monosyllables. He thought it was because she was snobbish and didn't approve his introduction to their close-knit group.

"She never said anything," He said in defense.

"Did you know that each of your friends have been going through problems of their own?" The old woman asked. "But you were so busy troubling them with yours that they never told you about all the predicaments they themselves were facing."

Aksh was no longer struggling with the hair bind around his throat. The words of the old woman hit him hard and he wondered if he had been selfish and needy all this time.

"I'll try to be a good friend to them," Aksh said. "Please let me go and let me be a good friend to them. I'll change... promise!"

The old woman scoffed. "You expect me to believe you will reform?"

"Yes!" Aksh screamed. "Don't kill me!"

The old woman tapped her chin thoughtfully. He saw her face lose its ferocity and turn softer. Her face morphed back into a human's but her hands were still claws and her hair was still winded around his throat- though not as tightly as before.

"No," She replied and Aksh felt his heart sink. "I'll have to take your soul."

Aksh sank to his knees and the hair strands tightened around his neck. "Please, I'm begging you." He said, clasping his hands together.

"I need a soul..."

"Take Maya's soul!" He cried. "Take her but spare me!"

The old woman closed the distance. "From all your friends, you choose her?"

"Yes!"

"Is that your final answer? Hers and no one else's?"

"Yes! Yes!" Aksh felt his hope grow. The old woman looked like she was willing to make the exchange.

She lowered her head to his and he could smell the stench of burning wood and rotted meat. She opened her mouth and it widened more than a human's was capable of. Her teeth elongated into sharp needles and her ribbon tongue lashed at his face, painting his cheeks with sticky burning liquid.

Her hair unraveled from around his throat allowing him to breathe freely before she put a clawed hand on his neck.

"Not her!" She roared. "I see my daughter in her and do you know what a mother does when she senses her child is in danger?"

"No!" Aksh gasped, not realising what he was saying.

The old woman let out a roar again and a few droplets of the sticky liquid sprayed on his face.

The old woman's grip tightened around his throat, then she pushed him back with force. "But no! I won't kill you!" She screeched. "I'll let the person you wronged take revenge."

The old woman cackled. "Then I'll take your soul to hell myself!"

Chapter Twenty-Nine

Preeti tried to get Rudra to release her wrist, but fighting against the stronghold was futile. Rudra was behaving like a deranged animal—a bull, she had once seen in the news toppling over a matador. She imagined that if anyone or anything came in his path, he would trample it the same way that maniacal bull had.

"Let me go!"

But he was no longer listening to her. Something was going on with him that she couldn't understand. One minute he was being his usual considerate self, the next he was screaming at her and treating her like dirt. This wasn't the Rudra she had known for years and she couldn't imagine what had gotten into him. The wind was pushing back his hair from his face and revealing the pinched look on his face. His eyes were narrowed as if searching for his target and his hands were clenched too tight.

Preeti saw her hand turn blue and even though she hadn't wanted to, she used her nails to scratch his arm. Rudra winced and let go, examining his arm.

"What the hell is wrong with you!" he bellowed.

Preeti started to cry and hated herself for doing so. She massaged her hand until it turned red and she could feel the numbness wearing of. Rudra noticed her movements and his face softened.

"I am sorry," He said, keeping his eyes averted.

"What has gotten into you?"

Rudra pressed his lips together and finally looked at her. "We need to find Nisha and bring her back to the tree."

"The one where all the corpses were hanging? Why, Rudra?" Preeti asked, but he was already turning away and walking with long strides.

Preeti chased after him, finding it hard to match his rhythm. She heard the rustling of leaves and turned her head to see the ghost couple staring at her from under the tree. Even though their eyes were just glowing white orbs, they seemed judgmental and discerning. They had saved her once and let her out of the forest and they were obviously chiding her in silence, but there was nothing she could do.

She passed by them, hoping that when the time came, she would find them again so that they could show her the way out. In the meantime, she could only hope that she could find her friends alive. She took a step forward when the couple suddenly approached her.

Their form was blurring and their faces were contorted. Their mouths opened wide and Preeti felt a gush of wind as they screamed.

"Get out now!"

Preeti let out a whine and ran as fast as she could, away from them. How foolish of her to think that she no longer feared them.

Rudra was still walking at the same pace and she had to lunge to grab his arm. "You need to explain to me what's going on."

"There is nothing to explain," He replied, sullenly.

Preeti saw a movement behind a grove of trees and paused, giving Rudra the opportunity to slip from her grasp and continue walking. She put a hand out and pushed away the drooping branches of an old tree. When she saw a small cottage in front of her, she gasped.

"Rudra!" she called. "I found a house!" She slipped through the narrow opening and stood in front of the cottage. The roof had sticks tied together with rope and she spotted hay sticking out of the edges. There were two windows in the front that had no curtains or glass and a wooden door that looked like it would tear down and break into pieces with the smallest brush of wind.

There were five steps leading to the door and Preeti wondered if this old rustic house would have a telephone line.

"Rudra!" she called. He came to stand by her side, his face devoid of any expression. She was almost startled by his sudden appearance but tried not to show him how terrified she was getting of him. "Maybe there will be a phone inside."

Rudra remained unmoved, though his brown eyes were piercing as they studied the cottage.

"We could call for help."

"No," He replied in a numb tone. "We have to find Nisha."

Don't be stupid," Preeti argued. "We have to check to make sure that…"

Just then a phone rang and Preeti gasped. The ringing continued and Rudra stood motionless with his back turned toward her. Preeti felt a vibration in her pocket and reached inside to bring out her cell phone.

"Where did this come from?" she asked. The last time she had seen her phone was when she was outside the forest and near the car. She had received eerie calls on it and had dropped. After that she couldn't remember the fate of her phone. Had she put it in her pocket?

The phone flashed Abhi's name and she clicked on the green button. "H-hello?"

"You cheating bitch!" Abhi screamed at her. "You hypocrite!"

"A-abhi…"

Rudra whipped around in anger. His face was red and his eyes dark and stormy. He didn't walk, but charged towards her and she gripped the phone in her hands, certain that Rudra was going to either hurt her or toss the phone away.

Instead he stood right next to her, trying to hear her conversation. She could hear his harsh and rapid breathing as he fumed.

"What the hell are you doing with Rudra! You said he was only your friend!" Abhi yelled.

"Abhi, listen to me," She said calmly. "I'm lost in the forest near Darkwood Road. You need to get help. Please."

Abhi muttered an obscenity and Rudra grabbed the phone from her hands and put it near his ear. "Now listen, you bastard! If you call Preeti again I'll rip off your limbs one by one and I'll shred your skin to ribbons."

"Rudra!" Preeti said, horrified by the violent outburst. She had never seen him so enraged and she found herself stepping away from him.

"Fuck you!" Rudra yelled and switched off the phone in anger.

Preeti felt her mouth go dry. "We needed his help."

"We don't!" Rudra said. "I can't believe you went out with him. I can't believe you rejected my love for that asshole!"

Preeti took the phone from his hands and started to dial the emergency number. Reasoning or talking to Rudra at this point was useless.

"Hello, police?" She heard someone pick up on the other line, but heard no voice. "If you can hear me, we need help. My friends and I have lost our way in the forest near Darkwood Road. Could you please help us? Hello?"

She heard a whisper and pressed the phone closer to her ear. "Hello?" There was some more inaudible and incoherent whispers before she heard a click.

"Hello?" Preeti looked at her phone and saw it was disconnected. "Dammit." She dialed again and received the 'No Signal' notification on her screen.

"I really hope someone heard my message," She said. "Or hopefully someone saw our abandoned car and called the police."

"Or more likely stole it, in this case."

Preeti frowned and kept trying to make a call. She tried her parent's number and then her cousin's. When she couldn't get through, her shoulders slumped and looked ahead. "We have to go into that house."

Rudra grabbed her by the shoulders and shook her. "We need to find Nisha. No more distractions! Understood?"

Preeti dropped her phone and said nothing as Rudra resumed walking. She picked up her phone and looked up to see a face staring at her through the window. She turned and saw another face at the second window.

Stepping back, she saw that the faces were of two girls in their teens, staring at her. They had bushy brown hair and were dressed in white. Their faces were brownish-blue and they had deep lines on their faces.

Preeti felt the breath being sucked out of her as she continued to stare at the two girls with same features.

Twins!

The two girls tilted their head to the side and she could hear a sharp creaking sound as they moved.

"Rudra?" she whispered. The girls didn't blink and continued to watch her as she took another step back. Even though their mouths weren't open, she heard them whisper.

"Why don't you come in, dear?"

Preeti felt her heart turn cold as a smile spread on their faces. Their faces still tilted, she continued to hear the creaking sounds that reverberated all around her.

Preeti turned on her heels and ran as fast as her strength would allow.

"Don't go!" she heard them, even though she was no longer near their house.

"Come in and we'll never let you feel lonely."

Preeti put her hands over her ears and kept on running. Her feet splashed on the puddles and she could hear her own rapid breathing. There were finally some sounds in the forest, though she yearned for the silence again as the girls continued to beckon her.

"We'll be friends forever!" their voices were strung together until they were one and their tones were without any emotion. She couldn't wait to get as far from there as possible, but no matter how much distance she had put, she could still hear the twins whispering.

"We have secrets to share with you," They kept saying.

"Stop it!" she screamed. "Rudra! Where are you?"

She saw him walking up ahead at a fast pace and ran after him.

"Your friend likes us too," They said. "He wanted to stay with us forever."

Preeti ignored the voices. No doubt they were tricking her to stop so that they could drive her insane. "Rudra!"

He turned then and she ran right into him. Putting her arms around him, she sobbed. "Please don't leave me alone."

Rudra didn't move for several minutes and they stood there in the misty rain until she could feel her heart stop palpitating so hard. Then she felt his hand on her back and Preeti felt a smile tug her lips. His hand on her gave her comfort and the assurance that everything was going to be fine.

She could feel his hand through her jacket and then suddenly he grabbed a fistful of the material and yanked her away from him.

A gust of wind blew against him and she saw his glaring at something ahead. His eyes narrowed, his nostrils were flared and his mouth pressed together. Preeti followed his gaze and saw a girl sitting under the tree with her knees propped up.

She had long straight hair, an oval face and long neck. She was dressed in a red sequined tank top, shorts and matching boots. Seeing her, Rudra stomped toward her with clenched fists.

Preeti grabbed his arm, but he easily pulled it away. She ran and came in front of him and put her hands on his chest.

"Rudra, stop! Just stop!" she turned to see the girl watching them with fright in her large brown eyes.

"Is that her? Is that Nisha?" she asked. Rudra wasn't even looking at her. There was rage in his eyes and all his muscles had become taut. He started to charge again and Preeti put her hands on his waist and tried pushing him back with little success.

"Rudra, don't!" she screamed. "Stop it!"

But he still wouldn't listen and struggled in her grasp.

"Listen to me!" she screamed. The wind was making it harder for her to talk or breathe. It seemed as if a storm was coming. "You said she was your friend. You don't want to hurt her!"

"Move!" Rudra screamed back at her.

Preeti gasped, but continued to push him back. She was afraid that Rudra was going to hit the girl or creature, whatever Rudra thought Nisha was. She may have not harmed him before, but if Rudra provoked her, who knew how she would react.

"No!" She reached over to slap him hard on his cheek.

Rudra looked stunned for several seconds before his eyes narrowed with rage again and he grabbed her arms. "Get out of my way!" he bellowed and pushed her aside.

Preeti lost her balance and fell hard on the ground, hitting her head against a large rock. She clutched her forehead and yelped in pain, but Rudra paid her no heed as he went over to Nisha.

"Rudra...stop..." she tried to scream, but all her energy had been consumed. She saw dark clouds in her vision and fought to stay conscious.

"Don't hurt her!" she said. Her eyes closed and the next thing she sensed was a sinking feeling of falling into a pit of darkness.

Chapter Thirty

Dhiraj had always prided himself for not deigning to trickery while playing sport. He had seen many players resort to unfair plays to rattle their opponents so that they could score points.

His conscience would simply not allow him to find a way around the strict rules of badminton even though his coach had often offered to share a few tricks with him.

Dhiraj wished he had listened to the coach, now that he was in this predicament.

When alive, Sumit was had always been hotheaded and every single thing had seemed to push him over the edge, but his ghost was unpredictable. Just when Dhiraj thought he had figured out how to get under his skin and make him lose concentration, Sumit would surprise him with a calm demeanor and smooth returns in the rallies.

A quick glance at the scoreboard showed him that his opponent was not far behind.

Dhiraj served and the shuttlecock landed easily on the other side. Sumit emitted a low growl and clenched his hand around the racket.

"Game to Dhiraj," The umpire said.

Dhiraj didn't react nor look up at the phantom crowd. While adjusting the strings he thought about all the plays he hadn't learned from his coach because he had deemed them unfair.

Sumit was walking all around the court with unbridled rage, muttering to himself. Dhiraj tried to hear the words, but couldn't from his position and wondered if Sumit was conjuring a spell to make himself win the game.

When the next game started, Dhiraj's fear was confirmed. Sumit played effortlessly, his racket moving in smooth strokes. When the shuttlecock fell on Dhiraj's side, he felt his heart skip a beat.

Looking up, he saw Sumit smile at him as he took the shuttlecock. Dhiraj readied himself for the return, afraid that his opponent might gain the upper hand. He was right again as he missed the shot.

"Now isn't that a pity." Sumit sneered.

Dhiraj turned away from him and toward his phantom parents that possessed black smoky eyes and pale yellow skin. They weren't his parents, but a trick Sumit was playing to make him nervous.

Despite his earlier resolve to play the game fairly, Dhiraj silenced his conscience and planned what he would do next. He had to consider the possibility that Sumit may not keep his word and let him go if he won. On the other hand, if Sumit did let him go, it would only be because he won the match and to ensure his victory he had to rile up his opponent so much that he would lose his concentration.

"I hate this," He whispered to himself. But in order to survive he had to do this.

Turning, he grinned. "Let's go."

Sumit frowned at his sudden perkiness but served nonetheless.

Dhiraj stepped on the side and let the shuttlecock fall near his feet. "Nope, sorry. That was a fault."

"What? No it wasn't!" Sumit said.

"You served near your chest; not the waist. That's a fault," Dhiraj said.

"You're lying!"

Dhiraj laughed inwardly at Sumit's outburst.

That was easy.

"Dude it was a fault," He provoked and Sumit looked mad enough to snap his racket in two.

"Don't lie to me!" Sumit pointed an accusatory finger at him.

"Ask the umpire."

The umpire had a stony face and hollow eyes from which black smoke wafted. When Sumit turned to him, the umpire quivered with fear.

"What was it, was it a fault?"

The umpire remained motionless and silent.

"Only trained him to read score, huh?" Dhiraj taunted.

"Shut up! Just shut the hell up!" Sumit screamed.

"Whatever man, I'll let you serve again," Dhiraj said in a casual tone. "Come on, try again."

Sumit didn't waste another thought. He positioned his racket near his waist and hit the shuttlecock hard, making it fly into the net.

Dhiraj hissed. "Yikes!"

Sumit thrashed the racket on the ground and put his hands on his hair.

"Do you want to take a few minutes?"

"No I don't want to take a few minutes!" He said and picked up his racket. "Come on, just serve."

"Okay." Dhiraj glanced at the digital board where the time seemed to be stuck at two-fifty-nine. Though the numbers under the players' names had changed, the time still hadn't.

He smiled as another idea came to him. Positioning himself for a serve, he twirled the handle of the racket in his hands.

"What the hell are you doing? Serve!" Sumit called.

"I will, relax."

Sumit assumed his position again, but Dhiraj continued to dawdle. He stopped rotating the racket and picked at a thread on the hem of his T-shirt.

"Hey!" Sumit said, straightening. Dhiraj took that opportunity to serve quickly and pumped a fist when he scored an easy point.

Sumit stood in a daze, with his mouth open and his eyes fixed on the shuttlecock lying near his feet.

Dhiraj bit down on his smile and rejoiced when the digital numbers increased under his name.

For the next serve, Dhiraj employed the same tactic, doing everything but hitting the shuttlecock.

Eventually, Sumit let out a frustrated scream and then pointed. "Hey! You broke a freaking rule!" He grinned, displaying his sharp pointed teeth.

"You took more than five seconds to serve and that..." His grin grew so wide that all Dhiraj could see was the large pointed tips of the teeth that no doubt possessed the strength to tear off human skin easily from the bones.

"That is a fault!" Sumit finished.

Dhiraj splayed his hands. "I have no idea what you're talking about. I didn't take more than five seconds."

"Don't lie to me!" His opponent said, the grin disappearing. "It was more than five seconds."

Dhiraj pointed at the board. "It doesn't show on the board. Look at the time."

Sumit growled louder. "You're cheating."

"You're going to have to prove it. If anyone's cheating, it's you," Dhiraj said in a condescending tone. He came to a realization that while he was playing his favorite sport, he had been so distracted by his thoughts that he no longer feared Sumit's ghost. He decided that it probably had to be the way he had gained an upper hand in this game that was giving him the confidence to shake off his terror.

"I thought it was going to be a fair game." Dhiraj tsked. "But you never played fair when you were alive, so to expect that you would do so in death..."

Sumit charged to the net that separated them. "How dare you."

"I'm not scared of you," Dhiraj said, a smile playing on his lips. "Now are we going to have a fair game or what?"

He looked straight into his opponent's eyes, challenging him and feeling the rush of power in his veins. It felt so good to beat Sumit again and it gave him the confidence to promise himself that he would walk out of all this alive.

Then he heard a click on the digital board and saw Sumit's expression change. A smile tugged at his lips, showing him a pointed tooth.

Dhiraj turned to see the object of his amusement and at first couldn't understand what had cheered up his opponent. The score was still the same, with him leading. The only thing that had changes was the time. It showed three o'clock and for some reason Sumit seemed to look victorious.

"Let's play," Sumit said and walked back.

Dhiraj looked at his back and then at the scoreboard, not understanding what was going on.

Focus, he told himself.

He squeezed his eyes shut and took a long deep breath. He could do it—he could get himself out of this quandary. When he opened his eyes, he found Sumit standing with his head raised up and his arms by his side with his palms facing out. He opened his mouth and started to chant something that wasn't audible.

Dhiraj lowered his racket. Though there was pin-drop silence, he thought he could hear the sound of footsteps behind him. He turned to see the spectators seated behind him standing with their mouths wide open and their form becoming yellow and fuzzy. He looked straight ahead to see that his parents had reappeared and were standing too, with their mouths wide open and the black smoke expelling through their eyes.

The people around him started to chant with Sumit in a strange language Dhiraj had never heard before. Their chants grew louder and louder, and he whirled all around, certain he was going to go mad if they didn't stop soon. Their chants turned shrill and Dhiraj clasped his hands over his ears and let out a cry. He could feel their words drive into his ear canal and pierce his brain.

He bent over as the pain became excruciating and he was hardly aware that he was screaming. Then all of a sudden, the silence reemerged and for the first time since he had entered the forest, he was glad for that. Removing his hands from his ears, he watched as the spectators walked down from the stands and headed toward Sumit who still appeared to be chanting. Dhiraj watched his lips move but heard no sound and became wary as the spectators formed a line in front of him.

He saw his parents' illusion standing first in line and when Sumit stopped, they turned to give Dhiraj a vacant look before stepping inside Sumit. The other spectators followed suit—disappearing inside Sumit's body right before his eyes. With each of the spirits entering his body, Sumit's form started to glow with a bluish-white light and turned his eyes from black smoke to an orange fiery glow. He could see Sumit's skin scarred with red lines that glowed and pulsated. When the last of the spirits had entered Sumit, his opponent let out a satisfied sigh—as if he had just quenched a dire thirst.

Sumit lowered his gaze and snickered at him. "Let's keep playing."

Dhiraj felt the energy zap out of him. All his hard work and trickery had gotten him nowhere as he now found himself face to face with a man who looked too powerful.

Whatever had just happened had in some way benefited his opponent and Dhiraj found himself getting nervous.

"Nephew, you haven't forgotten us, have you?"

Dhiraj gasped when he saw the men he had encountered in the forest whose leader had turned out to be Sumit's uncle.

"Uncle!" Sumit said happily and went over to embrace him. "Your presence was terribly missed."

The uncle looked at the scoreboard and shook his head in disappointment. "This isn't going so well for you, is it?"

"No, but look at the time." Sumit gestured.

The uncle's grin grew wider. "Then your victory is assured."

Dhiraj watched the exchange between uncle and nephew with anxiety. He was overpowered and he imagined both uncle and nephew pouncing on him and finishing him off—after or during the match.

The uncle gestured to his goons and they came to stand behind Sumit in support. The six of them looked terrifying and all the hope Dhiraj had garnered to build back his confidence, abandoned him. There was nothing he could do anymore, except say his goodbyes.

The uncle whispered something in Sumit's ear that made him laugh and stare at him. The six men laughed and pointed, making Dhiraj even more nervous. He surveyed the stadium and looked for an exit door, but still could see no sign of one.

"Don't worry," The uncle said. "We're honest demons."

The goons burst into laughter at that, but Sumit watched him with an expressionless face.

"If my nephew promised he will let you go if you win the match, then we will keep that promise," The uncle said.

Dhiraj didn't reply and stared at the racket. It was better to keep his eyes on anything else except for the demons standing before him. He thought if he kept looking at them, his mind would snap and throw him into a delirium he would never get out of.

There was only one way to get over his fear. This was something his father had once told him when Dhiraj had come home crying when he was ten years old. The neighbor's kids had bullied him and stolen his football and then pushed him over. Dhiraj had been so scared of the teenage boys, that he had stopped going out to play, until his father had given him a piece of advice that Dhiraj had carried and adhered to for all these years.

"The only way to get over fear is to face it. If someone bullies you stand up straight, look them in the eye and show them how afraid you are not!"

That and along with some advice on how to excel in sports was what had gotten him through his sports training and school.

Dhiraj looked up at the men. The one thing he had had mastered with the bullies he had encountered thus far was to smile at them. A smile always intimidated the bullies.

"You know, I've always wondered how you managed to get into the team," Dhiraj said. "Considering how amateurish your plays are." He nodded at the uncle. "Now, I get it."

"What are you implying?" Sumit snarled. His eyes turned a darker orange and the red veins on his skin glowed.

"You're smart enough to get *it*," Dhiraj said, ignoring his heart thudding in his chest. "Oh wait....you kind of failed your semester, didn't you and had to repeat it? Have you graduated yet?"

"Lies!" Sumit bellowed. "All lies!"

His uncle put a hand on his back. "Relax, he's just trying to get under your skin. Focus on your game and win the match."

Sumit exhaled white smoke. Dhiraj turned his back to them, gathering up his courage and flexing his trembling hands. He kept looking for a door, but all he saw were blue walls and empty seats.

"Serve," Sumit said.

Dhiraj felt his throat getting dry, something he hadn't felt in all the time he had been in the forest. When was the last time he had even a sip of water to drink? Or food? When had he eaten last?

"Play!" Sumit commanded.

Dhiraj served and watched the shuttlecock fly over the net. He saw Sumit jump up and slam it down the other side.

"Point!" Sumit cheered.

With a sinking heart, Dhiraj watched the score increase under Sumit's name. The rest of the game turned out exactly as he had feared. His racket made no contact with the shuttlecock as Sumit delivered one perfect serve after another.

When he reached twenty one points, the umpire declared Sumit the winner of the game. Now that they were tied, there was just another game left to decide his fate. Dhiraj walked over to the empty stands and sat down with his head bowed and mourning the loss of the game. He thought he had the advantage and figured out Sumit's weak spot. How wrong he had been!

"The game starts now," The umpire said.

Sumit had been standing in position and waiting with a racket in his hands. "Ready to lose?"

Dhiraj didn't have a clever comeback and kept his mouth shut. He would give his best and if he was destined to die today, then there was nothing to stop him. All that he would be leaving behind would be disappointed parents who had longed to see their son with the national championships. All their hard work would have been for nothing.

With the gloom settling down on him, Dhiraj walked dejectedly back to the court and gave a silent apology to his parents.

Sumit was getting ready to serve when he paused suddenly. His orange fiery eyes turned dull and the red markings on his skin vanished.

"Did you feel that?" He asked his uncle in a numb voice.

His uncle shook his head. "What are you talking about?"

Sumit lowered his arm as his eyes widened. "She's here again."

"What? Impossible!" The uncle paused and turned his eyes to the side as if waiting to hear something. "Oh no!" his voice was a brush of wind.

"Why is she here? Has she come to take me?" Sumit asked, looking frightened.

"Perhaps she has come to take him." The uncle gesticulated at Dhiraj.

Sumit shook his head. "No, she spared him. If it was him, she would have taken him when she had the chance."

The six men stood in silence, waiting to hear something else. Dhiraj knew who they were talking about—the old woman with the silver hair who had given him truths and nightmares. She had let him go and he couldn't understand what made the demons so terrified of her. Where did they think she was going to take them?

"Who is she here for?" The uncle asked. "I think she's coming closer."

The uncle's goons receded to a corner and huddled together. The silence had returned—more powerful than ever, but it lasted for a few seconds. Dhiraj heard a whisper in the air and words that he couldn't understand. The voice was feminine and her words appeared to be garbled. He listened closely, but all he managed to hear was 'go straight and turn left.'

Dhiraj swallowed, aware his mouth had gone dry.

Then a door slammed open and the old woman with silver long hair entered. She brought along with her a gust of wind and an ominous sensation that weighed down upon him. When she stepped forward, the six demons pulled away from her.

Dhiraj eyed the door behind her that had just formed existence. He considered making a run for it, but his limbs were paralyzed with fear after seeing the woman.

"W-why are you h-here?" Sumit asked, hiding behind his uncle. "Who have you come here for?"

The old woman smiled. Her hair, Dhiraj noticed, was so long that it was still outside and beyond the door.

"Who do you think I am here for?" The old woman asked.

"Take them!" The uncle said, pointing at his goons who let out a frightened cry. "Or him!" He pointed at Dhiraj.

The old woman closed the gap and stood right in front of the uncle who trembled with fear. His mustache dropped and quivered, and his bluish skin turned white.

"How about I take you?"

"Please...don't take me to the tree!" He implored.

The old woman burst out laughing. "I am not here for you. I have found who I was looking for and it is none of you."

Everyone, including Dhiraj, heaved a sigh of relief.

"But there is another matter that must be resolved," She said and curled a hand around her own hair. She yanked at it and Dhiraj heard a swooshing sound. He saw a lump of silver enter the door and at first couldn't understand what he was seeing when the lump moved frantically.

Then when he spotted a pair of feet and felt the breath knock out of him. It was a body!

"Here he is." The old woman presented, and with another tug on her hair, unraveled the body to reveal a small man with glasses and short tousled wavy hair. He was wearing a blue shirt and brown pants that were smeared with dirt and blood.

Dhiraj's mouth dropped open when the young man adjusted his glasses and looked up with frightened eyes at the demons in front of him.

"Aksh?" He said.

His friend looked at him, but instead of mutual relief, he saw guilt blanket his expression.

"Ah, yes…your friend," The old woman said and turned to Sumit. "It's time you learned the truth."

Chapter Thirty-One

Rudra was having a tough time holding himself together..
His own voice was being suppressed by the whispers in his
head that was slowly taking control of his motor skills.
When he wanted to walk left, the voice told him to turn
right instead and his body obliged, ignoring his screaming
inner voice.

He was being taken over and there was nothing he
could do. Preeti was sadly unaware of what was going on
and he wanted to hold her in his arms and console her as
she regarded him with fright in her big brown eyes.

But he couldn't risk telling her anything in case the
demonic voice in his head kept his word and hurt Preeti.

Rudra started to regret making this deal to gain her
affection, but he was exhausted from trying to suppress his
love for her. No matter how hard he tried or how many
girls he dated, he had always felt something missing and
empty in his life.

He had to have her.

"And you need to find Nisha," The voice said.

Rudra winced when he felt a sudden ache in his
right shoulder. He stopped and realized Preeti wasn't
anywhere near him. He retraced his steps and heard the
sound of rustling leaves. It could either be the wind playing
with them or...

Pushing a gap through the hedges, he stepped in to
find Preeti on the other side, gazing at a cottage in front of
her. She was saying something to him with panic in her
voice, but all he heard was the impish voice telling him to
keep walking as fast as he could to find Nisha.

"Now!" The voice screamed in his head and then suddenly his feet had started moving quickly in the opposite direction from Preeti.

He had left her behind and there was nothing he could do about it. Rudra was walking all alone in the forest and he dreaded the silence surrounding him.

His ears were strained for any footsteps that would follow him so he could find comfort in the fact that he wasn't separated from Preeti.

He wanted to turn his head, but he could feel invisible hands on the sides of his face, making him look only ahead.

"Oh... it's happening," The voice said suddenly, its voice so strained and raspy that Rudra couldn't make out if it was fear or happiness that was laced in that tone.

There was a loud ticking sound then and Rudra paused, finding that he had regained control of his limbs. He looked down from where he heard the sounds and saw that his watch was ticking loudly.

When he had entered the forest, his watch had been frozen at two-fifty am, but it was working now and the big hand touched twelve. It was three o' clock and Rudra thought how strange it would be if be found out that he had been in the forest for only ten minutes.

A piercing pain in his chest made him bend over and scream. The pain intensified and flooded his entire body with massive prickles.

The voice in his head returned and he could feel its power tightening around his soul again.

"Find her!"

"I can't!" He gasped. "The pain... I can't!"

There was a sensation of something being sucked away from him only to be replaced with something heavier that had its hand around his heart.

"There we go. Better?" He heard impish laughter and before he knew it he was walking ahead in long quick strides.

A hand clasped around his arm but he barely felt it through the numbness.

"Rudra!" Preeti was screaming for him or at him, he couldn't bring himself to care. He heard her take Nisha's name and then something about how she was a friend and shouldn't hurt her. She kept tugging at him and came before him, jogging backwards. He looked down to see her hands on his chest, but he felt nothing.

The realization that he couldn't feel her touch suffocated him. He tried to fight the invisible restraints on his arms and legs, but whatever had taken control of him was more powerful. Before he knew it, he watched himself push Preeti away with a flick of his arm.

"No!" He screamed and found that his voice remained inside of him. He hadn't even opened his mouth!

"There she is." He could feel his mouth talking but those were not his words but the one who had taken control of his body... And now his voice. He had lost himself and that emotion was tiny compared to the feeling of accomplishment at finding his target.

He saw Nisha sitting under a tree watching him with wide frightened eyes. In her human form, she looked like an innocent girl waiting for someone to come save her, not harm her the way his possessor wanted to.

"I found her! I found her!" He felt himself say.

His movements grew quicker and he was barely eight feet away from her when he saw someone emerge from behind the tree. It was a girl with plaited hair right up to her shoulders and dressed in a blouse and short skirt.

"It's Maya!" He said to himself.

"What is she doing here?" The impish voice bellowed. "What are you doing here?"

Maya said nothing and kept staring into his eyes. He wanted to scream and tell her to run before he hurt her, but he had lost that control completely.

He could see himself walking faster and then felt himself slip and fall.

A cry emitted from his lips, but it was not his own. His body came in contact with a rock, but he felt no pain.

Looking around him, he found himself in a deep narrow pit. He gazed up to see Maya and Nisha look down at him.

"It worked," Nisha said joyfully.

Maya didn't look too happy. She glared at him and when she spoke, her voice was acidic.

"Let Rudra go you fiend!"

***

Nisha had been reluctant to act as bait and refused the plan outright the minute Maya had told her. She couldn't understand at first why a creature of the forest would be frightened of a jinn and then wondered if there was a weird food chain here as well and perhaps Nisha's other persona was right at the bottom of it.

Maya didn't want to know who was right at the top. The thought that there was a superior being out there in the dark waiting to pounce on her, had made her shudder.

"Please Nisha, that's the only way. We have to separate the jinn from Rudra." She had tried to persuade.

Nisha had begun crying and mumbling how she would be forced to go back to the tree and all the while Maya's eyes had skittered around her surroundings, hoping the noise wouldn't bring back the beasts who had barely spared her life. If it hadn't been for the white wolf, she would have been mauled to death by the black one—who must have been a hell hound.

"If you don't want to go back to the tree, you have to help me or Rudra will pursue and catch you relentlessly," She had said and then knelt and stroked Nisha's slimy arm. "Just one act of courage and you never have to be scared again. Just once, please. You don't even have to do anything."

Nisha had agreed reluctantly and then positioned herself under the tree. They had to wait a long time in silence, in case Rudra heard them both and their plan was ruined. She thought how fortunate it was to find a narrow pit dug near the tree and wondered who had done it. Beside the pit she had noticed freshly dug graves and two shovels discarded near them. Maya felt another shudder rush through her and willed herself not to imagine which creature must have done it to hunt another.

Beside her, Nisha started to move her legs restlessly but the minute Rudra came into view, she let out a small moan.

Maya who had been hiding behind the tree, held her breath. "I'm right here," She assured her.

Rudra stormed towards them and Nisha whined.

"I can't," She said. Maya knew if she didn't act fast, Nisha would run and lead Rudra away from the trap they had laid out.

So she had come out of her hiding place and Rudra had reacted in a surprised manner—just the way she had expected.

Watching her once genial friend now, she could only wish that once they escaped the forest, none of her friends would be scarred for life by what all had happened.

Rudra advanced, ready to lunge at Nisha and Maya tried not to cry out when she saw that the jinn was no longer sitting on Rudra's shoulder but was somehow inside of him. There was a shadow of horns near Rudra's head and red glowing eyes over her friend's. It looked like he was being split in two and she felt a rush of terror. She couldn't do this either and was about to grab Nisha and flee when Rudra slipped. His eyes grew wide with fear and for a fleeting second, it wasn't the maniacal animal that was going to attack them, but one of her best friends of ten years.

When he fell into the pit, he let out a hoarse cry and that snapped Maya back from her frightened thoughts. That cry did not belong to Rudra.

"Let me out!" He screamed in a demonic voice.

Nisha whimpered and then came to stand close to her. "Now what?"

"We... we have him trapped," Maya said, not wanting to peer down, but forcing herself to.

Rudra was grabbing and pulling at his hair while kicking at the walls of the pit.

"Let me out!"

Nisha gasped and then forced herself to look down to. Seeing her, Rudra grew even more frenzied. He screamed incoherent words and Maya felt a chill settle in her heart.

"How do we get the jinn out of him?" Nisha asked.

"We need Preeti. Seeing her and responding to his love for her is the only way to bring him back," Maya said, stepping away from the pit. She couldn't watch her friend screaming in pain anymore.

"Where is she?"

Maya looked up ahead. "She was with Rudra the last time I saw her."

Nisha circled carefully around the narrow pit and walked forward. "There's something there... is that her?"

Maya tore her eyes from the pit and carefully navigated herself from the edges of it. "Where?"

Nisha pointed at a pair of legs near a large rock. In the dark, that was all she could see.

"Maybe."

"Why is she lying on the ground like that?" Nisha asked, walking as closely as possible with her. "Is she dead? Did Rudra kill her?"

Maya paused as she said that and then ran to the shades of the trees. Falling to her knees, she turned the person over to find Preeti unconscious with blood dripping from the center of her forehead.

"Oh no, she's dead!" Nisha cried. "He killed her and now he'll kill us."

Maya clutched Preeti's limp arm and felt for her pulse. When she felt the slow throb under her wrist, she let out a long breath.

"No she's alive," Maya said and swallowed. "He would never hurt her."

Nisha bent with her hands on her knees. "Then why isn't she opening her eyes."

Maya wanted nothing more than to embrace her best friend. She had been so lost and scared and thought she would never see her friends again. But here they were.

"Preeti," She said, shaking her gently. "Preeti wake up. Please... Wake up. We need your help."

Chapter Thirty-Two

The truth. What was the truth of the moment?

The truth was that Dhiraj was scared that he was going to lose the badminton match—the one sport in which he had spent most of his youth training for. It was through sheer hard work that he had made the team and it was the proud faces of his parents that had made him persevere.

Dhiraj had been instilled with values that compelled him to be a decent honest human being. He had never hurt anyone on purpose and had always stood up for justice. Then Sumit had come into his life and he had been forced to alter his beliefs. Instead of using his parent's faith in him to motivate himself, he had applied competitive spirit.

When Sumit had raised a hand to bully someone, he had raised his too to stop him. Aksh hadn't been the first one to suffer Sumit's abuses.

Seeing his friend sitting on the floor in a disheveled state, Dhiraj thought back to that day at the hospital. The old woman was right—he wasn't completely innocent. He had known what Aksh had done—the look on his face had said it all. His usually meek friend had pulled off a perfect revenge plan, or so he must have thought.

Whether any human knew for sure or not, the old woman or whatever her true form was called, knew.

Dhiraj glanced at Sumit and saw him returning to his human form as well. His skin was still pale blue but his eyes had returned to their former grey ones. He looked frightened but also curious as the old woman grinned, showing her crooked yellowing teeth. This was her human form and after everything that had been going on, Dhiraj thought that if she morphed into her demonic persona, he would lose the last shreds of his sanity. He couldn't take it, he didn't want to be here anymore.

"Wh-what is he doing here?" Sumit asked.

The old woman pulled Aksh closer to her feet by dragging her hair and then caressed his tousled hair as if she were comforting a child.

"You do know how you died?" The old woman said.

Dhiraj felt the stranglehold of guilt around his neck. The door behind the old woman was still open. He had only to make a run for it, but now that Aksh was here, how could he leave him?

"I-I don't remember. The details are..uh... fuzzy."

Sumit's uncle cowered behind his nephew while his goons were bunched in the corner, eyeing the old woman warily.

Her hand grabbed a fistful of Aksh's hair and yanked. His friend let out a painful cry then sobbed into his hands.

"Tell him what you did," The old woman commanded.

Dhiraj imagined what would happen when Aksh told the truth and knew it wasn't going to go well for him. The picture of Sumit pouncing on his timid friend was too vivid. He had to save him; he had to try.

"Whatever happened, happened," He said in a controlled voice. "Just, please, let us all go."

Sumit nodded in agreement though his curiosity hadn't left him. His uncle came to her feet and clasped his hands.

"Please spare us," He begged.

The old woman snorted as if the most amusing joke had been told. She put one pointed finger under his chin and raised his head, not once losing her grip on Aksh's hair.

"I've been hoping to catch you," She said. "Your deplorable acts have earned you a special place in the tree."

"No!" He gasped. Rising to his feet, he ran to the exit, only for it to slam shut.

The old woman cackled. "Nobody gets to leave."

"Please forgive me!" He implored. "I'll do anything to make amends."

"Anything?"

"Yes, please!" The uncle had stooped so low that he had his nose to the ground.

"Can you bring the two girls back to life?" She asked.

"What? Which two girls?"

"The twins," The old woman stated. "The ones you threatened to harm and who were so scared for their dignity that they committed suicide."

Dhiraj saw his friend look up in astonishment at Sumit's uncle.

"It was you? The don? They told me..." Aksh started to say when the old woman pulled harder on his hair.

"You don't get to speak," She warned.

He had to stop this. Whatever was going on was going to end badly for Aksh. Either Sumit or the old woman was going to kill Aksh and his morals told him that he couldn't let an innocent die.

Aksh hadn't meant to kill Sumit and he shouldn't be punished so severely for that one moment of weakness. But what could be possibly do to save him?

***

When the old woman had told him that she was going to take him to the person he had wronged, Aksh had expected to be dragged out of the forest and back into the real world.

Sitting on the ground of what looked like a sports arena, he wondered if this was the real world or still his never ending nightmare.

He was dragged ruthlessly in and his back ached from the numerous scratches he had incurred because of it. The old woman refused to loosen her grip and his mind refused to let him keep his grip on reality.

He wanted to scream and sob and then beg to be let go. And then he saw Sumit and knew he wasn't going to survive. Everyone in the arena was cowering from the old woman, as if she was far superior than them and Aksh found himself wishing he was back in the twin's house looking for an easy escape rather than being bound by the old woman's strange silver hair that slithered like a thousand snakes around him.

Overhead he heard the old woman pass judgment on the people in the arena and when she accused a talk bulky man of being responsible for the twin's death, his eyes shot up and he made the mistake of speaking.

She rewarded him with a painful yank that showed him the other side of the arena. In his despair he hadn't noticed that there was a match going on and a digital board in the center showed him the score of two players—Sumit and Dhiraj.

It was only then that he turned sideways to see his friend standing in the corner watching the scene before him with a blank expression.

Was there a match going on?

The stands were empty but he spotted the waxed form of a man in an umpire uniform. The score on the board showed that both players had tied and they needed just one game to decide the winner.

Aksh looked back at Dhiraj wishing he would look at him and help him. Instead his friend stood numbly with a racket in his hand, watching the old woman apprehensively.

Despite the situation, Aksh started to get angry. His friend wasn't in binds and could easily pry him away from the demons and help him escape.

Was Dhiraj even going to try to help him?

He muttered a curse under his breath. And here he had thought that Dhiraj was a good friend to him, and would always protect him from bullies. How he wished he had asked the old woman to take Dhiraj instead of him. For some strange reason the old woman seemed to have a soft side for Maya and he couldn't understand why.

"He's the one who purposely prescribed the wrong medicines for you," The old woman said and Aksh realized to his horror that she had told Sumit the truth.

He gazed up, to see Sumit's eyes become stormy and his face darken to a reddish-brown. His eyes started to glow red and the only reason he was holding himself back was probably because the old woman scared him.

She returned to caressing his hair and Aksh looked up pleadingly at Dhiraj. When he still didn't make a move to help him, he turned away in anger.

He hated him—he hated Sumit and he hated all his other friends. If only the old woman would take them all in his place. He was about to open his mouth to suggest it when Dhiraj stepped forward.

"Sumit is not so innocent either," He told the old woman. "If you know the truth of everyone then you would know that as well. He harassed a lot of people and broke their spirits."

"Hmmm... yes," The old woman said and Sumit's eyes returned to normal and grew wide with fear.

"No one is innocent here, not even me." She cackled and started to walk to and fro, not once loosening her grip over Aksh.

"But how many people here have been the cause of someone's death?" She asked. "Come on, raise your hands."

No one raised their hands but Aksh could feel everyone's fear—especially his own palpitate.

The old woman had raised her hand slightly. "No? Oh..." She put her hand down. "What I hate even more are liars."

A sound escaped Aksh's throat and he knew he was close to bursting out in tears.

"Did you want to say something, child?" She asked lovingly.

Aksh put his arms around her ankles. "Please let me go! Please don't kill me!"

"Why does everyone do this?" She sighed. "It's my job to bring a wicked soul back to the tree, where its fate will be decided, and they will be sent to the underworld. Hell needs a lot of evil souls." While she said that, she kept stroking his hair as if she were comforting a frightened child.

"Not me!" Aksh begged. "Take anyone but me."

The old woman grabbed a fistful of his hair and pulled again. "Why don't you tell everyone here who you want to take your place?"

Aksh whimpered. If he took Maya's name again the old woman would get angry again and punish him. He looked up at Dhiraj and saw his friend looking like a scared little mouse who hadn't raised a paw to help him get away from the old woman. He could take Sumit's name but chances were she would remind him that he had already taken Sumit's life.

"Take Dhiraj!" Aksh cried. "He knew I had something to do with Sumit's death but remained quiet!" He pointed an accusatory finger at his friend. "He's not so innocent either. Take him, but please spare me!"

The old woman walked over to Dhiraj who stepped back instinctively. Her hair was still wrapped around Aksh and keeping him frozen to one spot.

"See?" She told Dhiraj. "And this is the friend you were trying to help. Look what that got you?" She laughed. "You must regret the day that you ever saved him from the bullies."

Dhiraj looked disappointed but he remained silent. The old woman shook her head while smiling and walked back to Aksh.

"While you were thinking how your friend was doing nothing to help you." She lowered her head so that her lips were near his ear. "He had come with a really good plan to help you escape. Too bad it would never come into play."

She straightened and snapped her fingers at Dhiraj. "You're free to go!"

Dhiraj was startled and watched the old woman warily, trying to see if she was joking.

"You've been tormented enough. Go find your friends. Your *real* friends," She said.

Dhiraj looked at Aksh with pity in his eyes and still wouldn't move.

"Do you want me to take Aksh's offer?" She asked. "He wouldn't mind you taking his place at all."

"Please..." Dhiraj said stepping forward but the old woman let out growl. Then with a flick of her hand, she pushed him with such force that Dhiraj flew across the arena and through the door that opened suddenly. Then it slammed shut, leaving a tremble that shook the ground.

Aksh started to cry. "Please don't kill me."

"I won't raise a hand... yet." She said and walked over to the stands to sit. "I'll just sit here and watch Sumit avenge his death."

Sumit let out an audible gasp of surprise.

"This is going to be fun," The old woman said gleefully. "Go on, Sumit. This may be your only chance."

Sumit too couldn't believe the old woman's words, but when minutes passed by and she hadn't lunged toward him. He took a step toward Aksh.

The old woman leaned forward, her hands under her chin and her elbows rested on her knees. Her eyes glowed with excitement and her hair slowly unraveled from around his neck.

Aksh pushed himself back with his hands as Sumit advanced. He clenched his hands into fists and lowered his head. His eyes glowed a fiery orange and when he snorted, Aksh was sure he had seen a wisp of smoke emit from his nostrils. A smile spread his thin lips, displaying his fangs.

Aksh whirled around to the old woman. "Please don't let him hurt me!"

The old woman smiled. "Sumit's soul would never find peace if he doesn't do this." Then she nodded at Sumit. "Go ahead. Do your worst."

Chapter Thirty-Three

She kept trying to swim to the blur of light, but something kept tugging her legs back. Preeti turned, holding her breath as she swam in the grayish water. What she saw almost made her open her mouth and let the murky water enter. Black spiky tentacles slithered towards her and twirled around her ankle, pulling her further down.

Preeti used her free leg to kick at it and winced when the spikes pierced her sole. Closing her eyes and mustering up all her strength, she stepped hard on the tentacles holding her down and then swam upwards.

It was while she was using her hands to push herself forward that she realized that she had no idea how she had fallen in the water. She stopped and used her legs to kick and stay afloat.

Where am I? I wasn't here. I was in the forest and Rudra...hadn't he just pushed me away?

All of a sudden she found herself back on the wet slippery road, looking at the forest in front of her. Preeti looked for the car that had brought her friends and her here and saw only the long road whose surface shimmered in the moonlight.

I'm in another dream. Why am I dreaming?

"Wake up!" she told herself, but the scene didn't change when she opened her eyes. She heard voices then, getting louder and rowdier as it came closer. Preeti saw flaming torches and gasped when a mob, consisting entirely of men dressed in white long shirts and pants, came into view.

"Find them!" The man in the front said. He couldn't be older than thirty and had jet black hair and a mustache. "Find my daughter!"

Preeti picked up another sound coming from the other side and saw a young couple holding hands and running. It was them—the couple she had met when she had come into the forest and who had thrown her off the cliff that had seemed to be the only exit out of the forest.

"We won't let them get married!" Three of the men in the mob said. The men advanced with their flaming torches and swords in their hands and Preeti let out a frightened moan. She couldn't figure out whether the men could see her or not and she couldn't understand why she was being shown this.

"Leave us alone!" she heard the young couple scream. "No one can separate us. Not even death!"

The words had been what they had uttered when she had encountered them. Preeti found herself torn between trying to figure out what she was doing here and helping the couple.

She had to try, she decided, when she saw the men slashing the trees' branches as they made their way through the forest. She didn't know how she was seeing all this from her position, but she was and it was terrifying.

Preeti started toward them, thinking of throwing rocks at the men to distract them, when she saw a movement in the trees. Then there was a soft sweet melody being played that sounded like someone humming—a woman.

Parting the shrubs, Preeti saw a tall woman take a step towards the mob. In the moonlight, she looked to be about ten feet tall, dressed in a black dress with lacy full sleeves and a silk skirt. She had her long hair tied up loosely, which allowed her ringlets to fall on her shoulders. When she turned, Preeti saw that the woman had fair skin and large brown eyes with long eyelashes. She had a straight nose and pale full lips.

The woman was extraordinarily beautiful and Preeti had to look away from her hypnotic looks. She could hear the woman give a short laugh and then walk forward. Her humming had stopped and Preeti heard her whispering something. Her words were like a gush of wind and the men immediately stopped in the tracks.

The woman, who looked to be young, walked past the mob and stood by a tree whispering something. This time, Preeti heard her.

"Turn left," She was saying.

Preeti looked down to see the young couple suddenly run left.

The woman in black smiled, satisfied that her order had been carried out. Preeti shuddered when she saw the woman grow taller until she was just the same height as the tree she was standing beside.

"Go straight and then turn left again," She whispered.

Preeti came forward and made her way through the crowd of men who stood frozen in their spots. Their eyes were glazed and their mouths were slightly open. When she accidentally bumped into a young man, he didn't move a muscle.

Preeti walked quickly and followed the woman in black who had resumed her humming.

"Good," She said, between melodies. "Keep going."

Up ahead, the young couple seemed to be following every command and they jumped over small hedges and rocks instead of going around them. The woman had after all not commanded them to walk around obstacles.

"Stop," The woman said, then hummed and waved her hands, as if she were a conductor of an orchestra. "Go forth, my children."

Preeti gasped. They young couple were standing right at the edge of the cliff. They looked at each other and held their hands. A look of sorrow shadowed their expressions and she saw tears roll down their faces.

"Go," The woman repeated. As if they had received their cues, the couple stepped into the emptiness and let them fall.

"No!" Preeti screamed, running to them. She stopped herself at the edge and knelt down to see the couple falling to their deaths.

"You made them jump!" she screamed at the woman.

The woman laughed without opening her mouth. She snapped her fingers and the crowd of men behind her collapsed on the ground. She walked over to them and knelt. Using a finger, she swiped a dribble of blood oozing from the mouths of one of the men.

Preeti expected the woman to taste it, instead, she used the blood to paint her lips bright red. Then she let her tongue run over it and made a satisfied sound. She got up and turned to her and Preeti instantly felt her muscles tightening.

"Who are you?" she asked. "What are you?"

The woman in black smiled widely and the blood on her lips started to drip. Putting one finger on her lips, she opened her mouth.

"Shhhh."

"A-are you going to kill me?"

The woman came forward and Preeti realized that she couldn't step back anymore. If she did, she would fall off the cliff and this time she didn't have the young couple to save her. The woman clasped her hands together and closed the distance between them.

She gave her a friendly smile and Preeti had to use all her willpower to try and not respond to her but the muscles in her mouth had a mind of their own and she was forced to return her smile.

"Don't hurt me."

The woman shook her head. Then put her hand under Preeti's chin and started to caress her cheek.

"I won't," She whispered. "Not when I have a mission for you."

Preeti was sure she had misheard the woman. *A mission?*

"You want me to do something for you?" she asked.

The woman nodded and Preeti felt her heart sink. She looked up at the woman and saw her giving her the kindest looks.

"And if I refuse?"

The woman looked amused. "Sweetheart, you don't have a choice." She said in a whispery voice. "Now here's what I want you to do...."

***

Seeing her friend lying motionless on the ground filled Maya with sorrow. This was her friend—no Preeti had been more than her friend. They had done everything together—played, studied in the same school and then college and had even gone out on their first dates together with boys who had been twins.

Even though their lives had drifted apart after college, Preeti had always been in her heart and the first person she would call whenever she had been depressed about her personal problems. Preeti had never invaded her privacy; she had always cheered her up without prodding into her affairs.

When Preeti had started to become distant, Maya had guessed what had happened and knew it was her cheating boyfriend that had gotten her depressed. However at that time she had been having her own problems with her mother and couldn't be there for her best friend.

Now, she regretted all the time she had never been there for Preeti.

"Please, don't die." Maya sobbed. Her hand was still around Preeti's wrist and at one point, her pulse had stopped. The fear that had engulfed her was too overwhelming. She wanted to cry and scream—but all she could do was shake Preeti harder.

"Preeti! No!"

But her friend remained limp.

"She's dead!" Nisha wailed. Looking up at her, Maya thought Nisha looked too young and innocent to be wearing such promiscuous clothes. The top especially revealed more than it should when she bent over Preeti.

"She's not dead!" Maya screamed at her. Nisha's lips trembled and Maya instantly felt sorry for her. "Preeti is not dead. She's like my sister and I'm not losing her!"

"Then why won't she wake up?" Nisha cried. "You said Rudra wouldn't hurt her, but what if the jinn had?"

Behind them, Rudra was screaming at the top of his lungs, cursing the two girls with the heaviest profanities Maya had never imagined existed. She heard him trying to claw his way out and failing and then yelling even more obscenities.

He was trapped in that deep pit, but that was not all Maya wanted to do. She wanted to save Rudra and for that she needed Preeti.

"That's why you can't die," She said, numbly.

Nisha clasped her hands and started to sob in them and her pessimism was making her angry.

"Shut up!" she screamed at the frightened girl. "Just shut the hell up. She's not dead! You got that! Preeti isn't dead!"

"I'm sorry." Nisha wailed and her skin rippled to show her true form. Then in a blink of an eye she was her human self again.

"Go make sure Rudra doesn't come up," Maya said, encouraged by the way Preeti's pulse resumed its normal pounding.

"I'm too scared," Nisha said. "I could help you wake her up."

"And just how are you going to do that?" Maya asked impatiently. She looked down to see Preeti's eyes flutter. "I think she's regaining consciousness."

Nisha put her hand on Preeti's forehead and closed her eyes. With her head raised to the full moon that was showing through the small patch among the trees, she appeared to be praying.

"She's dreaming," Nisha said. "I can see her...and the others."

Maya rubbed Preeti's hands to provide her with some warmth. "How can you do that?"

"Shh!" Nisha said, opening her eyes. "That's what she was saying."

"What?" Maya asked.

"I couldn't see anything else," Nisha said. "Except that she was talking to someone. A woman. A very tall woman."

"It was just a dream," Maya said. "We need to find her some water."

"There is no water here," Nisha said. "Only rain, but we've never drunk that because we are never thirsty."

Maya heard Preeti let out a soft groan and her hopes rose. Preeti was finally reviving!

She looked up at Nisha who was watching Preeti with curiosity, as if wondering whether or not she should be scared of her.

"Ever since I've come here, I haven't felt hunger or thirst either," Maya said.

Preeti's hand suddenly moved and Nisha pushed herself back. Her expression grew solemn and she suddenly grabbed Maya's wrist and turned it over to look at her watch.

"It's just after three," Nisha said in a serious tone.

"Yeah, so?" Maya felt Preeti's pulse grow stronger and her breathing resume to its normal rate.

"That is when the forest becomes powerful." Nisha looked far into the distance. "When *we* become powerful."

"What?"

Nisha looked down at her hands and Maya saw her trembling suddenly. Nisha grunted and morphed into her beast form and then back into her human one. Her eyes grew larger and glowed with white. She threw her head back and let out a shrill scream, before collapsing on the ground beside Preeti.

Maya let out a gasp and moved away, gripping Preeti's arm tight with fear.

Preeti let out a loud gasp and sat up straight. She put a hand on her stomach and groaned.

"Preeti!" Maya exclaimed and put her arms around her friend. "You're okay!"

Preeti hugged her back and Maya allowed herself to weep. She stroked Preeti's hair to make sure that this wasn't an illusion and that her friend was not only alive but also right where she was.

Then she had a coughing fit and Maya had to pat Preeti's back gently. "Are you okay?"

"I couldn't breathe." Preeti mumbled and then put her hand on Maya's cheek. "It's really you?"

Maya smiled and nodded, tears streaming down her face.

Preeti smiled back and hugged Maya. "I can't tell you how happy I am to see you."

"I thought you were dead," Maya said. "When I saw you lying. And then your pulse. You stopped breathing. "

"I'm okay now," Preeti assured her and then her face grew grave. "I was with Rudra. He wanted to find Nisha."

Maya pointed back at the pit. "That's where he is now. We had to trap him." She took a hold of Preeti's shoulders. "We need your help. You have to find a way to separate the jinn from Rudra. Remind him of all the happy moments you guys shared together…anything to bring him back."

Preeti's eyes turned to the side. "Who is that? Is it Nisha?"

"Yes," Maya said.

"He wants her," Preeti said.

Maya put a hand on Nisha's skin and winced when she felt how hot it was. "She's burning up. I think she fainted."

"We can't let him have her," Preeti said. "We have to protect her."

"Yeah, she'll be fine," Maya said. "I'll stay with her while you go to Rudra and make him see reason."

"No," Preeti said, brusquely. "I can't leave her or she'll take her."

"What are you talking about?" Maya asked. Preeti's eyes looked lost and hollow as if she were in a daze.

"The woman…the woman in black…she said I had a mission," Preeti told her.

"What mission?"

"I need to find an old woman," Preeti said. "That's what I have to do."

Chapter Thirty-Four

Under normal circumstances, Dhiraj would have been wounded severely as he was thrown out the door of the stadium and onto a thorny bush from which he had bounced and landed on a large rock.

But as he picked himself up, he found that he had sustained no injuries—not even a scratch from the thorny bushes. A drop of water plopped on his head and he looked up at the cloudy night sky to see heavy drops of rain. Putting his palm out, he was relieved to see it wasn't blood rain at least.

He brought himself back to reality and looked at the large white door through which he had been flung out. The door slammed shut and Dhiraj ran toward it.

"Aksh!" He screamed. He pounded on it with his fists and screamed for his friend again. Putting an ear to the door, he could hear nothing except for a whizzing sound that reminded him of the time his TV had started to break down and every channel he had switched to, had lost all sound and made that very same static sound.

"Aksh!" He pounded on the door again. Then he took a few steps back and ran toward it, bumping his shoulder against it.

The door pushed back slightly but didn't open. Dhiraj tried ramming it again and again until his shoulder ached.

He clutched his shoulder and moaned. With that pain, came more pain. He looked down at his arms to see deep welts appearing and a small thorn sticking out from his elbow. His chest felt heavier and when he coughed to clear his passage he saw speckles of blood in his palm that washed away as the rain fell harder.

Touching the side of his neck, he saw more warm sticky blood and in a flash he saw himself sitting in a car and listening to his music when suddenly there was a bright white light. Then there was the sensation of being shoved and his head coming in contact with the glass. He remembered how cold the glass had felt.

He felt warm coppery tasting liquid, fill his mouth and spat. Ignoring the splat of blood on the rock that was quickly washed away, he scrambled to the door and found it further from his reach. He took a few steps and the door pushed further back.

Dhiraj started to run as the door pulled farther and farther away. He had a dream like this once and he remembered how instead of the door, he had been chasing the badminton trophy.

When he blinked, he saw that the door was now twenty feet away from him.

"Aksh!" He screamed. "Dammit!"

He tripped and fell on the ground as tears sprang to his eyes.

"No!" He screamed and punched the ground. He couldn't save his friend. No matter what Aksh had said in there, he knew that his friend did it because he had succumbed to fear.

"What have I done?" Dhiraj sobbed. "I couldn't win the match and I couldn't save you."

He turned and lay on his back, letting the rain bathe him. He put his hands on his eyes and sobbed.

A failure... that was what he was.

He heard a low growl from afar and his heart clenched in his chest.

What was that?

He sat up and looked to the right from where he thought he had heard the noise. The growl turned into a scream and his heart started to beat faster.

Getting on his feet, he tried to see through the blanket of pouring rain, but could only see the silhouettes of trees.

Then he heard the cry of girl and Dhiraj froze on his spot. One part of his mind told him that he should run as far as he could from the noises, the other reminded him how he was unable to save his friend and was now going to back away from helping a girl.

Taking firm strides toward the cluster of trees, he parted the low branches to see a girl dressed in a small red sparkly dress, sitting beside a hole in the ground.

There was something inside it that was making those growling sounds. Suddenly, a hand emerged from it and moved around to grab at something.

The girl gasped and then let out another frightful cry.

"He's coming out of the pit!" She screamed.

Dhiraj turned all around him and when he didn't see anything he could use as a weapon. He put his hands on one of the branches and a foot on the tree trunk. Using all his force and ignoring his awakening pain, he tore off the branch and rushed to aid the crying girl.

He was about to swing the branch at the wet bluish hand when someone came in front of him.

"No!" She yelled.

Dhiraj skidded to a halt and breathed deeply. Wiping away the wet tendrils from his face he saw a familiar face looking up at him in amazement.

She had raised both her arms to block him and was still standing in that position with her mouth open.

The branch slipped away from his grasp and landed with a thud on the ground.

"Is that... really you?"

Relief washed over her face and Preeti lowered her arms. "Dhiraj?"

Without another thought, he took her in his arms and hugged her tight. "Am I glad to see you!"

***

"You have no idea how happy I am," Preeti replied. She could feel Dhiraj's skin under her hands, she could smell the faint scent of his cologne and she could hear his heartbeat. It was all real.

She was finally reunited with her friends and nothing could make her happier than this. The rain was still falling all over them, but Preeti didn't seek shelter. She relished the cool water that washed away some of her fear and anxiety. Then she remembered what she was supposed to do and got serious.

"We're all here," She said, stepping back but still not breaking contact with him. "Except for Aksh. Once we find him…"

Dhiraj lowered his eyes and looked sad. "I did find him."

"Oh? Then where is he?"

Maya came up behind her and gasped in surprise. "Dhiraj?" She ran into his arms. "You're really here?"

"Maya you're here too?" Dhiraj asked in a stupor. He looked dazed and distracted but Preeti imagined it may have been something to do with the horrors he must have incurred while roaming in the forest.

"Rudra is there, in that pit." Maya pointed to where Rudra was screaming about drowning in the hole.

"We have to get him out!" Dhiraj said, running to the pit.

"No!" Maya grabbed his arm. "He's been possessed by a jinn."

"What?"

"That's true," Preeti said. "Maya had to trap him in there because he was hell-bent on finding Nisha."

"Who is Nisha?" Dhiraj asked.

Maya and Preeti turned around and saw Nisha sitting up, clutching her stomach as if she were in pain.

"Was she lost in the forest too?" he asked.

"No," Preeti said. "She's one of them."

Dhiraj didn't ask any more questions. It seemed he knew exactly what she was referring to and he watched the girl in the red dress with caution.

"We have to get Rudra out of the pit or he'll drown in the rainwater," He said, still eyeing Nisha as if expecting her to lunge at him.

"The jinn won't let Rudra die. He needs a vessel to do his dirty work," Maya explained. "Once Preeti helps him, we'll get him out."

"Where is Aksh?" Preeti asked and turned to Maya. "He said he saw Aksh."

Dhiraj adopted a forlorn look. "I think he's…gone. I don't know. I tried to save him, but the old woman wanted to punish him and…"

"Old woman?" Preeti asked. "Was she dressed in white?"

"And have silver hair?" Maya asked.

Preeti looked at Maya. "You know who I'm supposed to find?"

"What's going on?" Dhiraj asked.

"I had a dream…or a vision. I don't know what it was," Preeti said. "I saw a woman, as tall as a tree and dressed in black. She said she wanted the old woman dressed in white and who had silver hair."

"What does Nisha have to do with it?" Dhiraj asked.

"Nothing," Maya said, a little defensively. "Everyone wants to send her back to the tree because she escaped from the alleged gateway of hell." She shook her head. "I can't seem to believe everything that is going on around here. There's a gateway to hell?"

"The tree?" Dhiraj asked, remembering the time the old woman had hung him from it. He shuddered.

"Anyway," Preeti interjected. "The woman said I had to bring the old woman to her, to the tree."

"Why?" Maya asked. "None of this makes sense."

"Where is she, anyway?" Preeti asked. "Is Aksh with her?"

"Aksh is gone." Dhiraj wiped away a tear. "He...." Thrusting a hand in his wet hair, Dhiraj looked distraught. "He may have had something to do with Sumit's death."

"Sumit's dead?" Maya asked, looking pale all of a sudden.

"He...and I got into an altercation and he had to go to the hospital and Aksh, he may have wanted to take revenge on him for bullying him." Dhiraj appeared distraught. "The old woman had him. She dragged him to Sumit and said he could do anything he wanted. Now Sumit's a demon, and he's powerful because he said the time was three a.m. I have no idea what he meant."

Preeti went over to Dhiraj and hugged him. She could hear his rapid heartbeat and his breathing quicken. Dhiraj hugged her back tight, sobbing. "I swear I tried to save him. But the door just went further and further away from my reach."

"We know you tried." Maya patted his arm. "Wait. What was it about it being three a.m.?"

Dhiraj wiped his face. "Something about the demons getting stronger."

Maya turned to look at Nisha who was standing and watching them—a numb look on her face.

"You think she'll hurt us?" Dhiraj asked.

"I don't think so," Maya said. "We have to keep her safe. If everyone wants her..."

"We should give her up," Preeti interrupted. "It's her or us."

"What? No!" Maya said. "We can't trust anyone over here except for us."

"Nisha belongs to the forest," Preeti said. "Look, I was the one who told Rudra not to hurt Nisha, but after the dream I just had, everything seems clearer. The woman said that I had to bring the old woman and that Nisha had to be brought back to the tree. She controls the forest. I saw how she does it."

"Preeti, it was just a dream," Maya said.

"It felt real." Preeti put a hand on her cold forehead. "When I came here, I met a couple and she showed me exactly how she had led them to the cliff."

"That's how they died?" Maya asked. "And you still want to trust her?"

"She said, she would help us all leave this forest," Preeti said. "I don't want to be here anymore and I can't leave. The couple helped me back to the road where the car was, but I couldn't go anywhere else."

"Are you listening to yourself?" Maya asked. "The woman is by all means evil. She could be lying, have you considered that?"

"I saw what she could do!" Preeti cried. She wanted to scream and cry and make her friends see reason, but she knew that Maya was obstinate and difficult to convince. Dhiraj on the other hand, looked confused, as if torn between the two girls.

"I think I know what happened to us," Preeti said. "I saw our footprints in the mud. We all entered the forest in a straight line and none of us knew that. She whispers and she led us away from everyone. Without her wish, we couldn't contact each other."

"I guess that's true," Maya said. "I saw you guys walking, but it was like an invisible wall was stopping me from getting to you."

"So you see?" Preeti said, relieved that Maya agreed with her. "Let us give her what she wants and get out of here. All of us!"

"Yes," Dhiraj said. "The old woman is evil. She delivered Aksh to Sumit. She could have saved him from that."

"I say we find the old woman and help Aksh," Preeti said. "I have faith that he's still alive."

Maya shook her head. "No."

"What? Why not?" Preeti asked, getting irritated.

"The old woman isn't evil. She's just doing her job. She had children," Maya said. "She killed them but…"

"She killed her own children?" Preeti said in disgust.

"Yes, but she…" Maya pressed her lips together. "She is trying to make amends for what she did. The old woman told me that she wanted to get out of here too and that if she couldn't find a soul to replace her children's' then she was forever cursed to roam the forest and do its bidding."

"What the hell is with you and the old woman?" Dhiraj said angrily. "Back there, Aksh offered Maya to the old woman instead of him and she acted like he had personally offended her."

"Aksh offered my soul?" Maya asked in surprise.

"Yes. And then mine." Dhiraj shook his head. "The point is that he was scared so he just took our names."

"And we're going to pick him over the old woman?" Maya asked. "Are you kidding me? He really said that the old woman should take me?"

"We know Aksh longer than you know that old woman," Dhiraj said. "He's our friend."

"I'm beginning to wonder if he really ever was," Maya rebuked.

"Will you both stop fighting?" Preeti screamed. "Dhiraj is right. Aksh is our friend and we have to save him."

"The old woman is just misunderstood." Maya seemed to plead.. "I met her when I came to the forest. She's not as evil as we think. Besides, she's dressed in white and the woman you saw was in black."

"Colors of clothes are unimportant here." Preeti scoffed.

"I was attacked by a black beast and saved by a white one," Maya told them. "The old woman said…"

"Oh," Preeti said, finally understanding why Maya was taking the old woman's side. "Now I get it. Maya, she's not your mother."

"What?" Maya narrowed her eyes at her.

"I know your relationship with your mom," Preeti said. "You never said anything, but your silence always said it all and the way Aunty showed little interest in you or your friends was evident enough."

"Shut up!" Maya said. "Just shut the hell up."

"You have to be reasonable, Maya." Dhiraj put a hand on her shoulder. "If the woman Preeti saw in her dream is offering us a chance to get out of here, then we should take it."

"I don't agree."

"Let's take a vote," Preeti said and was glad to see Dhiraj join her side. Maya looked disappointed and she did feel bad for her, but Preeti knew that she had taken the right decision.

"I think this is a mistake." Maya crossed her arms.

"Now how do we find her?" Dhiraj asked, turning to her.

Preeti shrugged. "I have never encountered her. You guys tell me. How did she come to you?"

They heard a shrill cry and turned around to see Nisha standing and pointing at something behind them. The fear on her face turned Preeti's heart to ice. She looked to where she pointed and saw Rudra's eyes peeking at them. His eyes were bright orange orbs that looked like flames. Using his hands, he hauled himself up and grinned.

Dhiraj pulled Preeti back and stood before the two girls.

Rudra seemed to find this amusing and laughed maniacally. He didn't look like the man they knew. His brown eyes contained disdain for them and when he flexed his hands, she saw spikes piercing through his skin.

"I'm going to kill you all!" He screamed.

Maya let out a scream while Preeti looked around her to find a weapon she could use. She saw a tree branch lying on the ground that Dhiraj had been holding and picked it up.

Rudra charged at them and Preeti readied herself. She would never have wanted to hurt Rudra, but this wasn't her friend anymore.

Please don't make me do this! Don't make me hurt him!

He was inches away when Nisha suddenly appeared out of nowhere to stand before the three.

"No!" she screeched and her entire body morphed into her creature form. Scales appeared on her back and her skin turned brownish-grey with minuscule bumps. Her hands turned long and when she turned sideways, Preeti saw she had a long snout like an anteater's, but when she opened her mouth, she had pointed teeth like a shark's.

Rudra stopped and snarled. "I was looking all over for you," He said. "Now you're all mine."

Nisha raised her head and laughed. "I'm not as weak as I was before." She lowered her head and bent her knees. "Let him go! Let Rudra go!"

Rudra laughed a demonic laugh. "Never!"

"Then you've given me no choice," Nisha said and pounced on him.

Chapter Thirty-Five

Sumit grabbed Aksh's throat and slammed him hard against the wall.

"You did this on purpose!" He screamed. His breath was hot and acidic against his face and he could smell the stench of burning wood and flesh. Aksh's gagged when Sumit pressed his face closer.

"Let me go! Please!" But his pleas fell on deaf ears. Sumit flung him on the ground and he screamed in pain. When he rolled over, he saw the old woman watching the scene before her with amusement in her green eyes. She brought her silver hair in the side and began combing it with the long nails of her fingers.

Sumit grabbed his shirt from behind and tossed him against the wall so hard that Aksh's glasses were thrown to the side.

"Don't kill me!" He said. "I didn't mean to. You kept abusing me and something inside me just broke. I swear I didn't know that you would die because of the allergic reaction. I thought you would only break into hives. Please believe me!"

Above him Sumit fumed and Aksh's could see black smoke wafting from his form. He growled and his pointed teeth made an appearance, sending chills down Aksh's spine. He put his hand out to look for his glasses and his hands closed over his golden frames. With quivering hands, he picked it up and wore them. With his sight clearing up, the horror that was before him also brightened. Sumit was joined by five burly men, all of them with charred skin and scarred bluish faces. They each grinned, their pointed tooth smiles and their hands grew nails that looked like daggers.

Aksh was sure his heart had stopped beating. He crawled away as fast as he could, the stench of burning growing stronger and heavier. He went over to the old woman and hugged her feet.

"Help me, please. Save me from them. I'll do anything."

The old woman grabbed the curls of his hair and raised his head so that he was face to face with her. The old woman's eyes changed color to a fiery red that glowed.

"Anything?"

"Yes, but please take me away from here. I won't ask you to take any of my friends. Please!"

The old woman pitied him and made him sit next to her on the bench. "There, there." Her voice was soothing. "Now that you've given me your word, I'll help you."

The smile she gave him however made Aksh think otherwise.

"I can save you from Sumit," She said.

"Really?" Aksh's hope grew. Behind him, Sumit and the five unknown men stood waiting. Apparently they weren't going to make a move with the old woman so nearby.

"I'll do anything." He clasped his hands together as if in prayer.

The old woman looked down at his hands and seemed pleased to see how desperate he was.

She resumed combing her silver hair with her nails and each time she did that, the strands glowed white.

"A long time ago, when I was human, I killed my own children because I thought they wanted to leave me," She said in a rueful tone. "After I died I found no peace because of the heinous crime I had committed. When I came to the forest I found that there was a way for me to escape this wretched place and find heaven."

Aksh listened but kept his eyes on the men behind him. He could hear Sumit breathing sharply and grunting with impatience.

"You could help me," She said, turning her red glowing eyes at him.

"How?" Aksh asked pushing himself closer to her when Sumit put one foot forward.

The old woman grabbed his wrist so sudden, that Aksh let out a yelp. "Come with me... voluntarily."

Aksh stared at her in stunned silence. His mouth dropped open and he could feel the heat from the woman's hands radiate onto his skin. He wanted to pull away but couldn't and not only because she was hurting him. Her words were raking through whatever sanity he had left.

"I...what if...?"

"What if you don't?" The old woman's eyes lost their reddish glow and turned dark- like drying blood. Then she let out a laugh and Aksh let out a whine. "Then I'll let Sumit tear your head off. Or maybe, he would like to tear your limbs first—one by one so that you feel immense pain before you die." She looked up at Sumit. "Is that what you would like to do?"

Sumit was flabbergasted that she was talking to him, but quickly regained his composure.

"He killed me on purpose," He said.

"I didn't!" Aksh cried.

"You did!" Sumit screamed and Aksh could feel a burst of wind that slapped his face. "She's right. I want to see you suffer before you die. I'll tear of each of your fingers one by one, then your whole hand then your toes..."

"Enough!" The old woman ordered. "He gets it, don't you?" Her voice was so kind but Aksh only felt his fear mounting until he was sure he would choke on it.

Sumit immediately silenced and stepped back into his corner.

"Now after Sumit is done mutilating you, your soul will be transported to the tree where you will have to wait a long time before judgement is passed on you. Then you'll go to hell."

"And if I come with you?" Aksh asked, sobbing.

"I'll be forgiven for my crimes. You'll still die but there's a chance you may not automatically be sent to hell."

"I'll die either way?" Aksh wept.

"You shouldn't have made that mistake." The old woman shrugged nonchalantly. "You shouldn't have killed Sumit or ignored the old man's warning."

Aksh remembered the old man who had tried warning him and his friends about proceeding further.

"He used to be my husband," The old woman said. "The poor man still tries to warn people from coming to the forest, but no one listens to him. I never did either, when I was alive." She smiled as if she had just shared an inside joke with him.

Aksh leaned back, letting his aching back rest against the bench behind him. The old woman was right— he had screwed up everything. If only Sumit had never come back into his life—he wouldn't have prescribed the wrong medicines and then been so troubled by his decision that planned this ill-fated trip. Of course it was Dhiraj's fault for punching Sumit in the first place that made him go to the hospital, but the old woman apparently didn't care for him blaming his friends for his predicament.

Aksh closed his eyes knowing that until he made his decision, Sumit won't hurt him. The old woman wouldn't take him until he said she could. He still had some time to decide how he wanted to be killed.

There wasn't another way, was there?

He was in the middle- the woman was on his right, Sumit and the other men on his left. Straight ahead was the door that he would never get through. All was lost. There wasn't another way; there was nothing he could do...

He dropped his head and clutched his hair. There was something inside him reminding him of a third way, but he ignored it. He was doomed. No matter how many times he had heard that there was always a way out, this time he was certain that there wasn't.

He had to make a decision and obviously being taken away by the old woman was far better than being torn apart.

Aksh opened his mouth to announce his decision when the voice in his head spoke up.

There is another way!

Aksh listened to that voice and suddenly there was a glimmer of hope. He straightened, looked at the door and hoped his hunch would be right. There was no other way and if he wanted to survive, he had to do this.

"Made a decision?" The old woman asked, her eye sparkling with excitement.

Aksh closed his eyes, said a silent prayer and hoped he was right. He opened his mouth and his eyes.

"Antara Meena!" He screamed. The door flew open and Aksh saw just who he wanted to see—his only chance to stay alive.

Chapter Thirty-Six

There was a flurry of movement and a blur of red. The force of the two creatures was producing a forceful wind that compelled the three friends to step back and watch one of their possessed friends try to take down a formerly docile creature.

When they broke away from each other, Preeti saw Rudra land with a thud on the ground while Nisha stood over him with a triumphant look on her face. Then in seconds, Rudra had jumped to his feet and raised his leg, executing a swinging kick that Nisha couldn't dodge.

Maya and Dhiraj stepped back further, but Preeti was mesmerized by the scene before her. Her eyes wanted to study Rudra's face as it turned ferocious and all she wanted to see was that one glimmer of her friend that she was coming to love.

Instead, all she saw was a growl on his face, the red fury in his eyes and the paleness of his skin. The Rudra who had professed his love for her was lost.

What have I done?

The words tortured her mind and soul. She should have just accepted his proposal in college. Then she wouldn't have been cheated on by Abhi and wouldn't have agreed to come on this road trip that had brought them into this wretched forest.

What if Rudra never returns to his former self?

That would be her fault too.

Nisha recovered from the attack and uttering a sharp cry, lunged at Rudra, wrapped her legs around his waist and beat him with her fists. Rudra picked her up by the waist and flung her to the ground but Nisha kicked his instep and made him lose his balance.

"What do we do?" Maya whispered in her ear.

Preeti wanted to answer that she didn't know but her mind wouldn't leave Rudra. She could feel Maya shaking her, but found herself incapable of any response.

Nisha and Rudra rolled on the ground, trying to strangle one another, before Nisha landed a powerful kick and Rudra was propelled towards a tree. When he hit it, he let out a grunt and got back on his feet. Nisha watched him, unmoved by his fury and bending her knees and readying her fists.

"This is never going to end," Dhiraj said, coming to her other side. "They are both too powerful."

"We have to go back to my original plan," Maya suggested. "Preeti is the only one who can shake Rudra off his trance."

"I can't!" Preeti said, finding her voice and turning to her friends. "He is not in a trance, he's possessed. He's not our friend anymore and Rudra is just...gone." She went to sit on a rock and held her head in her hands, trying to ignore the screams and the grunts of the two still fighting.

Maya came to sit beside her. "Preeti you know that Rudra loves you and that is the strongest emotion of all. It can cut through all the evil in the world."

"He doesn't love me." Preeti wept. "He's with someone else now and I'm just..." she shook her head at the black gloomy sky. "I'm just alone."

Rudra whirled around with such force that Preeti had to cover her face. When she parted her fingers to look at what was going on, she saw Rudra stomping towards them. Putting her hands down, she clutched Maya's arms.

Dhiraj came to stand before the two girls, but Preeti could see that Rudra didn't show any intention to hurt them. Rather, there was conflict in his eyes as he twisted his arms and head.

"You lied!" she heard Rudra's voice and her hope grew.

"You're all mine now!" His voice turned demonic again and his snarl returned.

"What is happening?" Maya asked.

"I think he's trying to fight the demon possessing him,' Preeti said.

Nisha pounced on Rudra's back and brought him down. She used her knee to press down on his upper back that constricted Rudra's breathing.

Rudra pounded the ground, then using all his power, flipped and with one hand, clutched at Nisha's throat.

"We have to help her!" Maya said, getting up.

"We have to help him!" Preeti stated.

Dhiraj looked at the two girls in confusion. "What could we possibly do?"

***

There was a loud crack heard in the air and the sky lit up all of a sudden.

"Was that lightning?" Maya asked, grabbing Preeti's hand.

"Thunder before lightning?" Dhiraj looked all around with wide eyes. Behind them, Nisha was angrily thrashing at Rudra's arms and managed to free herself from his tight grip.

Preeti felt a shudder rush through her when thunder boomed again followed by lightning. She had to admit that the reverse storm did nothing to alleviate her fear. Through the small mass of trees on a hill, she spotted movement and froze.

Icy rain started to pelt them, but Preeti couldn't take her eyes away from the shadowy figures on top of the hill.

When lightning flashed again, she saw two identical girls walking up the hill with stern faces and dragging something behind them.

Preeti narrowed her eyes and when lightning flashed again after the thunder, she saw that what they were pulling behind them was a person. Whoever it was, his head was slumped on his chest and his whole body was slackened. The twins were dragging him by putting their hands under his arms and pulling at him.

"What is it?" Maya asked, putting a hand on her shoulder.

"Do you see it?" Preeti asked through ice cold lips.

Maya's grip tightened as she nodded. "Who is that?"

"I can't see from here," Dhiraj said. "Is that a corpse they are dragging?"

They heard a roar behind them and turned to see Nisha lying on the ground near Rudra's feet who was growling at them.

"Shit!" Dhiraj screamed. He put his arms up to shield the girls, but this gesture amused the demon inside Rudra. He advanced with his arms outstretched and his face contorted into an ugly snarl. He grinned with his pointed teeth that had smears of blood on them.

The rain came down harder, but couldn't wash away the thick layer of blood stained on his face. Preeti looked down at Nisha who was lying near a rock and wondered if she was dead.

"Rudra….please…don't." she whimpered.

Maya stepped back further while Dhiraj was still trying to protect them with his body. Rudra charged towards them and Dhiraj pushed the girls behind him. Preeti saw the grotesque expression on Rudra's face and surprised herself by pushing away at Dhiraj's arms and standing before him.

"No!" she screamed.

Dhiraj tried tugging at her arm and pulling her back but Preeti wrestled herself free from him. Rudra raised his arm and Preeti caught it.

"You won't hurt me." Her voice was a command. "Rudra would never hurt me. I know that with all my heart."

The demon before her paused, but his anger grew. He snorted and she could see wisps of smoke emitting from his nostrils.

"Rudra loves me," She continued. "Even though we can never be together, because…because he's with someone else, I know that he would never want to hurt me."

Rudra opened his mouth and let out a shrill cry but he made no attempt to pounce at her.

"I knew he loved me," Preeti said, her chest getting heavier with raw emotion. "I always knew. But I was naïve and thought I was better suited with Abhi because he was so cool and dangerous and exciting." She felt the tears pooling in her eyes, but she didn't want to look away; not when Rudra was no longer looking enraged.

"I let the one person walk away from me who actually did care for me." Preeti let the tears fall from her eyes. "Abhi never did. He cheated on me and he treated me badly. When we broke up, the first thing I thought of was you, Rudra. I thought what an idiot I was for letting you go."

She brushed away a tear and looked overhead. The thunder had stopped but the lightning was still flashing and the rain continued to fall.

"I hated myself for being so glib and not understanding that someone could actually love me enough to let me walk away from him." Preeti took another step toward him. She heard her friends whisper her to stay back, but she had to take a chance. She took Rudra's hand and felt her throat tighten when he stiffened and uttered a low growl.

"You did this for me. You didn't pursue me and you didn't try to turn me against Abhi," She said softly. "You could have hated me and decided that you never wanted to see my face again. But you continued to be my friend despite it all."

Her tears fell faster, yet Preeti continued to keep her eyes on him and her hand in his. "And I love you for that. I love that you were my friend when you could have decided not to. So please, Rudra. Please don't let a demon take you away from me."

Rudra pulled his hand away with such force that Preeti stumbled back. Dhiraj caught her and Maya held her arm.

"I hate you!" he screamed.

Preeti felt her lips tremble. "No you don't."

Rudra walked back and threw a punch at a tree trunk. Small pieces of wood flew as his fist made impact with the tree. Preeti flinched but didn't step back.

"I'll kill you."

Preeti sucked in a breath. "Rudra would never hurt me."

Rudra paused. She saw his shoulders stiffen and his fists clench. He turned his neck slowly and then tilted his head. "Do you want to bet on that?"

He strode towards her and Preeti willed herself to stay calm.

"He won't hurt me. He won't hurt me," She murmured to herself.

"Come on," Dhiraj whispered in her ear. "Preeti that's not Rudra anymore."

"He won't hurt me. He won't hurt me."

"He'll kill you." Maya cried. "Preeti, let's go!"

But she wouldn't budge. "He won't hurt me," She said slowly. "He won't!"

Rudra raised his hand at her and then dropped to the ground and screamed. Preeti started to sob as he writhed on the floor, trying to fight himself. He got up on his knees then fell back again. The screams were louder than the thunder that resumed.

Maya was clutching her wrist so tight that Preeti was sure she would end up with bruises, but she couldn't let herself do anything but watch Rudra struggle with himself on the ground. The leaves swept all around them and the wind grew fiercer.

Rudra put his hands on his face and appeared to be tearing away at his skin.

"We have to help him," Dhiraj said. He moved forward when Nisha came in front of them out of nowhere.

"No!" she said. "He's already won."

Chapter Thirty-Seven

She walked through the forest without a care in the world.

The storm was worsening and the rain was falling harder, but she knew it would pass soon. It had all happened before.

Her white gown flowed behind her, as did her long silver hair that made a slithering motion. Her talons contracted and her hands returned to their human form. She could feel her face lose its scars as well. Taking in a deep breath, she relished the sweet smell of flowers that were blooming somewhere in the distance.

Nothing grew here and nothing smelled like fresh leaves or grass or anything. But very rarely, a flower or a plant would start growing from under a mass of undead plants.

The old woman touched a leaf and it jolted in her hands before turning black and powdery. A sigh escaped her lips and she reminded herself of another failure she had incurred today. Her only chance at redemption was snatched away by two girls, who didn't even possess as much power as her, but like her, they too were cursed, and that gave them the slight advantage.

"Things didn't go according to plan?" she heard a familiar mocking tone.

"Of course it would have to be you," She said, turning around to find a tall woman dressed in black, leaning against a tree.

"Of course." She smiled, her red lips stretching over bright white pointed teeth. "I was going to use one of them to bring you to me, but it looks like…"

"You failed too." The old woman scoffed. The woman in black frowned heavily and with a wave of her hand, brought forth two beasts—one snowy white, the other jet black. The two hounds growled menacingly at her, but she found them to be no threat.

The woman in black walked forward and her towering height lessened with each step until she was face to face with her.

"You were trumped by two newcomers," She said. "And a very easy target." She began to laugh and that sounded like daggers to the old woman's eardrums. Then she walked around her and touched her silver hair. "Do I spot another white hair in here?"

The old woman yanked her hair away from her grip. "How do I know you had nothing to do with it?" she retorted. "After all, you were the one who made me commit my sins in the first place."

The woman in black lowered her head and whispered in her ears. "It's that easy for me. I can make you do anything I want."

"You *could*!" The old woman glared. "But not anymore!"

The woman in black laughed heartily. "I rule the forest. I made those five crash here and walk into the forest. I made them walk in circles around each other without them knowing."

"You did a lot more." The old woman snarled. "You had the goons corrupted even more and used your whisperings to make them threaten the twins. And when they killed themselves, instead of taking them to the tree, you decided to use them as pawns."

"It was all in fun...sister." The woman in black laughed.

"I am not your sister!" The old woman snapped. "We were never sisters to begin with. You were always jealous of me. When you died, your malevolent spirit haunted us all and then you created this wretched forest into a plaything."

"But I did miss my sister so much," The other woman said. "That's why I had to bring you here."

"You told me my children wanted to leave me. You created that insecurity and fury in me so that I could be manipulated."

"Your accusations are ludicrous, sister." The woman in black cuddled the two beasts that were resting under a tree. "You were always mad and that is why our parents were so unhappy."

"They were unhappy because you were a terrible younger daughter," The old woman accused. "Had you not been born..."

"Enough!" The woman in black said and her height grew an inch. "I gave you power and a purpose. You are free to leave, provided you fulfill your condition."

"Which you make sure never happens!" The old woman denounced.

"Oh well," The woman in black said nonchalantly. "There is still time, perhaps I can use my whisperings to separate the friends again. You seem to have taken a shine to one of the girls—Maya was it?"

"Leave her out of this!"

"Or what?" Her height grew another inch as her face turned darker.

"I grow tired of this game." The old woman turned away. "They won their challenges fair and square. They should be allowed to leave."

The woman in black let out a melodramatic sigh. "I always keep my word."

The old woman pressed her lips together, knowing full well that the other woman never kept her word but it was futile arguing with someone who possessed more power than her. Someday...

"You still won't be able to beat me," The woman in black whispered. "I can read thoughts remember? Even yours."

"Then you knew the boy would call upon the twins."

The woman in black chuckled. "Of course. It was fun seeing you get your hopes up for that one second."

"You made the twins more powerful than me," The old woman said dejectedly.

"Oh, rest assured, everyone and everything in this forest fears you." The woman in black said. The beasts made whining sounds when she stepped further away from them. They followed her and nuzzled at her skirt. The woman patted their heads and grinned. "You are my sister after all. But every creature in this forest has a special skill and if the player decides to use it, I can't do anything about it, can I?"

"Players." The old woman scoffed. "You're still that young girl who likes to play with dolls, except now you play with real human lives."

"Oh don't tell me you preferred your married life with that drunk over this power filled one." The woman in black pointed out. "You hated him and you know it."

"I have no desire to share my marital woes with you," The old woman said. "Now will you let the rest of them leave or not?"

"You are that concerned for Maya?" The woman in black raised a pointed eyebrow. "She doesn't even look like your daughter."

"It's not about the looks. It's what I felt about her when we met," The old woman said. "You would not understand love or the yearnings for it."

"I suppose so." The woman in black picked up the two beasts by their necks with ease and tossed them away. "Very well, I shall not interfere in their matters anymore. If they find a way to leave, I'll let them."

"They will," The old woman said. She knew about the lovers and how they would try to help the people to leave the forest. They weren't powerful enough to block every path, but they had power that couldn't be manipulated by her younger sister.

"Must be that annoying emotion—love." The woman in black rolled her eyes. "I could make them jump off a cliff, but I couldn't separate them or stop them from hindering my plans." She gave another sigh. "I really wanted to play with that girl—Preeti. But she too escaped my grasp."

The old woman said nothing and walked away, hoping that her sister wouldn't pull out another trick. As far as she knew, her sister never gave up that easily.

Chapter Thirty-Eight

"Are you okay?" Preeti kept asking Rudra who was kneeling with his head slumped against his chest. Maya was standing next to Dhiraj and she was certain that he too didn't know what to do. Nisha was watching all of them with a stern expression, but said nothing.

Whether Rudra had come back to himself or was still under possession, none of them could tell. Maya could see the desperation in Preeti's face as she shook Rudra.

"Talk to me!" she cried.

Behind her, Nisha suddenly flinched and looked at her hand as if it was the oddest object she had ever seen. Then she turned her head to look at something above. Maya followed her gaze and saw that the sky was lightening just a tiny bit.

The pinkish clouds had dispersed and the inky black sky now had a tinge of grayish-blue. Maya took a step forward to where there was a bigger patch of the sky noticeable through the tops of the trees.

Was the sun really coming up?

So mesmerized was she by the sight of the sky, that at first she hadn't heard the whispers.

"Maya!" the voice repeated and she turned to see a lock of silver hair floating from behind a tree trunk. She muffled her gasps, gave her friends a quick glance and walked towards the tree behind a large rock. The voice in her head told her not to be so naïve and rush to the beckons of the strange old woman, but something inside her refused to acknowledge or entertain that thought.

The old woman peered through a branch to make sure she was coming and Maya thought she looked nervous and frightened.

"What are you doing here?" Maya asked through cold numb lips. She wanted to go back to her friends, but the old woman's gaze was captivating her and making her limbs immobile.

"You and your friends must go this instant," She said in a whisper.

"You're afraid of someone." Maya realized.

"All that isn't important. You must leave now!"

Maya turned to look at her friends and saw Nisha walking backward as if she were being pulled away by an invisible force. Preeti was still sobbing over Rudra's rigid body and Dhiraj looked torn between decisions only he knew about.

"Rudra is…"

"He's fine," The old woman said. "This is your only chance."

Maya flicked a tongue over her dry upper lip. The sensation of thirst and hunger was beginning to grow within her and reminding her that she hadn't nourished her body in hours. Suddenly she was overwhelmed by exhaustion and fought to keep her eyes open.

"We don't know how to leave," she said groggily

"Your friend there knows how." The old woman nodded towards Preeti. "Ask her to remember."

"One of our friends—Aksh—he's still here."

The old woman's jaw stiffened. "He's gone. He made his choices. You must leave before it's too late for you as well."

"What? Is Aksh…dead?" Maya could feel her chest tightening as her mind tried to grasp the news.

"No, but he has decided not to leave the forest," The old woman answered. "I say this again and with urgency, run and leave this forest as fast as you can."

"What are you afraid of?" Maya asked.

The old woman had opened her mouth to reply but she clamped down shut on her words. Putting a hand on Maya's hair, she stroked it. "You need not worry yourself about that. The forest is slumbering again and you'll be able to leave. If you don't go this instant, it'll wake without warning and then...then you won't be able escape

"I don't understand."

"You don't need to, dear." The old woman kissed the top of her head and Maya winced, expecting to feel something hot and evil. Instead she felt a feathery warm touch on her hair, one that coaxed her into comfort. She closed her eyes, thinking about how she wanted her mother to kiss her like that and make her feel safe.

She opened her eyes and saw that the old woman had disappeared.

"Maya?" Dhiraj asked. "What are you doing here?"

Maya turned to face her friend and put her hands on his arms. "We have to go. Now!"

"What?"

Preeti rose slowly, though she kept one hand on Rudra's shoulder. "Maya, who were you talking to?" her eyes were narrow and suspicious.

"Do you know that way out of the forest?" Maya asked, ignoring Preeti's question.

"I don't know. I think so," She said uncertainly.

"We have to leave." Maya pulled away from Dhiraj.

"Can we even leave?" Preeti asked, incredulously. "We've been going around the forest looking for an exit and we can't leave Aksh behind."

"I don't think we can find him," Maya said. She wanted to tell them exactly what she had learned, but her friends were likely to do the opposite of what the old woman had advised and Maya couldn't risk missing the only chance for their escape.

"We'll come back for him," Dhiraj said. "Preeti if you know the way, lead us out. Once we're out and away from this wretched forest we'll go find help." He turned back and then all around him, his eyes searching for any movement. "I'm not leaving my friend behind."

Taking a deep breath, Dhiraj yelled." Aksh! We'll come back for you! That's a promise!"

Maya tugged at Dhiraj's shoulder and led him to Rudra. "We have to help him up."

Without wasting time, Maya put one of Rudra's arm around her shoulder while Dhiraj did the same with his other shoulder. Both of them supported Rudra and made him stand on his feet.

"Preeti, lead the way," Maya said.

Preeti nodded with tears in her eyes. "Okay. I'll try."

Chapter Thirty-Nine

He had been standing in the arena when he had called the names of who he thought would be his saviors. They had arrived immediately and when his eyes met theirs, there had been a sudden chilling wind and then only darkness. Somewhere around in the black depths of his mind, he thought he had heard Sumit let out a disappointed scream and the shrill cry of the old woman.

Then there was nothing.

When he came to, he found himself staring at his feet and the moving ground. He still had his shoes on, he thought incredulously. After going through all that he had in the forest, there was not a scratch on them.

Aksh turned his head sideways and saw his arms were raised and that he was being pulled away like a rag doll by the twins. Overhead, he heard the boom of thunder and then the crack of lightning.

Wasn't it supposed to happen the other way around?

Then he heard the soft humming of a song and his mind dispelled the soft wisps of grogginess from his mind. The twins! They were going to possess his body and use him like a sock!

He grunted and began to struggle out of their grasp but they held on; not even unperturbed by his futile exertions. In fact they barely glanced at him as they dragged him up a thorny hill. Aksh prepared himself to feel the prickles of thorns and pointed rocks and at first felt nothing.

Then when lightning appeared followed by thunder, he knew something had changed around him. Looking down at his shoes, he found them tattered with the soles ready to tear off. His right shoelace was undone while the left one had no laces at all. His eyes traveled up and he saw muddy smudges and smears on his pants and when he looked down, he choked on his own gasp.

There was a large, dark splotch of blood on his chest and Aksh let out a cry. The girls dropped him unceremoniously and looked up at the sky with a deep frown. Lying on his back, he saw the sky beginning to lighten and thought he understood what was going on.

The dark magic of the forest was evaporating.

The twins looked down at him with snarls on their faces and then bending over, took his arms again and dragged him along the ground.

"We're almost there," They said together. "Once inside you can rest. In peace." They chuckled and Aksh lost all his hope of ever escaping. As his back was scratched further by the nettles and thorns, he prayed for this agony to end and for the twins to possess him pronto so that he wouldn't have to suffer any more pain, but his prayer went unanswered.

The twins dropped him again and Aksh heaved a shaky sigh. Looking up, he saw the view of the house that was to be his cage. The lanterns were still on even though the sky was now a lighter shade.

"Come in," The twins said sweetly.

Aksh preferred to stay on the ground and remain unresponsive. The twins let out a frustrated sigh and stomped over to him. "Come on, Aksh. Get up on your feet and enter the house."

"I don't want to," He said pettily.

"Stop being an insolent brat!" They berated. "You staying out here won't help you."

"Just get it over with," Aksh said. "Possess my body."

The twins sighed. "Of course we will," They said. "Be patient. We just thought you would prefer coming in first and washing up and having a meal with us. Your last meal."

"I'm not hungry," He replied childishly.

"Of course you are," They said. "Now that morning is coming, you're going to feel every single thing."

"You said there never was day," Aksh said. "I thought the forest didn't have a morning."

"There's a lot you don't understand," The twins said, their voices in unison. "We will explain it all. Now come on in."

Aksh looked up at the brightening sky and then touched the ground with his fingers. Would he ever feel the earth again? He wondered what being possessed would feel like. He would have no control over any actions, but would he be aware of them?

Aksh let out a tiny moan when he imagined all the distasteful and violent things the twins would make him do. Going out into the woods was clearly not all they wanted to do.

"We're waiting," They said, behind him.

Aksh got up dejectedly and dragged himself to the house. There wasn't any point prolonging his inevitable destiny. After all he had been the one to call them.

The twins stood by the door and smiled at him as if greeting a guest.

"We hope you like our home." Then they chuckled. "Think of it as your own!"

He stepped in with his eyes closed; certain that his first step in would result in him losing total control of his muscles. But when he felt nothing but the warm damp air of the house, he slowly opened his eyes.

In front of him was a round dining table he had been sitting at the first time he had been invited by the twins. The table was laden with bowls and platters of all his favorite foods. How the twins had guessed didn't bother him, rather he was acutely aware of how hungry he was.

Aksh turned and saw the front door ajar and the twins nowhere in sight. He blinked, sure that his sight was deceiving him. He opened his mouth to call for them then realized how ridiculous he was being.

There it was— an opportunity He could make a run for it and try to escape this horrible nightmare. At least there was a slim chance that the twins wouldn't find him and he had to take it. He took one step toward the door and waited, holding his breath. Nothing.

Another step and his courage grew. Aksh was at the door when he took one last look around him. The food on the table beckoned, but the will to flee quickly overtook his hunger. He had one foot out the door when he heard a thump behind him.

Aksh felt his heart stop and turn ice cold. Suppressing a gasp, he turned slowly, expecting to be punished by the twins for his audacity. However, when he didn't see the twins but something hanging out of the large cupboard in the room instead, his heart started beating again.

Swallowing, he clutched the doorway and realized that what he was looking at was a thin veiny hand and a lock of dry brown hair.

"It's not a snake," He told himself with a deep breath and then remembered the other occupant in the house. Or rather, occupants.

He reached for the cupboard door and yanked it open. Tina's lifeless body fell at his feet. He looked at the other bodies folded like clothes in the shelves and his panic grew. This was going to be him if he didn't escape from here soon.

He turned on his heels when he felt a hand clutch his ankle. Ash screamed and looked down to see Tina looking up at him. Her face was bluish and he eyes almost bulged from the sockets.

"Help me," She pleaded. "Please don't leave me here."

She was stick-thin and he guessed she probably weighed that much as well. He bent and took her hand away from his ankle. Tina gasped and Aksh wondered if he had accidentally broken her wrist.

"Help me." Her voice was a low squeak but it held the unmistakable desperation.

He glanced at the door and imagined carrying Tina over the threshold and into the forest. Though she wouldn't weigh much, she would hinder his progress.

"I'm sorry," He said. "I can't risk it."

Tina's eyes grew wide and large teardrops fell onto the floor.

"I promise I'll come back for you," He said and turned to go to see the twins blocking his way.

"Tsk tsk." They shook their heads in dismay. "That was your last chance."

Aksh felt his heart freeze into ice. He had lost his chance. And it was all because of Tina. He stared at her crawling on the floor, trying to hide from the twins. The twins regarded her with disdain and smugness then went over and pushed her back into the wardrobe.

"No!" Tina cried, but the door was closed on her face.

Aksh tried to make it to the door again, but it shut so suddenly that he was thrown back by the force of it.

"You really should have amended your mistakes," The twins said, and sat at the table. "Come sit and dine with us."

"What mistakes?" Aksh asked and came to stand by an empty chair. "If I correct them, is there a chance I could leave?"

The twins looked at each other. "You had your chance and you....um...how do you say....yes, blew it!"

Aksh looked at the doors of the wardrobe as it rattled. It was probably Tina who was trying to break it open. In her frail condition it must be quite a challenge but he had to laud her determination to escape.

"Wait...I should have helped Tina? Then you would have let me go?" Aksh asked, clutching the head of the chair tight.

"Probably." The twins giggled and started to pile their plates with the delicacies laid on the table. "That's what the forest is all about. It's like a purgatory of lost souls. Some of them find peace, some are cursed to roam it forever and others get to escape. You could have been one of them Aksh."

Their matter-of-fact tones peeved him and he threw the empty chair across the room. "I want my chance. I don't want to stay here with the two of you for the rest of my life!"

"Now that's just rude," The twins said together. "You lost your chance when you tried to pawn off Dhiraj's soul and put all the blame of Sumit's death on him."

"I'll apologize to him," Aksh said desperately.

"You already made your choice when you called our names," The twins said, smugly. "We were kind enough to offer one last chance before the daylight came and the decisions of you and your friends were made. You decided not to help Tina."

"I told her I would come back for her." Aksh sobbed.

"Would you have?" The twins folded their hands and put them under their chins. Their judging tones and raised eyebrows made Aksh wanted to kick something.

"Of course."

"Are you lying to us, Aksh?" They asked, sweetly.

Aksh walked over to a wall and punched it. Part of him expected to feel no pain, but when he saw the blood oozing from his knuckles, he yowled.

"Yes! I wouldn't want to come here, ever! I don't want anything to do with anyone in this wretched forest!" Aksh yelled.

The twins and smiled and picked up their forks and knives. "The truth at last. Now why don't you come and sit down with us. Have dinner, you must be starving."

Aksh wiped away his tears and picked up the chair. He was accepting defeat and he knew it, but he was tired of fighting. He placed the chair near the table and sat down. The twins started serving him all the food, one by one.

Through the blur of his tears he saw delicious looking food in the dishes. The aromatic smell of rice and vegetables made his stomach growl with hunger. One of the twins poured grape juice or wine into his glass.

Then they opened a large dish and Aksh saw hundreds of worms squirming around in it. One of the twins scooped up the wriggling worms with her hand and put it all over his food.

Aksh gasped and pulled his chair back, but the twins instead of being offended, offered him big grins.

"Eat up, Aksh. This is all for you and what you deserve."

Aksh felt his hot tears roll down his cheeks. He picked up his fork with trembling hands and started to eat.

Chapter Forty

"Do you think you can find a way out of here?" Dhiraj asked, grunting as he put Rudra's arm over his shoulder. Maya quickly came to his other side and grabbed Rudra's other arm.

"We've got him. Show us the way," Maya said, pulling Rudra up.

Preeti looked at her friends and saw how much they depended on her to get them out. After all she was the only one who had managed to get out of the forest though not out of this place. What if she couldn't help them?

She glanced at Rudra who looked like he had been slammed against the wall and made to stay awake for days. His head was resting on his chest and she could hear his ragged breathing. They had to get out of here and get him some help.

"Preeti, come on." Maya urged.

She nodded and walked ahead of them. "Hey! Are you here? Hello! We need to leave this forest!"

"Shhh, do you want to alert all the monsters of this forest?" Dhiraj scolded.

Maya looked up at the pale dark blue sky and shook her head. "No. They won't come, but we have to leave now."

"How do you know?" Dhiraj asked but Maya snapped at him.

"I just do. Preeti who are you calling?"

"There was a couple who committed suicide by jumping off the cliffs. They were the ones who led me out,"

She answered and then turned all around her. "Where are they?"

Rudra made an irritated sound and then his knees buckled.

"Here." Dhiraj made Rudra sit on a large rock. "Are you okay?"

Rudra coughed hard but nodded. "Just... need a second... to breathe."

Maya dropped his arm carefully and came to Preeti. "We have to move fast."

"I know!" Preeti could feel tears of frustration pricking her eyes. "I don't know where they are."

Behind them Rudra coughed and Maya went over to his side.

Preeti peered ahead and saw only trees and hedges. "I'm just going to go ahead a bit," She said in a watery voice.

She saw Rudra bent over and cough so hard that he fell from the rock and knelt further on the ground. He opened his mouth and coughed harder while clawing at his throat.

"Rudra!" Preeti was about to come forward when she saw him expel something from his mouth. At first glance it looked like a large black ball of fur, but when it started to crawl, she yelped.

Spiders!

Large spiders scuttled on the ground and ran towards the trees. Maya let out a shrill scream while Dhiraj pulled away from them in shock.

Rudra straightened then and pushed away a large spider from his arm.

"Oh shit!" Dhiraj gasped. "Are you okay now?"

Rudra spat on the ground then wiped his mouth. "Yeah, I could feel them crawling in my throat."

"Preeti, just get us out of here." Maya had tears in her eyes.

"I'll try," She said and with long strides, walked ahead. "I need your help! Please?"

The silence that greeted her pleas chilled her. Were they all alone? She stopped suddenly. It was too quiet. Why weren't her friends saying anything? Why couldn't she hear them?

She turned around slowly and let out a scream.

The ghost of the couple stood behind her, watching her with hollow eyes and contempt on their faces.

Preeti gathered herself and licked her dry lips. "Please help me and my friends get out of here."

"Who are you talking to?" Maya asked.

Preeti looked behind them at her three friends and felt relief wash over her. "They were the ones who helped me escape."

Maya took a step forward but didn't come to her. "Preeti... there's no one there."

Preeti looked at the couple whose form wavered and just for a second she thought she had seen their human forms.

"I'm the only one who can see you?"

The couple said nothing and turned around to walk.

"Are you leading us out of here?"

The couple paused but didn't say anything. Then they began walking again.

Preeti waved a hand at her friends. "Let's go."

Dhiraj and Maya put out their hands to help Rudra but he shook them away.

"I can manage." He rasped.

They walked behind the couple only Preeti could see. Beside her, Rudra walked in silence and when she glanced at him, he seemed preoccupied in his own thoughts. Behind her Maya and Dhiraj held hands and she thought she could hear Maya sniffing.

Rudra suddenly tripped and Preeti caught him just in time. With a hand on his chest, she thought there was no better feeling than to hear someone's heartbeat.

Rudra looked down at her and gave her a small smile. His hands closed over hers and then dropped it so that they stood with their hands entangled.

At that moment, Preeti felt a sense of liberation and euphoria. As if whatever had happened so far in the forest had not happened at all.

"Are we going the right way?" Dhiraj asked, breaking the moment.

Preeti looked ahead to see the couple standing ten feet away from them. "Yes."

Maya came forward. "Is that... is that the road?" She asked, then smiled widely. "It is!"

They walked faster and Preeti never left Rudra's hand. When they reached the edge of the road, Preeti turned to thank the couple but saw that they had already disappeared.

"We're here! We're finally out of the forest!" Dhiraj cheered.

Preeti smiled at Rudra and he squeezed her hand.

They stepped together on the road and Preeti thought she could kiss it. They had made it! They had managed to escape the evil clutches of the forest!

She looked down the road and suddenly frowned. "Where's the car?"

"What do you mean?" Dhiraj asked.

"When I came out, the car was right... here." She looked down at the empty road and her heart filled with fear.

Maya took a step forward and looked both ways down the road. "Maybe it was an illusion. Your nightmare."

Preeti shrugged. "I... guess. But we were in a car. So where is it now?"

Dhiraj suddenly pointed. "It doesn't matter. Look, headlights! There's a car coming."

True enough, through the darkness, came two glowing lights and the sound of an engine roaring.

Maya and Dhiraj stood in the middle of the road and waved their arms. "Hey! We need help! Stop!" They screamed.

Preeti frowned and felt an eerie sensation. Something didn't feel right.

Rudra squeezed her hand again and smiled down at her. "We're going home," He said.

Preeti felt that ominous sensation leave her when she saw the love in Rudra's eyes.

"Yes. We are." She joined Dhiraj and Maya and started waving her hands too. "Stop!" She screamed, never once leaving Rudra's hand.

As the car neared, Maya dropped her hands and her eyes grew wide. Dhiraj too paused midair and Preeti frowned.

"What's wrong? We need to stop them," She said.

"That car..." But before Dhiraj could finish, she saw what he meant.

It was their car.

They all stepped back instinctively, but not fast enough. The car came down and Preeti saw the shocked expressions of Aksh and Rudra sitting in the car. Behind them, she saw herself opening her mouth and screaming.

There was an impact, but Preeti felt nothing. She was engulfed in a bright white light and nothingness.

Before her thoughts left her mind and her hand detached from Rudra's, she realized that there never had been an escape.

Ends

About the Author:

Palvi Sharma is an avid reader who discovered her passion for writing at a very young age. Her love for horror movies and books is what propelled her to write her very own horror books.
When she's not writing, she loves taking long walks, listening to music and learning new languages.
You can read her blog here:
youngadultebooks.blogspot.com

Social Media Links:

Facebook: https://www.facebook.com/palvi.sharma.90

Twitter: https://twitter.com/Palvi_Writer @Palvi_Writer